KNIFE FIGHTER

The Omnibus Edition

KNIFE FIGHTER

The Omnibus Edition

TWO SHORT STORIES BY

LOREN W. CHRISTENSEN

KNIFE FIGHTER: THE OMNIBUS EDITION
by LOREN W. CHRISTENSEN

For more information, go to:
http://www.lwc.com

ISBN: 9798646598418
First Print Edition

Cover and Interior design by Kamila Miller: kzmiller.com

Disclaimer:
The author and publisher of this book will not be held responsible in any
way for any injury of any nature whatsoever, which may occur to readers,
or others, as a direct or indirect result of the information contained
within this book.

KNIFE FIGHTER

KNIFE FIGHTER 2

KNIFE FIGHTER

LOREN W CHRISTENSEN

BEST-SELLING AUTHOR OF OVER 60 BOOKS

ACKNOWLEDGEMENTS

As always, a big hug to my bride, Lisa, for her encouragement, enthusiasm and support.

And an awkward, manly hug to my friend and editor Kevin Faulk for his input.

He Who Pulls Out A Knife
By Knife
Shall He Die

~ Bulgarian Proverb

WEAPONS FEATURED IN KNIFE FIGHTER

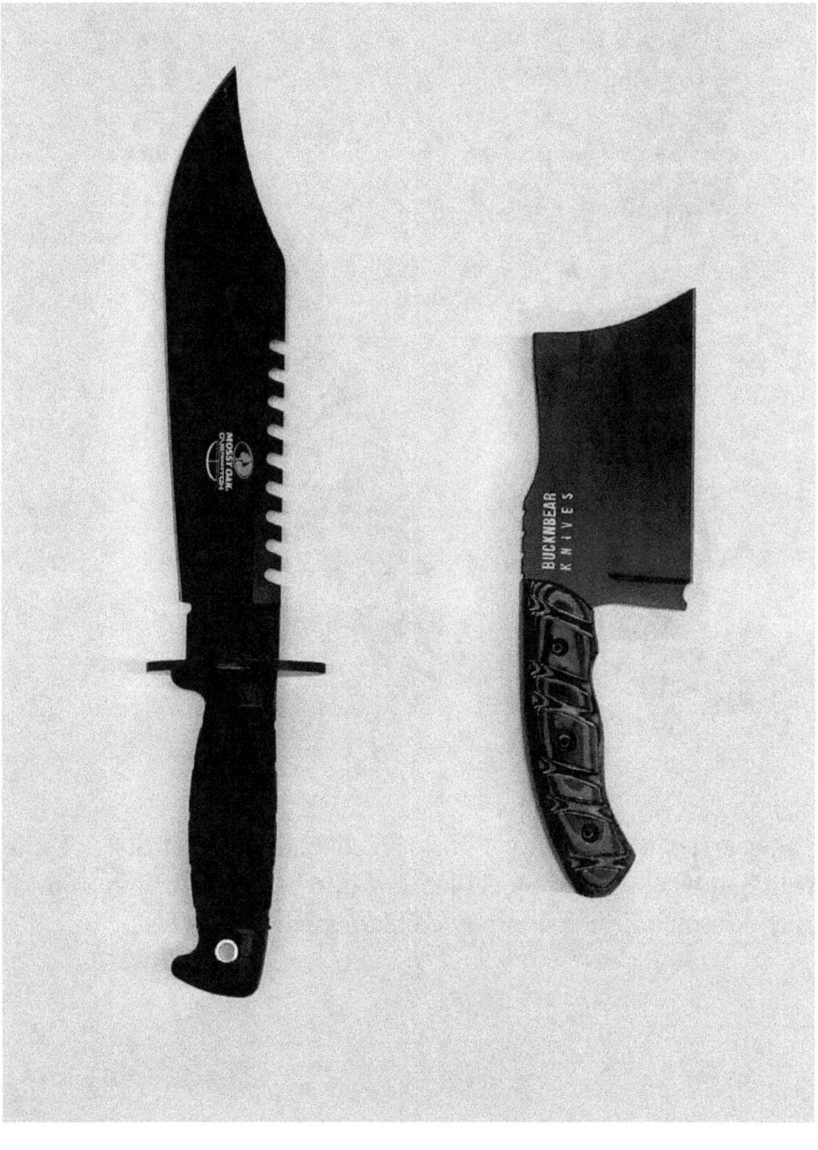

Grey carries a Mossy Oak Survival Knife, 15-inch Fixed Blade Hunting Bowie Knife (L) and a BucknBear Tactical Chopper Knife, Cleaver Fixed 6 Inch Blade, G10 Handle (R)

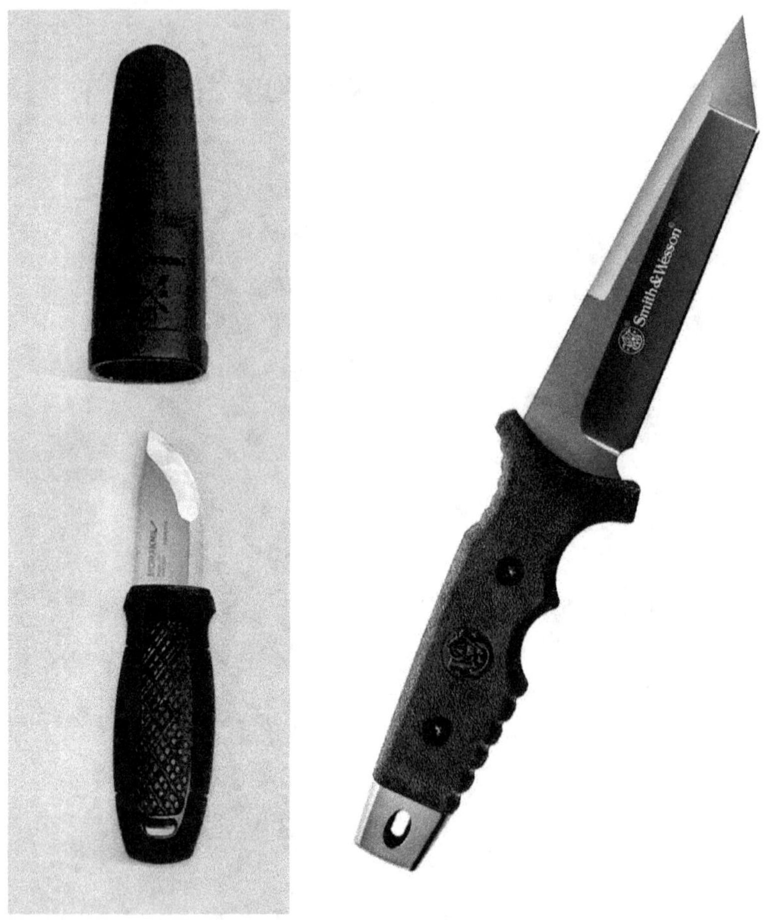

Tala carries a Morakniv Eldris Fixed-Blade Pocket-Sized Knife with Sandvik Stainless Steel Blade around her neck (L) and a Smith and Wesson 5.2-inch Tanto fixed blade on her hip. (R)

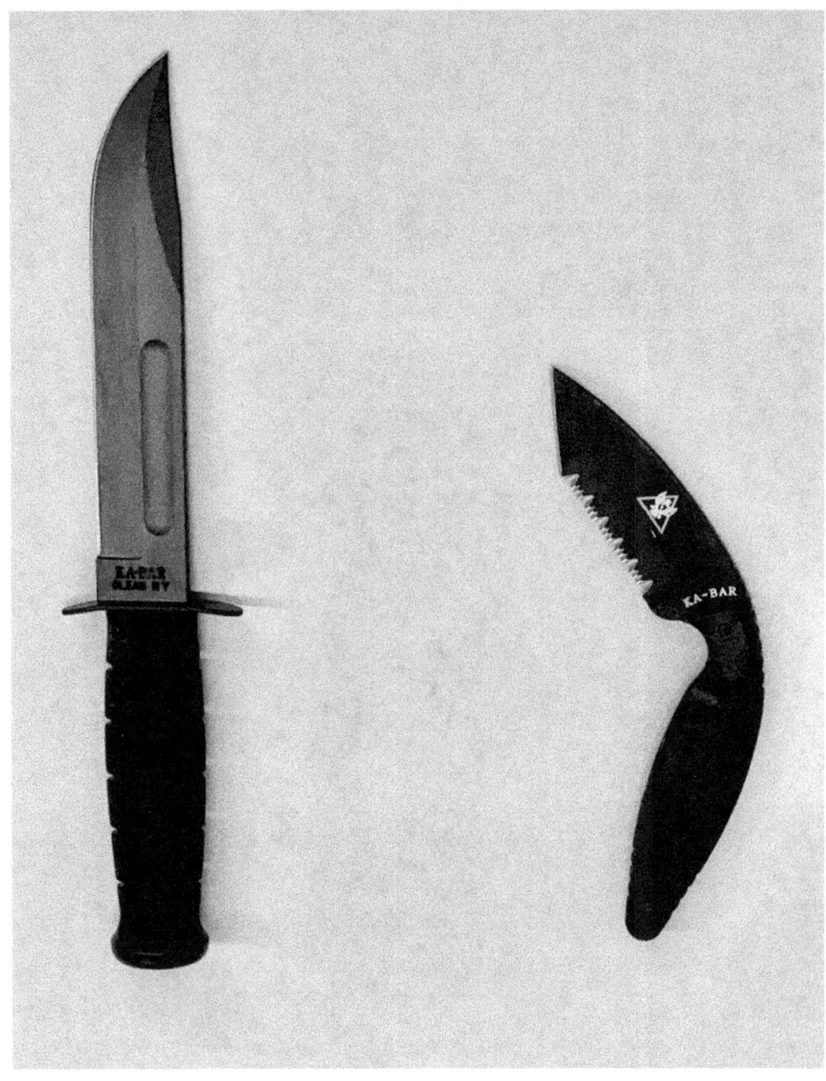

Leathers carries a 7-inch Ka-Bar (L) and a Ka-Bar TDI Law Enforcement Tanto Knife (R)

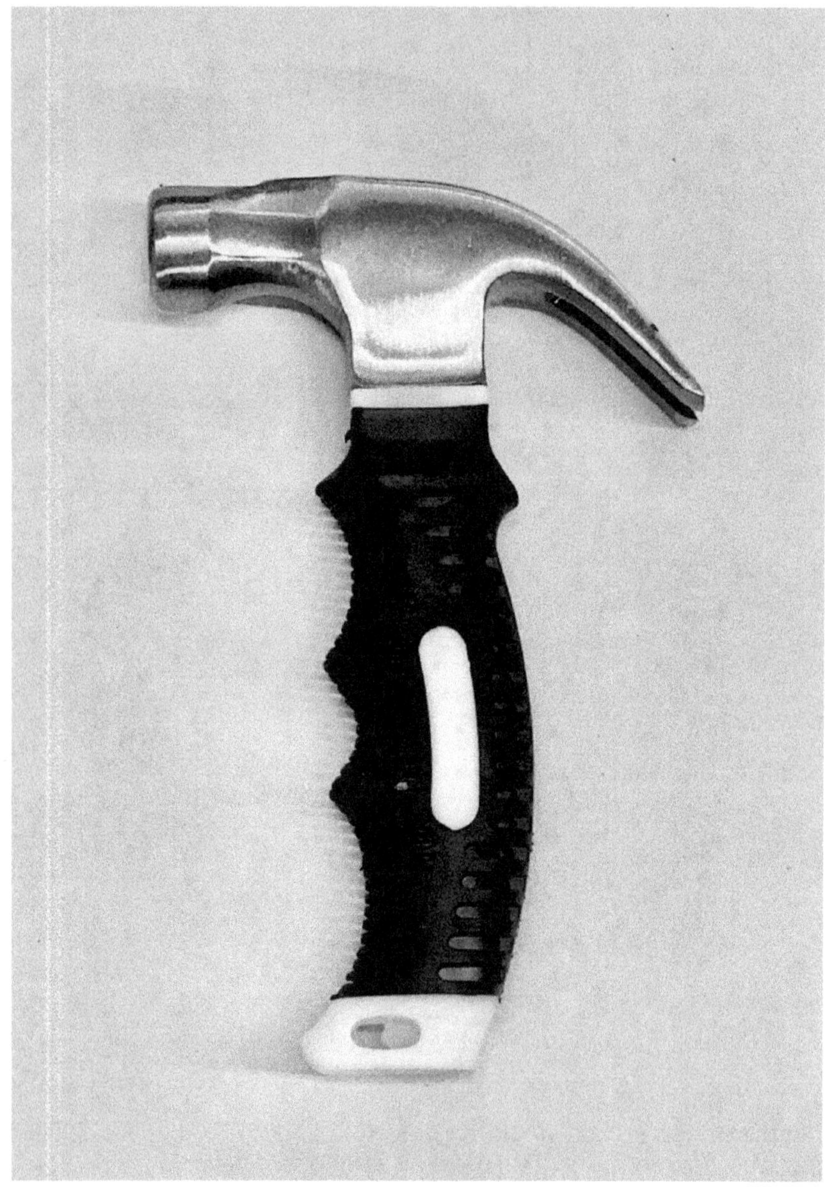

The Hammer Brothers carry two 8-oz Stubby Claw Hammers each.

THREE YEARS FROM NOW

CHAPTER 1

GREY AND HIS FATHER

Two, sometimes three nights a week, the sky dripped, not rained, dripped. During the days, it hung low, ashen and dense as if at any moment, the thick ceiling would rip open and dump its oily contents down on the new shitty world. But it never did; it just bathed the drab survivors in weighty gloom. But at night, the sky dribbled, like tall trees in a dense forest after rain. No one knew what was in the drippage. Many deaths were attributed to it. Why some people seemed immune was unknown.

Since The Change, much was unknown.

Grey was standing to the side of the window, peering out into the dark. Sector Four, where he had lived for the past few months, was near the core of the city, but the absence of lights that used to illuminate, reflect, dance, and give life to the streets and edifices were no more. Now only random fires, lanterns, and the rare lone light bulb struggled to illumine the thick, wet black.

It was quiet outside the window but in a minute or an hour, that would change.

Of course, the quiet didn't mean all was well. Not at all. Grey saw some graffiti scrawled on the gutted U.S. Bank building a couple of blocks over that read: "Just because it's quiet out doesn't mean people aren't dying."

He leaned back from the window. His reflection in the glass revealed his weight loss. He stood six feet at about 175 pounds and had lived 37 years, though he looked 40, some days 45. Gone was the 215 pounds of weight-trained bulky muscle of his early years. Now his physique was sinewy but still capable of tremendous speed. There were ugly puckers on his upper and lower arms, the result of novice stitching in the last three years. He had more of the same on his chest under his tattered shirt.

His features were handsome, but the distresses of surviving in the new life had pulled his skin taught and deadened his eyes. His thick dark hair bunched on his shoulders.

"Grey."

He took another step back and looked down at the old man lying in bed, his head sunk into a pillow. "You're awake, father," Grey said as he sat down on the upturned box next to the bed.

"You…" his father breathed in raggedly and let it seep out with a faint whistle, "have always had a keen grasp of the obvious." His glistening eyes twinkled before they drooped and closed.

Grey's father was 79 years old, and until a few weeks ago, he had looked 10 years younger. Now he looked older, 89, maybe. "Dying adds years to one's face," he said to Grey a few nights back. "It really takes a lot out of a fella."

The old man's left arm was gone, leaving a stump near his shoulder that protruded from his white T-shirt sleeve. His left ear was gone too, that absence a constant reminder of the assailant with the cleaver 15 years ago. The man was fast and accurate, as fast and accurate as the old man was, who everyone called "Knife Fighter." But because the first one to attack usually had the advantage, the man with the cleaver managed to hack off Knife Fighter's ear as clean as a whistle.

Witnesses said the man's attack beat Grey's father's attack by only a millisecond, but it was enough to do the removal. But Knife Fighter's blade still managed to impact a vital target; most would say it was the most vital of all. His father rammed his knife into the ax man's crotch all the way to the handle. Then he stepped back and kicked the end of it so hard that half of it penetrated into the opening the blade had made.

While the cleaver man might have eventually died from the invasive stab and kick, the sidewalk killed him quicker after Knife Fighter chucked him off the six-story roof. He liked the man's cleaver and kept it.

Grey's father squirmed to find comfort on the hard mattress. His sagging yellow complexion wasn't helped by the weak light emanating from the clown lamp perched atop an old dresser next to the bed. Grey found it lying on a sidewalk outside a children's group home. The last social worker had abandoned it by way of suicide, leaving the orphans to fare for themselves on the mean streets. His father had once joked that in his next life, he wanted to be a circus clown, so Grey brought it back to their apartment.

In the last few months, the old man had deflated, literally sinking into himself more and more each dreary day. He told Grey a few weeks ago that his time was near, but his son refused to accept the prognosis. That was then; this week Grey knew it was true.

This morning, his father said it would happen on this day or tomorrow.

The old man's face bore multiple long scars, two running at least five inches from his hairline on the right side of his face, down over his now sunken cheek. The others were smaller and were scattered about his forehead, left cheek, and the side of his neck. A few he had received in his youth. "It took me a while to grasp the notion," he said to Grey when he began teaching his son the blade, "that defense was just as important as offense. Without it, you might never get to do those more enjoyable attacking techniques."

Grey smiled at the memory as he covered his father's hand with his. As they had done so many times since Grey was a boy, they enjoyed each other's company in silence, finding words superfluous.

Whenever his father, a career Army man, was home, he went to Grey's martial arts training, beginning when the boy was seven years old until he got his driver's license at 16. Even then, his father would come to watch his practice whenever he could.

When Grey turned 18, the old man began teaching him the art of the blade. His father had learned knife fighting in the military, first during his years in the Philippines, where he studied with masters of kali, and during his four tours in Vietnam serving with the Green Berets. There he studied with two Vietnamese and a Laotian, all master level blade fighters who taught him how to survive in the hell of Vietnam.

Besides teaching his son what he called "the way of slicing and dicing," the old man also imparted awareness skills, alertness, surveillance, and counter-surveillance.

Neither son or father knew then how vital his training would be when years later, Grey enlisted in the Army and served two tours in Afghanistan. He was fortunate to have three Army buddies who trained in the martial arts. One practiced Hung Gar kung fu, another a street-oriented taekwondo style, and a rough kid from New Mexico, named Ortega, practiced what he called "street blade."

Learning hung gar improved Grey's hand techniques, taekwondo worked his kicks even when wearing heavy combat gear, and Ortega kept Grey's already impressive knife skills sharp and real. Ortega, who had grown up on tough streets, often said, "Thinking knife fighting is about fighting—like two drunks in a pub or kids on a street corner—will get you hurt or killed. Knife fighting is about survival. That is the mindset you must have to live."

Grey was part of a team that was sent on four secret missions in Afghanistan, jobs that didn't appear on paper, and would be denied any knowledge of by everyone involved. All of them required stealth and silence, and in the end, Grey killed 13 men with his blade. On the last mission, he was slashed across his left forearm and chest, and stabbed in his left thigh. He killed two men and a woman to make his escape, then helped a seriously wounded buddy across nine miles of rocky terrain in the dark to their pick-up point.

Grey didn't receive a medal, a word of thanks, or acknowledgment because, according to Army records or the lack of them, it didn't happen. His scars would argue that.

"I think I have been a good man," his father said in a voice so faint that Grey barely heard the words. The old man's eyes were still closed.

"Of course, you have been," Grey said quickly, his hand patting his father's. "And I think I'm a good man because of you. You were a wonderful father."

The old man opened one eye as if it pained him to do so. "Being a good father was important to me. I… I want—" he bunched his face and drew in a sharp breath.

Grey reached for the bottle of fentanyl next to the clown's oversized shoes. The drug was the most potent pain killer Grey could get on the street. "Father," he whispered, looking into the empty container. "You have already taken the last two tablets.

"Well, it hurts," the old man managed just before another thunderbolt of pain ripped through his lower abdomen. When his breath returned, he groaned, "I can handle anything but pain."

"Your scars would suggest otherwise," Grey said. "I'll get you some fentanyl from Doctor Feel Good."

"Wait, son." The old man opened one eye and quickly squinted it closed as another pain passed through him.

"You don't have to hurt."

"It's part of the experience, no?"

"No, father. It isn't."

"How would *you* know? But just wait." He extracted his thumb out from under his son's palm and rested it on top of Grey's hand. He inhaled, his face clenching as another wave rocked his dying body. "Tell me how I was a good father."

Grey lowered his head close to his father's. "You looking for a compliment?"

The corners of his father's lips turned up a little. "Mostly."

Grey straightened, looked at the tears of rain rolling down the black window, then back down at his father. "When I was a boy, you always took time for me when you came home on leave. Always. You came to my football games, you taught me Green Beret combatives to surprise my training partners, and we drank beer out on the balcony."

"Much to your mother's dismay."

"Yeah, but I think that was a front. Mom liked the idea of her husband and young son having a brew. But she didn't like us smoking cigars on the balcony that time, remember?"

The old man closed his eyes, and Grey knew this time it wasn't from the cancer gnawing on his pancreas. "Oh yes, she chewed my butt over that. She hated cigarette and cigar smoke." He smiled briefly. "My God, she was a beauty, wasn't she?"

"She was, father."

"And she was one tough cookie too."

"Oh, yes."

They sat in silence again.

Grey's mother was killed in the second wave of missile attacks three years back.

Grey had gone into his parents' backdoor and found a note she had written to his father. It said she had gone to EasyMart to try to get supplies. Grey had experienced the food line there twice in the past two weeks and knew things could get ugly.

Ugly described just about everything in the tense days after the first missile attack.

She had written the time on the note, 9:15; she had been there an hour. That meant she was still in the line just to get into the store.

He jumped into his pickup and stomped the throttle hard, his sense of agitation growing by the minute. Something was going to happen at the store—a riot in the line, a shooter, or worse, another missile attack.

Public radio, television, the Internet, and cell phones no longer worked. Ham operators couldn't agree if the attacks were from the Middle East, North Korea, or Russia. Some operators insisted it was all of the above. One conspiracy theorist claimed the attack came from our own government, and there was more coming until their sick objective was met. Whatever that was.

Grey was living on the other side of town from his parents, and he tried to check on them every other day, sometimes every day. They were both in their mid-70s, healthy, but the strain of recent events was showing on them. On Grey too.

Gas was no longer available at service stations. Grey's buddy, a prepper who had underground tanks, was getting more and more reluctant to share. Out of necessity, Grey was planning on moving in with them in a few days.

He was about five blocks away from the store when he heard the explosions, one coming from the east, one from the west, and another behind him. He couldn't see them, but the blasts shook his truck, though he was going 60 MPH. He was on 12th Avenue when he saw the black smoke tumbling into the air above a three-store building. The store was on the next block.

He skidded around a corner onto 13th Avenue, swerved around one pile of debris, but bottomed out on another before he could avoid it. The store was completely engulfed in flames and smoke, as was the devastated neighborhood that stretched out behind it; black smoke wafted everywhere.

Then he saw the crumpled bodies, at least a hundred of them, and limbs, torsos, heads, all burning. He saw only one living person, his clothing burned off, and his skin charred black. He was reaching upward with charred arms as he screamed at the sky, cursing God.

Grey found his mother, her thin frame curled around a fire hydrant half a block away from the market, the blast no doubt launching her along the sidewalk and into the yellow cast iron. What looked like hundreds of shards of glass had stabbed into the back of her head, neck, torso, and legs.

He cried out and fell to his knees, and he wailed as his bleeding hands angrily pulled the shards from her body.

He stayed next to his mother for the rest of the day and all that night. Missiles continued to strike, some distant, some closer, the ground trembling as if it were one extended earthquake. But no more landed in the same area as the ones that killed his mother.

In the afternoon of the second day, he carried her to his pickup and laid her in the back. But the truck wouldn't start.

That night, groups of people marauded through the streets searching through the rubble of the destroyed neighborhood. From inside his pickup, he watched as they picked through the clothing of the dead and stripped their fingers and wrists of jewelry.

How quickly civilization was breaking down, he thought.

Around midnight, he lost his fight to stay awake. Sometime later, he awoke, startled and confused as to why his truck was shaking. He looked out the windshield, but all was dark. When his vehicle shook again, he scrambled out the door, the interior light barely illuminating a man behind his tailgate—going through his mother's pockets.

Grey's cry was primal, his intent murderous, but after hitting the man twice, his strength and rage were gone, and he collapsed against the side of his truck sobbing. The man, middle-aged and chubby, his eyes wild with fear and confusion, said through his own tears, "Forgive me, son. This isn't me." He opened his hand and let his mother's coin purse drop onto the tailgate. "This isn't… God help us…" And with that, he ran off into the dark.

Deciding he would have to temporarily leave his mother in his truck, Grey commenced walking back to his parent's home, a journey of horrors and sorrows that were similar to ones he witnessed in bomb-wasted villages in Afghanistan. The block where he had grown up—the street, the sidewalks, the park—were gone. He wouldn't have recognized his family home if he hadn't seen his father digging through the rubble.

He looked up when Grey called to him, his dusty face tear-stained, his eyes distant. "Don't worry, son. Your mother's fine. She called my name twice. It sounded far away, but I know it came from under this stuff. She's always been a tough cookie."

That night, when Grey went back to where his mother had died, the truck, his mother, and several of the bodies were gone. He never saw her again.

The distant sound of gunfire brought Grey back to the small room with his father. The old man was sleeping, his hand still gripping Grey's forearm. Gunshots—single shots and automatic gunfire was night music since The Change; it was only a concern if it was occurring nearby.

He looked up at the window from where he sat just in time to see lightning illuminate the low sky for a moment and a dark helicopter moving beneath the black, tumbling canopy. He looked back down at the old man.

Grey's father served 18 years with the United States Army Green Berets, his last tour in Vietnam cut short when a grenade destroyed his left eardrum and blew off most of his left arm. A few years later, the man with the cleaver sliced off the same ear.

His father fought his forced disability retirement, but in the end, he lost. He had been home only six months, when a midnight phone call asked him to meet a man dressed in a Hawaiian shirt at the Lucky Lady Bar, four miles from his home. "We have work for you," the caller said. He told him that his superiors were fully aware of his exemplary work in the hairiest parts of North Vietnam and Laos. They knew of his ability to work covertly and keep his mouth shut after. The private contractor didn't elaborate on how he knew about his military record, but in the world of shadow operatives, reputations got around.

The contractor said, "The work is ethical, we can promise you that. It requires a man of your skillset, experience, and knowledge.

The pay will take care of you and your family far better than your disability payments."

Already bored with civilian life, Grey's father took the job, which kept him away from home for six months. When he returned, he had changed, physically and in deportment, more so, according to Grey's mother, than when he came home from Vietnam for the last time. He was distant, at times, almost zombie-like, and there was a new hardness in his eyes that had begun to soften during his six months healing from his injuries in the war. He never told his wife what he did, other than to vaguely comment that he had rescued U.S. government people taken prisoner. One night, years later and after his father had been drinking, he told Grey that he had terminated people who would have harmed America.

Grey never saw his father apply his skillset in a real confrontation. There was one time when young Grey thought he was about to, but the moment turned into a better lesson.

He was riding with his parents when a pickup abruptly pulled in front of them and stopped. The driver, a potbellied bearded man stormed out of his cab, grabbed a 2 X 4 board out of the bed of his truck, and stomped toward them. "Stay in the car," his father said barely above a whisper. He got out and moved up to the front fender where he stood motionless, his lone arm down at his side, the hand empty.

The road-rager stopped about ten feet away, his board at the ready, his eyes studying the man he assumed would jump back in his car and cower. After a few seconds, the bully's face visibly paled, his eyes blinked rapidly, and he stumbled back a step, though Grey's father hadn't moved or said a word. He simply watched. The man retreated another step, spun about, took a couple of strides toward his truck, and looked back; his face perplexed as well as frightened. The man tossed the board back into the bed of his pickup, scrambled in behind the wheel, and burned a little patch of rubber as he left.

Months later, when Grey asked him about the incident, his father said simply, "Sometimes there's power in silence and a look." Twelve-year-old Grey was disappointed he didn't see him in action, but when 18-year-old Grey thought about how composed his father had been when facing an armed threat, how the calm intensity in his gaze must have looked to the bully, he decided it was about the coolest thing ever.

Someone yelling down on the street brought him back to his father's bedside. The old man stirred and looked up at him. "It was one of my greatest pleasures to add to your martial arts journey, son."

"Thank you for that," Grey said.

"It was all I had to share with you."

"No father, you taught me much more than just the martial arts. Most of all, you taught me to be a man, to be humble, and how to love. I hope one day to love a woman as much as you loved mom."

"I can see how you love Tala."

"It shows?"

"Very much. Treat her like a queen."

"Yes, sir."

The old man took a deep breath and exhaled it slowly. "I am proud you absorbed the few things I taught you so well." He winced in pain. Then, "You took so quickly to the martial arts, what you learned from your teachers and from me. You know, everyone in my unit in 'Nam always talked about my speed, but I wished they could have seen you move. Extraordinary."

He scrunched his face again, but a smile quickly took its place. "Remember when we went to that Krav Maga school across town? You were just sixteen, I think, but you had been training for what, ten years or so? I asked the teacher if you could spar with him or one of his advanced students. I must have violated some protocol because the instructor took it as a personal challenge."

The old man grinned, chuckled, which made him cough. Grey wanted to tell him not to talk, but he knew he would anyway.

"You took it easy on him at first, but when he started landing some hard blows, you looked over at me, and I nodded. Remember?" He squeezed Grey's arm as his shoulders shook with constrained laughter. "You handed his swaggering ass to him, you did. Then his senior student came to his rescue like he thought he was in a Chinese chop-socky movie defending the Shaolin Temple."

Grey smiled at how the memory seemed to energize his father.

"He started out like it was a real fight, but you quickly showed him what *real* meant. He was unconscious for several minutes, remember?" His shoulders shook again. "That was a good time for me."

Neither spoke. Grey was the first one to sniff.

"I wasn't sure—" A hard cough reddened the old man's face. When he finally stopped, "I wasn't sure if I wanted to teach you the blade. But in my gut, I knew that the world was turning bad. The wars, the crazy things politicians were doing, the way countries were turning on one another, all of it. I had to teach it to you because I knew, I *knew,* you would need it."

"I'm here because of what you taught me," Grey said when his father didn't continue. "It saved me in Afghan and several times since The Change."

"You're thirty-seven now. So you were seventeen when you began learning the weapon."

"Eighteen, father. I remember because you said at eighteen, I could go to prison if I used my knowledge for anything but self-defense." He looked at the old man's powerful hand that still held his forearm. "You said in prison, I would have to take showers with muscular men with tattoos, and they would like me—a lot."

The old man chuckled. "I didn't say that?"

"You know you did," Grey said, laughing. He raised his closed first. "I remember your ten precepts." Grey lifted his thumb. "One. You can cut anything. If the question is 'Can I cut here?' The answer is yes." Grey raised his index finger. "Two. Keep moving. It's hard to detect movement from movement." His middle finger went up. "Three. Vary your attacks: the type and the angle. Don't form patterns." His ring finger lifted. "Four. Drill on timing and footwork. Without them, you can't get to the target." He raised his little finger. "Five: If you have a choice, run away from an attacker with a knife."

Grey raised his other fist. "Six—"

"Okay, stop kissing up to the teacher. You were a good student."

"Good?" Grey teased.

"Alright. Very good." The old man smiled, but it quickly turned into a grimace. "The times necessitated that I teach you—" he snapped his head from side to side. "To…protect yourself and…

"Oh, my—" The old man groaned loudly and arched his back. He squeezed Grey's forearm so tightly that he thought his bone might snap. The years of knife training had given his father a great hand and forearm strength, even in death.

Grey tolerated it and whispered, "Shall I get the fentanyl?"

The old man, eyes squeezed shut, nodded almost imperceptibly. "Just three. I won't need more."

Grey stood and turned away quickly to hide the tears streaming down his cheeks. He slipped on his brown jacket and picked up the sheathed Mossy Oak Survival knife with a 15-inch blade from atop the dinette. He pulled it partway out of its sheath the same way a handgun enthusiast would check that his magazine was in place. The blade was black, razor-sharp on one side, serrated on the other. The handle was full-tang, non-slip rubber.

His choice of knives always included a guard to prevent the hand from sliding down over the blade. A person might get away with one thrust into a human body without a guard, but a second one would be dangerous. When the knife is slick with blood, the stabber's hand will likely slide down over the blade and slice deeply into the fingers and palm.

Grey had seen it happen nearly a dozen times, often on the first stab when the blade was abruptly stopped by bone, but the hand kept moving down the razor-sharp steel. Once in high school, he saw a punk kid thrust a large double-sided knife into the principal's car tire and nearly cut off three of his own fingers.

His father once said that while man has reached great heights of warrior achievement, knife makers still create cutting weapons without guards that do more harm to the stabber than the one stabbed.

"I'm off to see Doctor Feel Good," Grey said, looking back at him. The old man's eyes were squeezed shut as another wave of pain blasted through him. "I'll make it as quick as possible." Either his eyes were closed from the pain, or he had fallen asleep. Grey wiped his eyes, unlatched the four locks on the door, and slipped out.

He worked his way down the stairwell from the fourth floor, stopping on the second landing to see if the man lying next to the bottom step, his head haloed in blood, was dead or alive. Dead.

Grey bent down and looked closer. It was Jacobs who lived on the same floor as he and his father. His skin was cool. Two sets of bloody rat prints led away from the pool and disappeared into a fist-sized hole in the peeling wall. It must have happened in the last hour or two because if it had been longer, there would have been dozens of bloody prints.

He looked up the stairwell. The poor bastard must have dived headfirst the 20 steps to the marble floor. Suicides in these times were as common as the rodents who fed on them. So were natural deaths and murder. They bodies dotted the streets and sidewalks every day.

Grey was no long affected by finding the dead.

He held onto the handrailing as he stopped over the dead man. He would tell the landlord when he got back.

He stopped on the ground floor and listened against the door that led outside. The streets were always dangerous, more so at night.

When Grey was in college a lifetime ago, a professor lectured that even if there were suddenly no laws, humankind would remain lawful. "Humans want and need order to survive as a species."

Grey wondered how that theory was working out for him now.

Those who believed that people were inherently law-abiding quickly discovered after The Change that without government, law enforcement, or military, people—hurting, hungry, angry, and hopeless—found violence to be the way. Those who refused to adapt quickly became victims and are mostly all gone now.

Improvise, adapt and overcome. Hang on to the old way and perish.

There were no windows in the door that led outside. Three weeks ago, Grey had opened it without listening first and literally bumped into a man beating another with a tire iron. The man spun around, cocked the bar back over his shoulder, but never got a chance to do more. After Grey's powerful fingers speared into his insane eyes, the man dropped the tire iron and ran off, screaming and banging into things.

With the door open, a new set of gunshots sounded louder than the previous ones. They were coming from his left about three blocks away. Maybe closer. He heard shouting coming from the next block over, at least a half dozen voices. A fight, Grey figured. An attack. A killing.

He eased the door open wider.

Hard panting and the sound of rapid clicks.

He pushed the door partially closed, leaving just a crack to see a pack of wild dogs charging past, five, six, seven of them. No, there was one more, a dog limping badly, whining as it tried to keep up with the rest. They were all big dogs, emaciated and matted with filth. In two days, maybe just one, the first seven would make a meal of the slow, injured one.

He felt a tug at his heart as he remembered Sampson, his white, lovable seven-pound Maltese he had as a boy.

Little dogs didn't survive The Change.

He opened the door again. No dogs, no people. Since Grey had gone upstairs earlier in the evening, a warming fire in a 50-gallon drum had been knocked over, its ashes and embers scattered about the street, a curl of white smoke disappearing into the dark. He wondered what happened to the three men standing around it. When Grey had unlocked the door to go in, one of them had demanded where he was going. Grey answered by flipping the flap of his jacket back to reveal the big handle of the Mossy, and that was that.

He scanned the empty street and sidewalk across from him and to the left. Except for a dimly lit intersection a block and a half to the right, it was impossible to see far in any direction. The dog pack moved into the lit intersection, sniffing the ground, the air, and looking into the darkness. Two of the animals began to fight, howling, rolling and thrashing, and then just as quickly stopped and went about sniffing the pavement again. Abruptly, all of them jerked their heads in the direction opposite of where Grey was. The biggest dog headed out first, followed by the rest, the injured one trailing.

Doctor Feel Good was in that same direction. Hopefully, the dogs were heading beyond it.

Grey moved along the wall of the building, his feet crunching on debris, glass, and something soft and squishy. A dead rat, probably.

More gunshots, a rifle. From which direction he couldn't tell.

Flashlight batteries were rare, but even if he had one, a moving light in the thick blackness would make him a target for dog packs, gangs, and anyone wanting the light for their own.

When someone had something, others wanted it; many would kill to get it.

He was a few steps short of the first dark intersection when he felt a presence. He had learned to trust his gut instinct because more times than naught, it was right.

It felt like eyes on him, watching.

He stopped at the edge of the building and observed. He noted everything to his front, the street behind him, and across the way where the mass of a six-story building made the darkness even blacker. His senses were telling him that he was being watched from there.

The feeling weakened…and was gone. It was probably an animal, curious about Grey for a moment, then losing interest. A rat or dog, possibly. The dog packs liked cats, so there weren't many around anymore.

Grey watched the intersection for several minutes before his senses told him it was safe to cross.

CHAPTER 2

LEATHERS

Leathers watched Grey from inside the abandoned check-cashing business across the street. He could see him through the broken window, but he knew Grey couldn't see him in the totally dark room. He had tested it earlier from where the Knife Fighter's son stood now. He had been waiting in the room for four hours.

He heard the rattle of gunfire from somewhere a few blocks away. He watched Grey hesitate at the building's corner, look behind him, over where Leathers was secreted, and then press himself flat against the building again. Now he heard several people shouting, but it was difficult to determine from what direction. All were the usual night sounds made salient in the dark silence.

Leathers was a big man, six foot two, 180, hard, and experienced in violence. He was 44 years old, and while he had lived a fierce existence, he was scar-free. Fear the handsome, unblemished man in a vicious world, his only friend had once mused. He had been talking about himself, but Leathers thought it fit him too.

Grey looked in all directions, then again toward Leathers. He knew Grey couldn't see him, but he seemed to be trying to concentrate. Might he be feeling my eyes? Leathers wondered. My intent? He had known men who could do that; he wished he could.

Just in case, Leathers looked down at the floor and thought of his feet, though he couldn't see them in the dark. He visualized his boots, the creases in the aging leather, the scuff marks on the top, how the heels were worn down on the right sides. A few seconds later, he looked up.

It worked. Grey, apparently no longer sensing him, was moving toward the intersection, his eyes checking every direction. He wondered how many knives he was carrying. Two? Three? He watched him move quickly across the street and blend into the darkness. There was a faint light down the block in another intersection. He would wait until he saw Grey pass through it before he moved out.

Five minutes later, he did just that, his head virtually rotating on his shoulders as he disappeared into the darkness again. He knew of Grey's skill, and he hoped he would never have to face him blade to blade.

Leathers moved to the left side of the window to check the red door Grey had exited. The sidewalk was clear. The only indication of the bloody fight the three men had earlier was the overturned barrel in the street. He didn't see what caused the brawl with sticks and stones, nor did he care. There were a thousand acts of violence going on every minute of every day in the destroyed city.

He didn't mind it; Violence fed his belly, and it gave him pleasure.

He stepped out onto the sidewalk. A single shot rang out from somewhere, but not close enough to worry about. He looked over at the paint-chipped red door and lifted his eyes to the fourth floor. The dim, yellowish light gave shape to the square window as it had all night. Leathers wondered if that was apartment 415.

He headed toward the door for the second time this night.

CHAPTER 3

GREY

Grey was about 15 yards from the dimly illuminated intersection when he heard movement from behind him. He quickly flattened himself against a door, only to grab the facing to keep from falling into the room. Thankfully, the partially open door didn't squeak or bang against something. He backed into the room, his hand on his sheathed knife as four people passed by the window. The last one looked into the windowless frame, but the dark was too deep for the passerby to see anything. They were teenagers, all walking with purpose and a perceived strength in numbers.

Grey had faced many such gangs before. Some of those times, the attackers fled with one or two fewer members. On one occasion, there were no survivors to flee.

He listened until their footsteps and laughter died away, then moved over to the door and peeked out. The parking lot across the street looked clear, though it was too dark to know for sure. He stepped out into the inset and looked around the corner in the direction the boys had gone. They were past the lighted intersection and disappearing into the dark. One of them was hooting like an owl.

Grey heard the whisper-quiet of a helicopter somewhere to his left, its interior lights off to reduce its visibility. A spotlight from the craft fell to the ground, swung forward and back for two seconds, then extinguished, leaving only blackness where it had been. It was about five or six blocks over, Grey guessed.

About six months ago, he was in his apartment watching a man down in the street shoot at a helicopter that left its spot on too long. The round blew out the light, but the craft moved on, its props barely audible. The man's friends, about half a dozen of them, cheered.

Twenty minutes later, Grey heard two helicopters approaching his street. He knew there was going to be payback, but before he could take cover in his bathroom, his room lit up brighter than the noon hour. Bursts from multiple automatic weapons fired from overhead, while down below, people shouted and screamed. He stayed in the bathroom until dawn. When he dared to look out his window, he counted seven dead, men and women. Fresh chunks of shot up asphalt and cement combined to the usual garbage.

No one seemed to know who flew the helicopters or why they shined their lights down on people. Many thought they were some form of government; others said they were a Gestapo-like police force. Asking questions was dangerous, so most didn't talk about it and survived the best they could in their own space.

Grey was close to Doctor Feel Good now, but he paused to look at the empty dark street again. He let his eyes move up the building straight across from him. Twelve stories, but only two of the windows were dimly lit, one on the third floor and one on the 12th. Others were probably occupied, but they were using something to blackout their windows.

People didn't stay in one place too long; the lack of sewage made any dwelling uninhabitable within a couple of weeks. Grey was thankful that he and his father found an apartment building with occasional electricity and a way to get water and get rid of sewage. Three years ago, such amenities were taken for granted. Today they were rare luxuries.

He never strayed far from the neighborhood, or "sector" as they were called now. He didn't know who labeled them as such or how the areas were apportioned. For the first year after The Change, he hiked all over. At first, he only did day hikes, later two-days, eventually working up to a week. He just wanted to see with his own eyes what had happened to his city and, if possible, beyond it. But no matter which direction he went and no matter how far, all he found was death, destruction, hunger, illness, and brutality.

One time, he hiked what he thought was about 15 miles and found a neighborhood where there wasn't a living soul. The homes were undamaged, but the dead, thousands he guessed, lay spoiling on the streets, sidewalks, in crashed cars, and inside homes.

It had been more than he could absorb, and he ran from the neighborhood, and he didn't stop until he fell from exhaustion about four miles from his apartment.

It was unknown who sent the missiles three years ago. After a while, it didn't matter. If the United States responded simultaneously, it was likely that much of the world, or all of it, had been sent back to the early 1800s.

So much was unknown. Why did the skies drip black muck three years after the attack? Why was there heavy destruction in some sectors and others were untouched? Why were some people blown into a fine mist, while others were hit with germ warfare?

With so many unanswered questions and no way to get them, most people preferred to expend their depressed energy on survival. But that just raised another question: Why? Why continue to survive? Hope? Faith?

Faith in what?

The alley was about 20 yards from the intersection where the flickering streetlamp cast a dim, eerie light. Why this light worked to some degree, Grey never understood, but he was glad it did because its existence served to mark distance at night. He passed through the intersection without issue and hurried to where the weak streetlight didn't reach. There was comfort in the black. "Darkness is our friend," his buddies in Afghanistan used to say.

He paused for a moment, looking back to ensure no one passed through the light, then he quick-peeked around the edge of a building and into the alley; he saw only deep black.

He paced out seven strides, stopped, and slid his foot around until he felt the manhole cover. He bent and rapped his knuckles on it two times, paused, rapped three times, paused, four more times, and waited.

"Who's your daddy?" came the echoed voice.

"You are, always," Grey said, giving the proper response. The raps and pauses were Grey's signature, but Doctor Feel Good always wanted further authentication.

"What do you need, Grey?"

"Fentanyl. Three pills," Grey said, kneeling and talking to the manhole cover.

"I'm sorry," the echoed voice said softly, understanding why the small number. "I still got to charge you, though. The usual three nine-millimeter rounds per tab."

"I have them." Two shots rang out, and Grey reflexively turtled his head. They sounded close, maybe two blocks away.

"Standby."

Grey stood and walked over to the entrance to the alley. He leaned out a little and looked right and left. It was too dark to see anything to the right, but to the left, the lighted intersection was empty. He brushed his wrist against his sheathed Mossy Oak knife attached to his belt on his right side. The 15-inch blade was ultra-sharp and serrated on the top. The serrated part caught on his clothing occasionally, but the psychological power of the knife had stopped many threats in their tracks.

So had its sharpness.

"Grey?"

He looked back into the dark alley and saw Doctor Feel Good's bald head sticking up out of the hole. The light was shining upward out of the old sewer line, casting an evil glow on the man's face, accentuated by his Fu Manchu mustache that hung down past his jawline. "Here you go," he said, extending a palm with three dark capsules.

Grey took them and dropped nine 9mm cartridges into the man's grimy hand. "Thanks. Are you doing okay, Doc?"

"Hell no. Are you?"

Grey smiled faintly. "What options do we have, huh?"

"I'll be here next Wednesday at the same time for two-hours." He lowered his head and scraped the heavy cover back into place.

Grey pocketed the pills and moved back over to the edge of the alley. All clear in both directions, at least as much as he could see. He went left, moved quickly through the flickering streetlight, and back into the darkness again.

I'll be here next Wednesday. His father wouldn't need them then.

He was about 50 feet from his apartment building when a gaunt man emerged from the darkness, his image dimly lit by a haze of light from somewhere. Grey bladed his body, his right side forward. He scratched his chest with his left hand to draw the man's eyes to the movement as his right hand pushed aside his jacket flap.

"Excuse me, sir," the man said, his voice thin, hoarse. "Do you have any food? Anything."

Grey looked into his face but watched his hands in his periphery. He appeared ill, malnourished, and his clothes were tattered and dirty. He seemed too feeble to be a physical threat, but real hunger makes people desperate, dangerous.

"What's your name, sir?" Grey asked, violating a rule of the street. People could volunteer their name, but it was best not to ask because it was considered an intrusion of personal space.

"James Davidson. My wife was murdered two months ago, and two of my children too. The same people did it." He spoke without self-pity. Might that mean he was acting?

Grey's instincts told him the man had accepted his cruel fate, a vital part of survival.

"Where are you staying, James?"

"Walnut and Watkins Place. In a basement. My nine-year-old is there. I'm afraid if he doesn't get food…"

That was the direction in which Grey had twice heard the helicopter this night. "Did you hear a helicopter?" Grey tested.

He nodded. "Twice tonight. It seemed like they were right over my head. They didn't shoot, though. I saw them shoot before. Once at night and one time during the day. So frightening. No one knows who they are. Do you?"

Grey eyed him for a moment. He believed him. "No. Listen, two blocks over in the old Barnes and Noble bookstore, you can buy food from a guy named Fat Phil. He's not fat now, but word is he used to be. There will be other people out front. Some are desperate, so watch yourself. You got something to trade?"

"Only matches. Wooden ones. I got three boxes."

"That might help." Grey reached across his body with his left hand, leaving his right one down at his side by his Mossy Oak, and went into his jacket pocket. He retrieved three 9 mm bullets. "Here. This might get you some meat if he has it."

"Sweet, sweet, Jesus," the man gasped, his trembling hand accepting the bullets. He closed his fingers around them, covered it with his other hand, and brought both to his chest. "Thank you," he whispered. "I haven't experienced kindness for a long time. I'm so afraid for my son."

"Watch yourself, James," Grey said, backing toward the door.

"Pay it forward when you get the opportunity. I hope we meet again."

"Yes," James managed. "Yes." He moved off and was soon absorbed by the dark.

Caring, kindness, and generosity were often taken advantage of now, but Grey's gut told him that James was truthful.

His father said, "New days mean new rules. The war isn't 'over there' anymore, it's here. But you still must live with morals and ethics and compassion. Rockets have fallen and devasted our people, our cities and, for some, our humanity. You're a survivor, and you should contemplate that you might have been saved for a reason. So don't be like so many other survivors who have turned into rabid beasts. Hold onto your dignity. Be a warrior for good, for yourself and for others."

Grey took his father's words to heart. No matter what the circumstances, he would honor those who didn't survive by being the best man, the best human he could be.

He waited until he could no longer hear the man's footsteps before retrieving his key ring. He quickly unlocked the two lower bolts, all the while listening for anyone approaching from behind. Then he unlocked the two top locks. He looked to the right and left and slipped into the lobby and secured all four bolts again.

He thought of James as he took the first set of stairs. Not his legitimacy, Grey was good with that. But he should have sensed the man before he came into the light. Grey was usually so highly tuned to everything around him that he could feel someone near before the person made themselves known. Earlier, he felt he was being watched from across the street. Whatever it was—someone taking shelter or a frightened animal—they or it moved on without revealing themselves.

I can't slip up again, he thought.

On the second-floor landing, his neighbor Jacobs was still lying below the bottom step, but now he was closer to the wall, his head under the handrail. Someone had pushed him aside.

And there was a blood trail on the steps that continued to the next landing. Grey hurried up the stairs, stopped at the third-floor landing, and followed the blood around to the next set of stairs.

"Father," he said aloud, then ran up the rest of the way to the fourth floor. As he feared, the blood trail led to his apartment.

The half-open door was destroyed, the heavy deadbolts unable to withstand the force that smashed it. He heard a moan from inside.

"Father," he called, squeezing through the opening. "What—"

The old man was lying on his side on the floor, his knees drawn up to his chest, his white T-shirt soaked with blood, as was the sheet he had probably pulled down with him as he fell. Or when someone pulled him from the bed.

In his hand, his cleaver, the Bucknbear chopper knife that he got from the man who had cut off his ear. He often slept with it under his pillow. The rectangular-ish-shaped six-inch blade was red with blood.

His father's eyes were closed, his breathing wet and labored.

"It's me, Grey," he said, dropping down onto his knees next to him. "I…" He didn't know what to say. His father's blood oozed through his T-shirt in two places, over his chest, and his right side.

"S-s-son," the old man managed weakly, his eyes still closed. "I got… a ch-chunk of him…but not good enough to make him less da-dangerous."

"What can I do? I don't know what to do."

"Just si-si sit with me." He inhaled raggedly and eased it out with a faint whistle. "I thought I would go to-tomorrow. But the… b-b-bastard cheated me out of a few hours. That's…that's not right to do t-to a man."

"Who did it, father? Do you know?"

"A man named Leathers. Be…be careful, son. He's dangerous…"

The old man stilled.

Five hours later, another murky day had dawned on those still living. The dripping had stopped, and while there had been yelling down on the street earlier, it was quiet now.

Grey had wiped the blood from his father's bare torso—noting two 1½ inch long stab wounds, one an inch away from his heart and one on his right side. He had a few cuts on his wrist that Grey hadn't noticed when he first came in, which meant that even in his fragile state, his father had fought as well as he could with only one arm. A warrior to the end.

Grey dressed him in the blue sweatshirt and sweatpants he wore so often, combed his white, thinning hair, and wrapped him in a burgundy blanket. He scrubbed the blood from the bare floor, rinsing his rags in a water bucket. He stuffed the bloody sheet in their toilet bucket.

His next task was to go to Washington Street and see when Undertaker could take his father. The man so named lived in an old funeral home with a working cremation furnace. Because death on the streets was an everyday and every night reality, he stayed busy.

Grey suddenly felt drained, depleted. He wished his girlfriend, Tala, was here, but she was sitting bedside with a very ill sister who was about to pass. Grey sat down in an old brown leather chair. He sprawled his legs out in front of him, leaned his side against the chair's arm, and rested his head in his palm. He was instantly asleep.

He and his father were sitting on a park bench under a huge Weeping Willow tree. A light breeze cooled the shade, and Grey's sweat was beginning to dry after he had demonstrated several of his favorite fighting techniques.

"You look good, son," his father said. He had just returned after being gone for six months. Grey told him that besides the sessions with his sensei, he also trained three days a week with a friend who studied kenpo karate.

"Outstanding, troop. You're fast, explosive, and you have a grace that adds a distinctive beauty to your moves."

"Thank you, father."

They sat in quiet, the wind rustling the limbs of the umbrella-like Weeping Willow tree. It was a happy moment that had remained with him all these years.

The park was replaced by the image of his father dying on the floor of their apartment.

"Son."

Grey looked into his face as life ebbed from his eyes. "I thought I would go to-tomorrow. But the…b-bastard cheated me out of a few hours."

"Who did it, father? Do you know?"

"A man named Leathers. Be…be careful, son. He's dangerous."

Grey jerked awake. He was dripping sweat though he had forgotten to close the window, and the room was chilly. He looked at the blanket roll next to the bed, the shape of his father's body within. On the nightstand, next to the clown lamp, lay his cleaver, the Bucknbear chopper knife. Grey had wiped it clean.

Fully awake now, he thought of his dream and how happy he had been that day in the park.

On Grey's 18th birthday, his father went into his bedroom, returning a few minutes later carrying a lumpy manila envelope. He extracted a knife from it: USMC was engraved on the blade. Grey didn't know what kind it was then, but years later, he would learn that it was a Ka-Bar with a seven-inch blade and brown stacked leather handle.

His father looked down at it, his face hard. Grey reached for the knife, but his father pulled it back and shook his head, but not before the boy managed to see scratches on the blade next to the handle. At least a dozen of them.

"What do those mean, father?" he asked, though even in his 18-year-old mind, he knew.

His father looked at the knife for a long moment, his eyes glistening. "They mean nightmares for the rest of my life."

When his father went to the bathroom, taking the knife with him, Grey slid out a half dozen photos that extended over the lip of the envelope. They were typical military-type shots he had seen in the news and in magazines. But these were of his father sitting on a stack of sandbags, standing by a vehicle holding a firearm of some kind, and one of him in a fighting stance holding a big knife that looked like the one he just showed him. Written on the backs of all of them was, "To Knife Fighter, good luck on your next tour. Thanks for saving our sorry asses." Grey never saw the knife again in his parent's house, and he hadn't seen it since he and his father had been living together for the past six months that he had been sick.

When Grey was about 25, he and his father were having beers on the back deck of his parent's home. Grey asked, "Why did you let me see your Ka-Bar that time? Why so briefly, I mean?"

His father took two swigs before he answered. "I've asked myself that a few times. I guess… I think I wanted you to see what a killing blade looked like. Feel its aura. Its presence. But as soon as I pulled it out of the envelope, I no longer wanted you to see it, to know it existed.

"A blade that's killed is at once a hideous thing and a thing of beauty. Until it has killed, all the time you spend with it training, is all theory, play.

"Facing a deadly threat with a knife is a moment like no other. Suddenly you're no longer pretending as you have been in your training. Shit is real now, and to come out of it alive, you're going to have to ram that blade deep into human flesh. And you're going to *feel* that sensation in your hand, and that *feel* is going to remain in your hand, and in your mind, and the sight of him dying is going to stay in your eyes, even when you're asleep.

"I didn't want you to touch it or ever see it again."

CHAPTER 4

GREY AND UNDERTAKER

"Double damn. Sorry 'bout yur daddy." the man everyone called Undertaker said, opening the door a little wider so Grey could slip inside. He was a black man, about 70 years, slim, with arthritis of the neck and spine so bad it bent his torso forward about 45 degrees and forced the side of his head down onto his shoulder. Without the benefit of a tailor, the sleeves on his black jacket stopped about mid-forearm, accentuating his impossibly long arms and skinny fingers. Though his appearance would have been perfect in a low budget horror movie, his personality was that of a kind, caring man. "Come on to my sittin' room. Fella yesterday paid me with some tea. Believe that? Tea. Want some?"

"No, thanks, sir," Grey said.

Undertaker led him down the hall. "I always enjoyed your daddy's visits. Liked his stories. 'Course you know they called him 'Knife Fighter' over there in Vietnam. Had some excitement, he did. Going deep, sneaking around in the jungle to neutralize a leader, or to free American POWs. Mostly he had to do it real quiet-like, so he would use his 'Tennessee Tickler.' I can't recall what he called his knife, but Tennessee Tickler is what people called theirs when I was growing up in the Great Smokies. Anyway, I was in the Army, too, what they called Mortuary Affairs Specialist. That's where I learned my trade. I had to learn it fast in Vietnam because they kept us busy."

Undertaker turned around slowly. "I'm talking a hundred miles an hour because I don't want to cry in front of you. I will sure as hell, miss your daddy."

Grey nodded. "Me too."

Undertaker picked up a scrap of paper and a pencil stub. "Tell me where he is."

"Four blocks west. On Fourteenth, between Harney and Acorn. It's the four-story brown building with the name 'BAKER' engraved up near the roof. Room four fifteen."

"Know the building. Been there a few. Bob Marshall still running the place?"

Grey nodded. "Check with him first. They destroyed my door, so Bob is letting me move down the hall to Jacobs' place. I don't know Jacobs' last name. You'll find him lying on the second landing. I thought suicide at first, but with my father being… I'm thinking Jacobs might have gotten in the way." Grey squeezed his eyes shut. When he opened them, he said, "I'll pay for both."

Undertaker had stopped writing. "Are you saying your daddy was killed?" Grey nodded. "Damn, damn, damn! I know his health had been poor these last few months, so I just assumed he passed natural. A fine man like that!" He closed his eyes for a moment. "Your daddy was my friend. No charge. But I'll take something for Jacobs. It costs me to run the furnace."

His first thought was to offer Undertaker bullets. His father had worked some kind of a deal a year ago and brought home several cases of 9mm rounds. It had been a blessing, though Grey had the occasional moments of guilt about it. He usually got over it by convincing himself that people used them to save their life and the lives of their families.

"Would you like one of my father's knives?"

The Undertaker turned away and covered his eyes with his forearm. After a moment, he dabbed each eye with his palm and turned back. "It would be an honor."

"Before he passed, he said it was a man named Leathers that did it."

Undertaker nodded as well as he could with his ear resting on his shoulder. "Know the sumbitch, I do. Not personally nor even seen him in the flesh, but I've heard of him. Cremated seven of his victims over the past several months. Probably more, given the types of wounds, but there was no one at the scene to name him."

"Did my father know him?" Grey's voice was tight, his face too.

"One time, he came to visit, and I was about to cremate one of his victims, and I mentioned it to your daddy. He nodded like you would if you knew someone."

"What do you know about the man?"

Undertaker knuckled a tear off his cheek. "Let's see, heard he was in the Marines over there in Baghdad, Afghanistan, or some such. One of those elite outfits, but that might have been someone just inflatin' the story, you know. Me, I was just a 92-Mike, a Mortuary Affairs Specialist, but I guess I told you that. Anyway, I heard he was good with a knife. Heard he attacked his CO one day." Undertaker lifted his eyebrows. "That will sure as hell get you some time to cool off in a military prison. I don't know how long he was in, but I heard he got out a few months before The Change."

"'Good with a knife,'" Grey repeated under his breath. He had to have known about his father's skill, but did he know he was dying? Did father have some dealing with him before? Was Leathers avenging him? Was he hired? "You know where he lives? Where he goes? Where I can find him?"

The black man looked at Grey for a moment. Then, cupping the younger man's shoulder, he said, "An African proverb goes, 'The ax forgets, but the tree remembers.' This Leathers animal will forget what he did, but you'll always remember. So maybe the best revenge is to leave him be. Let him live to always be lookin' over his shoulder, always sweatin' that you're there in the dark comin' after him."

Undertaker stepped directly in front of Grey and looked up at him the best he could, the strain making his head tremble. "I don't want to be puttin' *you* in the cremation oven, son. Move away and focus on survivin' the best you can."

CHAPTER 5

GREY

Grey's father would be cremated the next afternoon. Undertaker said there were 22 bodies ahead of him, and that he had to take them in order so as to keep the odor of decay down. Grey would be there for it and bring with him one of the old man's favorite blades.

Undertaker had heard that Leathers hung out at a place called "Hades." He didn't know what it was or why it was called that, but he did know it used to be an old night club on Cleveland. He also heard Leathers frequented Bamboo Tunnel by Lincoln Park, not too far from Hades." Grey knew of it. His mother had taken him through it once as a child, a fantastic place made of towering bamboo. Undertaker said it was a jungle now full of predators.

After he left Undertaker's, he returned to his apartment and moved his and his father's few things down to Jacob's former place at the end of the hall. While he was at the funeral home, Bob, the landlord, covered Jacob's body with a blanket and moved his possessions out. Bob knew Grey's father had been sick, so his death wasn't a surprise. Grey had thoroughly cleaned up the mess, and he had disposed of the bloody water, crap bucket, and bloody sheet before he contacted him. Not wanting to get kicked out of the building for bringing violence to the place, Grey told him there was a break-in, and the burglar must have seen the body and left. Bob allowed Grey to leave his father in their old apartment for Undertaker.

The new one was a few square feet larger, and it had a slightly different view to include the intersection with the fluttery light. Grey liked the idea of seeing three streets from one vantage point.

Now, two hours later, he was standing at the corner of 20th and Fir, about a mile from his apartment. Grey decided to check Bamboo Tunnel first.

He proceeded along the sidewalk, mindful of doorway insets and any other structure that could conceal a threat. Had there been parked cars, he'd have to worry about threats hiding behind or between them. But it was rare to see a vehicle as most had long been stripped to non-existence. There was no need for them anyway since gasoline was as scarce as peace and happiness in the new world.

Grey felt uncomfortable, and he knew why. In the past year, he had stopped traveling more than 10 blocks from where he lived. He and his father had most of what they needed to survive—food, water, "currency," and contacts—within less than a mile in any direction. It was risky to go farther because he didn't know how things worked in other sectors. He was still in Sector 4, but he hadn't been this far east in a long while.

The streets here were similar to where he lived, but even a mile away felt foreign, and it made him feel naked. He sensed eyes peering out at him from the shadows and from windows in the broken high-rises above the sidewalks. Some lookers were just curious; others wanted whatever he might possess.

When Grey was about 10 or 12, with The Change more than 20 years in the future, he and his father would trek in the forests about a two-hour drive from where they lived. His father always told him that no matter how far they hiked, it was only half the journey because they still had to walk back out.

That was true today too, he thought, looking around at the eerily quiet city block. Fires had blackened some of the edifices, explosives turned others to crumbling shells, and of those still whole, bullets had perforated the walls and shattered windows. The asphalt streets and concrete sidewalks were broken, and debris-covered. Trees that once lined the streets had been cut flush with the sidewalks by survivors collecting fuel for fires or heat.

Graffiti was everywhere, most of it faded and chipped. Fresh scribblings were rare because markers and spray paint hadn't been manufactured since The Change. When there were new ones, they were often done in blood that had dried to rust/red.

He stopped just short of the intersection. Frequently stops prevented him from missing the small things overlooked when focusing only on the destination. Things like people trying to look nonchalant, usually just before they attacked in some way, or projectiles deliberately dropped from the floors above.

Three months earlier, he would have been struck by a dropped toilet if he hadn't stopped and looked in all directions. When he looked up, he saw the heavy commode rocketing passed the sixth floor. He managed to step a millisecond before it exploded against the concrete, sending a piece of porcelain shrapnel to slice open the back of his hand.

So many close calls, he thought, looking around at his new surroundings. He started to lean against the wall when his eye caught what looked like fresh longhand writing in rust-red next to him.

The earth is our mother
She gives birth to all living things
We must honor her to be worthy
She is sacred, beautiful, strong, and vulnerable
She must be protected from her greatest enemy
Her children of the human race. Signed, Black Elk

"A little late," Grey thought.
He sensed the man before he saw him.
Grey turned and stepped next to the wall to reduce the person's options. But the man was about 30 feet back, peering around the edge of a doorway. Grey looked at him for a few seconds to ensure the man knew he had been seen, and then he continued the rest of the way to the intersection, cognizant of everything around him.

He quick-peeked around the corner of the building. People, a dozen give or take, were gathered halfway down the sidewalk. Twice as many loitered across the street in front of the Bamboo Tunnel.

He flashed to when he was 12, and he and his mother were on this very street. She loved bamboo, and she wanted to see the block-long tunnel that city gardeners had designed, and that had been a big news story for several days. The area was crowded with people walking in and out of the green passageway formed by impossibly tall bamboo that extended for two blocks. As they walked it, his mother lectured him, and anyone else within hearing, on the types of bamboo, its history in Asia, and everything else. Grey's only thought was how cool it was.

Now, even from half a block away, it was apparent it was still a tunnel, its overgrowth having been crudely chopped back.

Grey turned about to face the man, now less than a dozen feet away. He startled as if he had intended to catch Grey by surprise. Then his mouth formed into an ugly smile, revealing dark, broken teeth. Above them, his eyes were as lifeless as a trout's. He started to step forward, but Grey's commanding voice stopped him. "Remain there."

The smile disappeared, then returned bigger than previously. "No, no, no," the man said quickly, extending his left palm. "You have nothing to fear from me." His eyes quick-scanned Grey from head to toe. The right side of Grey's jacket covered his sheathed Mossy Oak. The left side hung lower, and anyone with tactical savvy would suspect the difference was the weight of a possible weapon. When the man took a single step forward, Grey did the same with his right foot to blade his body, his right arm hanging loosely along his side, his left palm flat against his chest.

"No, no, no," the man said again, his left palm gesturing that all was well. "You got me all—"

"You need to move on," Grey said, his voice barely louder than a whisper. "We have nothing to talk about."

The man leaned forward a little. "I just never saw you before around here." His eyes had transitioned from a dead fish to radiating an internal hysteria indicative of a mind that was quite insane. The guy was a rocker, Grey thought, a word taken from an old expression meaning someone was "off their rocker." After The Change it was used to denote people who had gone mad. Grey and his father had often discussed how the name applied to about a third of the survivors.

The man giggled, and took a half step forward, almost in range of Grey. "I'm guessing you're here shopping. Yeah, you're looking for something. Food. A weapon. A woman." He leaned forward. "What you got for currency, newbie? Food? Seeds? Gas? Huh? What you got—"

"I said *go,*" Grey hissed, his eyes burning into the man, his right arm scooting the flap of his jacket back.

Grey's sudden intensity startled the man, and he stumbled back a step, his eyes flashing. He held his right hand along his side as did Grey, but his trembled and twitched.

Grey subtly scanned the area around them. Street brawls were common as the flies and rats, so most people ignored them or gave them only a passing glance. But the man might have friends, so this had to end now.

"Look," Grey said. "Let's end this. You head back down the sidewalk, and I'll continue in the other direction."

The man's hand snapped behind his back, to which Grey responded by taking a half step back as he gripped the handle of his still holstered Mossy. The man's hand came around holding a red-handled screwdriver, a Philipps. The head looked to have been ground to a needle-like point. He aimed it toward Grey. "Your c-c-currency," he said, his voice shaky. "G-give me your c-currency."

Grey let the flap of his jacket fall back over his Mossy, his eyes never leaving the man's face.

"I'm serious, man. Serious as a heart attack."

Crazy and untrained, Grey thought. The man was standing flatfooted, full body forward, and his empty hand was hanging at his side, instead of at the ready by his chest. He jabbed the screwdriver forward a few inches but three feet away from Grey, pulled it back, and jabbed it again, his white-knuckle grip so tight his arm was trembling. It was time to end this and do so without hurting him.

"I'm not giving you anything," Grey said calmly. "So that part of this conversation is settled. What happens next is up to you. Walk away, and the moment is forgotten. Force your demands, and the outcome will not be a good one for you."

Grey seldom made threats, but he wanted to give the rocker a way out.

The man lunged forward with respectable speed, thrusting his screwdriver like a fencer with a foil.

Grey sidestepped outside the extended arm and executed four moves in rapid succession.

He grabbed the man's wrist with his left hand.

Hammered his right bottom fist into the man's tender biceps muscle to numb the arm.

Yanked it straight again.

And slammed his forearm into the locked elbow joint, detonating a thousand nerves up and down the limb.

Grey kicked the dropped screwdriver into a pile of debris. "Now go the other way," Grey said, spinning the howling man around and kicking him in the butt. "Go!"

He watched the rocker stumble down the sidewalk, his hand cupping his injured elbow, his curses bluing the air. After a moment, Grey moved back to the edge of the building and quick-peeked around it again.

All remained the same: a few people still clustered halfway down the sidewalk on his side, and twice as many hung around the tunnel entrance across the street. He would walk partway down the block to see how much of a visual he had of the tunnel. Then he would cross over—

He felt the presence an instant before he heard the footsteps behind him. He spun around his hands up in front of him. The rocker was walking hard, his head bent forward with determination, his left hand gripping a carpenter's awl. Grey's father had one in his collection of "nasty pointy things," as he called them. This one looked to have a 7- or 8-inch stabbing point.

Grey waited until the man lunged—his body stretched out and off balance. He smoothly stepped to the side, so the awl's straight trajectory missed him by six inches. Then he cupped the back of the assailant's neck between his thumb and index finger and drove him down onto the filthy concrete, his nose and chin collecting a nasty road rash.

But the rocker acted as if he didn't feel it, and he slashed back at Grey's legs with the awl. Grey snapped up his closest one to avoid the weapon and then stomped down, aiming for the man's wrist. He missed.

The attacker retracted his hand and slashed back it at him again.

This time Grey jammed the arm's arc with his shin and stomped down on his forearm with his other foot, pinning it against the sidewalk. The rocker cursed and struggled to free his limb, but Grey's weight was too much, and the man's hyperextended right arm couldn't assist him.

For an instant, Grey thought about stomping down on the man's left elbow joint, but he quickly nixed the plan. He didn't want to disable the guy.

Not as thoughtful, the rocker twisted his body hard, his head close to the leg pinning his arm. Grey saw what he was about to do, and jerked it away, so the man chomped only into his pant leg.

The rocker swung the awl again.

Grey managed to catch his wrist before the pointy end, and its seven cold inches, punched through his tender calf muscle. Trying not to seriously hurt the guy was proving to be difficult.

"Okay, no more Mister Nice Guy," Grey said, not showing the slightest emotion as he slammed the man's fingers into the concrete. "Let go of the weapon," he commanded softly. When he didn't comply, Grey rubbed the man's knuckles back and forth on the sidewalk's rough surface, sanding off his skin and making a bloody smear on the walkway.

The man screamed, and the weapon rolled free.

Grey grabbed it with his other hand, placed it between his teeth, then dragged the man over to one of the tree stumps. He pinned the man's left palm on top of it, grabbed his right hand, and stacked it atop the left one, pressing down to keep them from moving.

Grey retrieved the awl from his mouth, gripping it like an icepick.

The man might have been a rocker, but he caught on. "Noooo! Wait, wait, wait… You can't…" Grey lifted the awl high in the air. The rocker bellowed this time: "NOOO!—"

The nasty pointy thing punched through the back of the man's top right hand with enough force that it exited the palm, speared through the back of his left hand, out the palm, and sunk its remaining inches into the old tree trunk.

Movement in Grey's peripheral. He jerked his head to the left.

"Tala," he breathed, smiling as the woman he had loved for the last two and a half years walked confidently across the street. Her long, shiny-black hair flowed behind her, and her smile brightened the gloom of the ashen sky.

"This is what happens when I leave you unsupervised," she said, walking up to him. She looked down at the man writhing like a trapped snake, both hands excruciatingly pinned to the stump. "Okay," she said, nodding. "That's original. Yup."

CHAPTER 6

LEATHERS AND THE HAMMER BROTHERS

Leathers was pissed and in terrible pain as he climbed the stairs past the second floor where he lived and up to the third floor where the Hammer Brothers and their wife had an apartment. The electronic, bone-numbing house music from Hades on the first floor usually soothed him and helped him sleep at night. But now it throbbed intensely into the terrible wound the old man had chopped into the side of his shoulder as if he were a woodsman and Leathers were a tree. He had tied his jacket around his armpit and shoulder as best he could, but it was a poor tourniquet that only minimally stopped the flow of blood.

He knocked on the door of apartment 333. "It's Leathers. I need some assistance."

He heard footsteps approach on the other side, stop, cloth brush against the door as the occupant looked through the peephole, and then the metallic clicking of a half dozen locks. The taller brother, Carlos, peered out through the narrow opening. "You alone?"

"I'm hurt, and I need Christina to help me. I also have work for you and Raul."

"What's the work?"

"I'm bleeding bad, Carlos," Leathers said, turning his shoulder toward him to let him see his blood-soaked sweatshirt sleeve. "Need some stitches."

Carlos opened the door far enough for him to extend his head out to check the hall both ways. He looked back at Leathers, his dislike for the man evident. "Yeah, come in."

Leathers stepped into the apartment and nodded at Raul, who was standing behind his brother. He was heavier than his younger sibling and half a foot shorter. Still, they looked eerily identical. Both men were Christina's common-law husbands, which Leathers thought was funny, especially considering that she flirted with him. "Hurt, huh?" Carlos asked rhetorically.

"Christina!" Raul called. "Bring the First-Aid kit." Then to Leathers, "How are you hurt?"

Leathers eyes stopped on a table next to a green, beat-up sofa on which lay four stubby claw hammers. The hammers' mirror-polished heads with short, black and yellow rubber-coated grips were the brothers' weapons of choice. It wasn't terribly original since "Hammer" was their last name. Everyone said the boys were as stupid as a box of them, so that explained it too.

"How are you hurt?" Raul asked again.

"Knife cut. More of a meat cleaver than a knife. Something's loose in my sleeve too." Leathers said all this without a grimace.

"Good day, Leathers," Christina said, smiling shyly at him, a small red case in her hand. She was Russian with a slight accent. "Oh!" she said, noticing his blood-sopped sleeve.

Leathers smiled at her, which didn't go unnoticed by Carlos. A few months earlier, Christina had subtlety flirted with Leathers when she and Raul had bumped into him on the second-floor landing. Raul only glared at them at the time, but when Leathers saw her two days later, she was sporting a black eye and swollen cheek. When she noticed Leathers' eyes flash anger, she quickly touched his arm and warned him to let it be.

"Help remove his jacket from his arm," she said to the brothers. "Very smart of you to make a tourniquet, Leathers. Careful, Raul. We don't want him to bleed more."

Leathers saw the brothers glance at each other in a way that said they wouldn't mind him bleeding more.

Leathers sharply inhaled as they removed the jacket. "Something fell into my sleeve," he said.

She stepped over to him. "Hold your arm straight down, please. Yes, like that." She used both of her hands to spread the sweatshirt sleeve wide. "Oh!" she said as a chunk of bloody flesh, about four inches long, an inch wide, and two inches thick dropped to the floor.

"That's why it hurts," Carlos said in a funny voice. Leathers glared at him

"Now remove his sweatshirt," she said to her husbands. "Gently."

Stripped to the waist, Christina and the brothers unabashedly stared at Leathers' torso. The wedge out of his shoulder did indeed look as if it were chopped away by a woodsman's ax. But what held their eyes was the cluster of old scars that formed a four-inch diameter circle around his navel.

"Shanking in juvenile detention many years ago," Leathers said by way of an explanation.

"Sit down here," Christina said, indicating a wooden chair by the window. "Carlos, please wet a rag and bring it to me." She looked at Leathers. "I don't have anesthetic or pain pills, but this needs to be stitched. The opening is so large it's going to be difficult, and it's going to hurt. I'm sorry."

"Understood," Leathers said, enjoying the feeling of her hand on his shoulder.

The pain was terrible, but he relied on a trick he learned from a cellmate when he was in his mid-20s. He would imagine a huge circle with a tiny dot at the bottom of it. The dot was his pain; the rest of his circle was his ability to carry on.

Thirty minutes later, Christina was about done, which was a good thing because his imagined dot had grown to half the size of the big circle.

"You mentioned a job," Carlos said. He and Raul had remained in the room, their eyes watching for any elusive communication between Christina and Leathers.

"Do you know of the one they call Knife Fighter?" Leathers asked, his voice strained a tad as the big stitching needle plunged in and out of his shoulder.

Raul nodded. "Yes, but we don't know if Knife Fighter is the father or the son. We saw the son once when we ventured into Sector Four looking for water. We only know it was him because we asked someone after we saw him cut a man many times who had tried to rob him of his food."

Carlos said, "The man we asked said some people called him Knife Fighter, but other people said it was his father's name."

"The father is gone now," Leathers said. "He attacked me, but I fought back hard. It was a long fight, and he cut me once, but I finally killed him." Leathers looked from Carlos to Raul to see if they were believing him. "Now his kid wants vengeance." He nodded at his shoulder and the ragged stitch work. "But I'm not at my best now."

"And you want…?" Carlos asked.

"To stop the son. Permanently."

"We'll do it for a gun," Raul said, looking at his brother. Carlos nodded.

"So rare to find," Leathers said. "I have a source I'm working on," he lied, "but until then, all I have are bullets. Forty-five caliber rounds. A hundred of them."

"Two hundred," Carlos said without hesitation.

"One hundred fifty is all I have."

"One hundred fifty it is then," Raul said.

"You two are tough negotiators," Leathers said, fighting not to smirk.

Carlos told Leathers they would do the job right away.

As he left their apartment, Leathers caught a glimpse of Christina over the shorter brother's shoulder from where she was cleaning up by the table. She shot him a quick smile.

Leathers translated it as a promise.

The acute pain throbbed in his shoulder and skull, and it made his eyes water as he made his way down to his apartment. Inside, he carefully and painfully put on a different sweatshirt, then gathered 150 rounds out of his stockpile of 600. He would give them to the brothers upon completion of the mission.

He stretched out on his bed and propped his injured arm on a pile of dirty clothing. He closed his eyes and reflected on how the hit on the old man had gone down.

When he did his reconnaissance, Leathers figured he would have to force his way into Knife Fighter's apartment building. But just as he neared the red door, a woman walked out, and he was able to slip in before it closed. She called through the door that he wasn't allowed in, but he ignored her.

On the third landing, a man confronted Leathers, who said he was a friend of the landlord and demanded to know what he was doing in the building. Leathers told him he was looking for his brother's room, but he wasn't sure if he even had the right apartment building. The man must have been oblivious to Leathers' muscular neck, thick chest, and broad shoulders because the smaller man grabbed him by the back of his collar as if to force-walk a street drunk off the premises.

Leathers swung his closest arm up and over the man's elbow, trapping his limb, then slammed his fist into the center of the man's face, exploding his nose like a water balloon. When the man bent over clutching his face, Leathers hip-bumped him, sending him tumbling down the stairs head over heels until his head clanked into the metal post at the next-to-last step.

Leathers stood fast for a long moment to see if anyone would come out into the hall. When all remained quiet, he stealthily moved up to the fourth floor. Noting that 415, Knife Fighter's apartment, was halfway down the hall, he hurried back down the stairs, stepped over the stupid man and his death rattle, and left the building.

Five minutes later, he was standing in the dark of a former check-cashing office less than 75 feet from the red door across the street. He was hoping he wouldn't have to wait too many nights before Grey left, but as it happened, he exited the apartment building about four hours later.

As soon as junior was out of sight down the street, Leathers hurried over to the door and jimmied the locks with his knife and a piece of wire.

The fourth-floor apartment door, however, was as secure as Fort Knox—when there had been a Fort Knox—so he kicked it open, sending chunks of the doorjamb into the room. He double checked the hallway, ready to decapitate any head that looked out of the other apartment doors, but everyone wisely kept to themselves.

The old man remained in bed, one hand resting on his belly, the other under the sheet, his eyes closed. Leathers was told the man was ill, so the job would be easy. The son, though, would be a big complication, so he had to hurry, not knowing how much time he had.

Grey looked at the frail man who seemed so small and insignificant in the bed. This is the famous badass? The one they called Knife Fighter? He looked like he couldn't peel an apple. It seemed ridiculous to kill the old fart since he looked like he was about to draw his last breath anyway. But a job was a job, and this one would give him six months of free rent.

He walked up to the side of the bed and removed his Ka-Bar from its belt sheath. He wasn't going to slash his throat, his usual way of killing. Leathers wanted to *feel* the blade enter the famous one called Knife Fighter.

He moved the man's hand away from his heart and lifted his blade in the air— A barely detectable movement from the side of the old man's body.

Something impacted Leathers' left arm and wetness splattered across his face and mouth.

Just as his eyes saw and his confused brain struggled to comprehend the slit in his jacket, Leathers felt an intense burning sensation in his left shoulder.

On pure reflex, he rammed the Ka-Bar into the frail chest.

The old man's eyes bulged as the blade punched through his flesh. Then he cried out as Leathers rotated it back and forth to enlarge the hole. He yanked it free, splattering himself, the old man, and the window with red. It was then he saw the weapon in the man's hand, a cleaver. Somehow, he moved his injured arm and jammed the man's weapon hand against the mattress. He whipped the Ka-Bar in an arc and drove it into his side, deep into his liver, the second most blood-rich organ in the body. The first he had already stabbed, the heart. Or close to it, anyway.

The old man arched up, and his eyes widened for a moment before they closed as his body settled back onto the mattress. Leathers wiggled the knife free and stepped back.

He wiped the blade clean on the sheet as he glanced around the room looking for something to stop his bleeding. He grabbed two shirts from atop a table and pressed them against his shoulder. He needed to get away before Grey returned. He looked back at his target.

The man was looking at him.

Leathers heart skipped a beat. He was still alive.

"He will…come for you," the old man wheezed. "And there is… going to be holy hell to pay." He inhaled weakly.

The old man released a long sigh.

Leathers hurried out the door, his heart thumping like a trip hammer.

CHAPTER 7

GREY AND TALA

"What are you doing here? How did you find me?" Grey had pulled Tala into the doorway of the corner building and was hugging her hard. "I'm so happy to see you."

She was nearly as tall as he was at six feet, long-legged, intelligent brown eyes, and high cheekbones popular among supermodels before everything ended. Tala was half Filipino and half Irish, the Filipino half dominating her appearance, except for her height, which she inherited from her father, Billy Flynn. She told Grey that she got her fighting skill, especially her knife handling, from her Filipino mother's side and her fighting spirit from her daddy, who boxed in his 20s under the name of Fightin' Billy Irish. She was wearing her usual threadbare black cargo pants and a white T-shirt under a tattered green bomber jacket. At 29, Tala was lean as most people were now, but hard from her regular training.

In the new savage times, beauty was a curse to women, so Tala did her best to conceal her looks with dirt smudges on her cheeks and forehead. Still, what Grey called "her exquisiteness," showed through, which made every venture out in the daytime dangerous for her.

"It gets annoying," she once told Grey, "but it keeps me sharp." Then she did that mischievous grin that always weakened his knees, "But it can dull my blade."

As a young girl, her mother had enrolled her in a martial arts system taught by her brother, a blend of karate, kali, and jujitsu. Later, her uncle taught her the basics of knife fighting, and her mother, an accomplished blade woman who had defended herself several times in the mean streets of Quezon City, Philippines, taught her the necessity of what she called "fierce mindset."

"Without the willingness to slice and stab another human being," her mother taught her, "your technical skill might not be enough." As it turned out, Tala had a fierce mindset in spades.

Two and half years earlier, Grey had been returning to his apartment with jugs of water when two men approached him from the front, distracting him from a third man hiding in a doorway. Grey's radar picked up on the third one a second too late, and he was struck in the head with what Tala later told him was an old rusted carburetor. Grey went down, and the three men commenced to kick him.

But only for about half a dozen seconds.

As far as the men were concerned, Tala appeared out of nowhere to thrust her 2-inch, Morakniv Edris Fixed-Blade knife through the smiling man's gums who was about to slam the carburetor down on Grey's head again. He backed away, blood and teeth flowing from his mouth, and dropped the car part.

She spun about and rammed the little blade into the biceps of the man swinging a section of car bumper at her. He dropped it, and when he went to grab his perforated upper arm, she ripped the blade vertically down his forehead, over his nose, and across his upper lip.

Tala ducked before she even saw the pipe wielded by the third man that flashed over her head, agitating her long hair in its breeze. She lunged from her crouch and whipped a roundhouse stab through the left side of his thin nose.

After that, the three men took off down the street, their hands covering their bleeding wounds.

"I had a passing thought about yanking the blade I put through the third guy's nose back toward me," she told Grey later. "You know, to slice his schnoz in half. But I didn't think the situation called for that kind of brutality. So I just pulled it out in the direction it went in."

"What?" Grey said, shaking his head. "What kind of a situation do you think would justify 'that kind of brutality?' I mean, the three men were beating me with car parts."

She winked at him, "Easy question. When three dudes are beating *me* with car parts."

Grey loved her smart-ass answer and right then knew he wasn't going to let her go. And though he was dizzy from the carburetor blow to the head, he decided even before she helped him all the way up the stairs to his apartment that he was in love. Two and a half years later, he still was, and she loved him equally.

She was fast that day she saved him, but not as fast as she would become over the next 30 months training with Grey and his father. The old man had liked her immediately, and to show his affection, he gifted her with the nastiest knife fighting techniques he knew.

At that time, Tala was carrying a second Morakniv Edris fixed blade in its sheath that hung from a leather thong around her neck. When Grey had tried to get her to pack something larger, she refused. "I saved your cute butt with it, didn't I?" He reluctantly stopped trying when on two other occasions, he saw how fast and deadly she was with the little blades. But a few months later, Tala acquired a Smith and Wesson 5.2-inch Tanto fixed blade. "I got it from a dude who doesn't need it anymore," she told Grey. Within three months, she became quite adept with the longer blade. She carried it in a sheath on her pants belt and continued to carry her little knife on her neck thong.

They hugged each other for a full minute in the doorway before Grey leaned back to look at her.

"I saw him," she said, her eyes tearing. "When I saw the damaged door, I was scared and went in, but you weren't there and your father… I'm so sorry."

Then her words came faster and faster. "I didn't understand. I mean, the place was so clean, so I thought he had passed naturally. But I didn't understand why he was on the floor. So I went down to Bob's apartment to see if you were there, and Bob said you went to Undertaker's place, but when I went to see him, he told me your father had been murdered… Jesus H, Grey. Then Undertaker said you had been there and left. He told me about Leathers, that your father said Leather's did it… Damn… I mean … Anyway, he told me where the guy might hangout. Undertaker didn't know if you were going back to the apartment. So since I had just come from there, I decided to look around the tunnel because it was closest. Then I saw you fighting that guy—"

Grey touched the side of her face. "Come up for air, Tala." She frowned, then nodded. They peered around the edge of the inset. The man with pinned hands was weeping like a child.

"Does he have anything to do with it?"

Grey shook his head. "Just a thief. I'll release him in a minute."

Tala held his arms. "Are you, uh, okay. Stupid question, I mean, your dad just—"

"I'm better now," he whispered and pulled her into him.

"Are we going after him?" she said, her voice muffled because Grey was holding the side of her face so tightly against his chest. "I can't breathe," she said. He relaxed his hug. "Thanks. This Leathers asshole. Are we going after him?"

Tala had fought by his side many times, so the thought of telling her that it would be unsafe would be a waste of breath and to mention insulting. Besides, she was a skilled fighter and better than most with a blade. "Yes," he said simply.

"Your father?"

"Undertaker is picking him up tomorrow as well as Jacobs, the man on the second landing."

"Poor Jacobs. Do you think Leathers did him too?"

"I didn't at first, but now…" He shrugged.

"What's the plan? Are you sure you're up to this?"

"Very," Grey said without hesitation. "But first, let's release my prisoner."

The rocker heard them coming and tried to twist around to look at them. "Ooooh, damn, it hurts," he managed, his face knotted in pain.

"What's your name?" Grey asked, taking a knee next to him.

"Greg." His grimy face was wet with tears. "I'm sorry. I'm not a bad person, I—"

"Your weapons would say otherwise."

"They're for my protection. It's the first time I've used them. I'm just so hungry."

"Stick your tongue out," Grey said, reaching into his pocket.

"What?"

Grey extracted a pill. "Fentanyl, a powerful painkiller. It will help you through the next few hours." He dropped it on the man's tongue and looked up at Tala. "What do you have?"

She patted her jeans pockets. "Matches and water purification tabs."

"Could I get one tablet?"

She smiled and handed him one. "You're such a softy, Grey."

He patted the man's back. "Greg, move your head out of the way and bite your jacket collar. This is going to hurt."

"Wait, mister. I—"

"Listen, Greg. Life is about choices. You decided to hurt and rob me. I *chose* not to kill you. Now I've *chosen* to free you. But if you'd rather that I *choose* just to walk away…"

"Okay, okay," the man cried. "Oh, lord, this is going to hurt." He bit down on his jacket.

Grey yanked the awl out of the tree stump and up and out of both of his hands.

Greg screamed and pulled his hands into his body. "Ooooooh!"

"Think of the holes as stigmata," Tala said.

"Stig … Not funny, lady. Ooooooh, it hurts!"

"The pain pill will kick in shortly," Grey said. "Here is the water purifier." He dropped it into the man's jacket pocket. "Now, get up and go and make better choices."

"Leathers is tall," Tala said. "An inch or two taller than you." She and Grey were across the street from the tunnel, both leaning against the side of a building. A dozen people were milling around them, all shabby and emaciated. When Grey and Tala had first walked confidently into their midst, the people started to close in, looking them up and down, sizing up the newbies, almost sniffing them.

"Zombies," Tala whispered, "but not as lovable."

When two of them invaded their space, Grey pulled his jacket flap back to expose his Mossy Oak, and Tala tugged on the handle of her sheathed necklace knife to reveal the little blade.

The crowd backed away and returned to moping about, giving the two only occasional glances.

"You said he's tall," Grey said. "You know him?"

She shook her head. "No. I was with my sister a few weeks ago looking for water, and we saw this guy thumping a couple of people on Fifteenth Avenue. He was punching these two guys who weren't fighting back. I was about to jump in because it looked so one-sided, you know, but then the two guys took off running. The guy didn't chase them; instead, he looked around at the other people as if to see if there was anyone else who wanted a shot at him. He looked at me for a beat or two longer than the others. It gave me the creeps."

"But what makes you think it was Leathers?"

"Some people near us were talking about him after he left, calling him Leathers and saying he hurts people for hire."

"I've never heard of him. But father had."

"Someone said they heard he was from down south. He hasn't been up here long. Got to be the same guy."

Shouting from across the street in front of the tunnel entrance.

The zombies turned to look toward a brawl on the sidewalk in front of the tunnel. At least a dozen people were punching and kicking, some on their feet, others thrashing around on the concrete.

Grey eyed a 10-foot-high pile of trash next to the curb a few feet away. "Let's move down behind that. With so many people involved, there is bound to be someone with a gun and—"

Semi-auto gunfire.

At least six rounds. Then two more, followed by another two.

Grey and Tala made it to the pile of junk before another burst rattled off on full auto.

"Where are they coming from?" Tala asked, quick peeking around the side of garbage. "Whoa! There are people down everywhere by the tunnel, Grey. Some are moving, some aren't."

Another burst of rounds, the sound reverberating off the buildings.

"Up there," Grey said, pointing. "The sixth floor of that building, corner window. I saw a barrel and flashes."

Single shots from the direction of the window, high caliber.

Then silence.

A man appeared in the window, black, bald head. He extended his arms and lifted his thumbs. "I think he's saying everything is okay now," Grey said. The man disappeared. "Stay behind pile. It could be a ruse."

A bloody-faced white man fell across the windowsill. He twisted to see behind him, then tried to push himself back inside the room, but he couldn't.

People were coming out from behind their cover and looking up at the show. Others were hurrying over to the wounded.

Grey thought he heard a voice from the window. "Did you hear—"

"Pleeeease!"

"It's the guy hanging out the window," Tala said. "Look. The black guy is lifting his legs. "Is he going to…?"

The white man struggled to push himself away from the sill, but the black man was lifting his legs higher and higher—

He slid over the ledge, and dropped—his arms waving, legs bicycling, a screeching "Noooo" traveling with him all the way to the cement. Where he bounced.

The bald man appeared again at the window, arms raised, hands clasped and pumping in a winner's gesture. The survivors down on the street cheered and waved.

Tala exhaled a gush of air and shook her head. "Another visual to haunt my dreams."

"I'd feel better if the shooter's automatic weapon had been destroyed. Hopefully, the new owner is a good guy." Grey looked behind them, then pointed to a doorway. "Let's step in there to get something solid behind us."

They pressed their backs to the door and watched people across the street carrying away the injured and dead. Tala leaned against Grey. "I wish we were in bed holding each other."

"Yeah." He kissed the top of her head, his attention on the tunnel.

Twenty minutes later, the casualties were gone, and fewer people were hanging around the entrance. Except for the blood here and there on the sidewalk and street, everything was nearly back to the new normal. "How is Angel doing?" Grey asked. Tala lived with her sister two blocks from Grey's building.

Angel was the antithesis of Tala: frail, slight, and timid. Weeks earlier, she had been out in the late afternoon when she saw a group of men stroll around a corner a block ahead of her. Frightened, Angel quickly stepped into an alley, failing to see the open manhole. She toppled into it, striking the side of her head on the rim, then falling about eight feet into knee-deep black sludge. She was still conscious as a colony of rats swooped over her, gnawing and chomping and squealing. The men heard the commotion and climbed into the manhole. By the time they pulled her to the surface, the rats had bit her nearly three dozen times. The Good Samaritans even helped her up to her apartment.

There was no way of knowing if she had contracted the plague, salmonella, or hantavirus. Doctor Feel Good said it was probably rat fever and apologized that all he had for it was fentanyl.

"She's not good," Tala said. "I don't know how much longer she has." She drew a ragged breath and wiped her sleeve across her eyes. "Adam, that guy who used to be a nurse, said he thinks she has just a few days. But he also said he might be wrong." She shook her head. "Am I a bad person because I had to get out of the apartment for a while? Adam is with her, though."

"I don't think you're capable of doing anything bad. Does it make me bad that I want to catch my father's killer?"

Tala pushed herself closer to him. "I'll answer my question. Yes, it makes me bad. And it's doubly bad that I'm out here doing this with you where I could get hurt and not be there when she… passes." She was silent for a moment, then, "But my gut says I'm supposed to be with you, and it also says I should stay with Angel." She shook her head. "My gut is a pain in the ass."

He turned his head and kissed her forehead. "Do what feels right, not what you think is right."

She leaned the side of her head on his shoulder. "I'm with you then." He kissed her head again. "Now you," she said.

He looked back out at the street. "I don't feel I'm wrong to go after Leathers. Father had hours left to live—hours, and this man stole them from him and from me. I don't care why he did it. He saw that my father was weak and dying. But he killed him anyway. This Leathers is evil for doing that. I…"

Grey's hand found hers and clasped it snugly. He shook his head. "Evil. It is all around us, everywhere, nonstop. I've been out here only part of the day, and a man tried to rob me and stab me. And just now, someone was randomly shooting people. The shooter might have been a rocker, but sometimes it's hard to see the difference between crazy and evil. Then a man caught him, tried him, and sentenced him to death in under three minutes. He saved lives, but it's all so…"

Grey's eyes were far away. Tala waited for him.

Across the street, two women were engaged in a tug of war over a blanket, both cursing.

Grey said, "If I don't stand up to someone who wronged my father, evil wins. He often talked about that before The Change. Especially those last few years when the criminal justice system was in chaos, government corruption was out of control, and human decency was viewed as a weakness. He and I knew that the way things were couldn't continue, that all was about to explode and implode for better or worse. Well, fate, or whatever, chose worse and rained rockets on us. And here we are now."

"Here *we* are," Tala repeated. "*We,* that's what matters to me in this new world."

Across the street, one of the women punched the other, knocking her down, her head striking the cement first. The hitter took off with the blanket, leaving the other motionless on the sidewalk.

"See?" Grey said, nodding toward the assault.

After a moment, Grey said, "My father told me his killer's name was Leathers. That's all he had time to say. But he wanted me to know so I could go after him. Not to avenge his death, which I must admit that for a moment, I thought of it that way. But I'm convinced now that he wanted me to show Leathers, and others like him, that evil doesn't get to win. Not always, anyway."

Grey looked up at the window from where the shooter had fired his deadly rounds. "That man with the bald head up in that window just showed all of us that evil doesn't always win. Those on the ground saw it, and some of them will fight back too now. When we get Leathers, others will see that, understand it, and hopefully, they too will be empowered to fight back."

"That man you just pinned to the stump?"

"What? You think that was wrong?"

"Not at all, Grey. I didn't see what all happened, but I know you were defending yourself. Then you gave him a pill because he was hurting. Maybe he learned something about good and evil."

Grey nodded.

"Do you know why Leathers killed your father?"

"Not specifically." Grey looked up at the rapidly darkening sky. The dripping would start soon. "Father was 'Knife Fighter.' I have some idea of what he used to do, his work. But I don't know all of it. Maybe Leathers or maybe someone he is working for wanted revenge for something Father did in the past.

"I don't know what all he did, but someday I hope to find out. But this I know for sure: He fought against evil. He fought it during all those tours in Vietnam. And I know he was doing good on those missions, or whatever they were after he got out of the Army."

Grey pressed his forearm against the big Mossy under his jacket. "Father had a shotgun when I was growing up, and an old Army forty-five cal. I had a Glock nine that I had loaned him because he was planning on going to the range with a buddy. Looters got all three before my father got to the destroyed house."

He took a deep breath, remembering his father looking through the rubble of his home and convinced he heard his wife under it.

"Father used firearms when he was in Vietnam, of course, but he said he preferred the blade for his clandestine work. And for daily self-defense since The Change."

"He was amazing," Tala said. "Like eerie amazing."

Grey nodded. "He taught me, but I'm not even a quarter as good as he was."

Tala squeezed his hand. "You underestimate yourself, Grey. I have never seen anyone move like you. And you both taught me. It's me who isn't a quarter as good."

"Yeah, but you're so damn cute doing it." She elbowed his side, her mouth trying not to smile.

She pointed at a naked man emerging from the tunnel. He looked around as if wondering where he was and then dashed down the sidewalk and disappeared around the corner. "What the hell. What kind of place are you taking me to, handsome? Is it clothing optional?"

Grey smiled for the second time in five minutes. He never smiled or laughed when he wasn't with her. "Have you ever been to the Bamboo Tunnel?"

"Not long before The Change. My mother took me through it. It was amazing, and it really was like a giant green tunnel. You couldn't see through it because it was so dense, but I knew it stretched between two high-rises for a couple of blocks." She looked across the way at its entrance. "I heard it's hellish now."

He looked at her. "I think you should check on your sister, and I'll come by later."

"Yeah? Well, I think you should kiss my butt."

Grey smiled for the third time. "Okay."

"Promises, promises," she said with a smirk. "You know what else I heard?"

"That, of course, would be a no."

She elbowed him again. "Some people were talking out in the hall at my place yesterday, and a man was saying he heard there was an army somewhere. Sector Five or Six, someone said. A real army, not a gang like around here. You think it's true? You think there's a government or something? Maybe they have to do with the helicopters."

Grey shook his head. "The helicopters have been around a long time. I don't know what they are, but they aren't the military, at least a benevolent one."

"That would be something, wouldn't it? I mean a military, a good one. They would probably bring us food and medicine. And order to all this chaos."

"Can we talk about it later?" Grey said. "We need to be in the moment, alert, aware."

"Good idea." She looked at the darkening sky. "It looks like we got just a few minutes before total black. When do you think it is the best time to go in?"

Grey looked at the tunnel entrance for a long moment. "Best?"

The sidewalk and street in front of the tunnel were bloodier than it appeared from across the street. The dozen or so people milling about the entrance eyed Grey and Tala with suspicion, which was no surprise given a gunman had been firing down on them not that long ago.

They walked around one side of the small crowd, making eye contact with those nearest. Grey had taught Tala what his father taught him: "If you have to walk through hell, walk like you own the place." More times than not, an attitude of confidence gave strangers pause. Some of them, anyway. This time it worked, and they proceeded to the lip of the tunnel and stopped.

Grey decided to go through at twilight. In full light, they could see better, but any threats could easily see them too. If they went when the night was at its darkest, threats couldn't see them, but he and Tala couldn't see anything either. As it turned out, there was sporadic artificial light here and there inside, at least in the first 50 feet or so.

"Gaaaawd!" Tala blurted, cupping her palm over her nose and mouth. The stench emanating from the tunnel—garbage, rotting vegetation, human waste, rats—was thick and ripe, and it intensified as they grew nearer. The bamboo that formed the tunnel at one time was now hard to discern, so overgrown were the sides and high ceiling with ivy, thorny vines, and every other type of creeping growth. There was still a tunnel-like shape to its sides, but the vegetation that formed the 30-foot ceiling—long-dead vines, some living greenery—was too high to trim, so it dangled, in some places just out of arm's reach.

The tunnel—half alive and half dead—was a metaphor for all of us who survived, Grey thought.

Tala nodded toward a bald-headed man sitting cross-legged along the left side of the entrance. He was bare-chested, his ribs prominent, and he appeared to be meditating. An old-fashioned lamp, kerosene maybe, burned next to him. Grey was surprised someone hadn't stolen it from him. Maybe he stole it.

"More lamps," Grey said. "See about twenty feet in on the left? There's one hanging from a vine."

Three men carefully stepped around garbage, clumps of vegetation, and roots as thick as a man's forearm as they made their way out of the tunnel. One man, who Grey thought looked familiar, made eye contact with him. Grey nodded a greeting as they passed, but the men only glared back and continued on.

"Look there on the right side," Tala said. "Someone is lying on the vines about halfway up the side. But on what? A board or something?"

Grey squinted. "A mattress, I think."

A middle-aged man, a sleeping bag strapped to his bent back, looked up at them as he exited the tunnel. "Gawkers or goin' in?" he asked. His eyes were sunken from fatigue and living, his mouth bruised and blood scabbed.

"Going in," Grey said, noticing he had a black eye too.

The old man nodded. "There's a rocker about halfway. Crazy as a loon, aggressive too. Clobbered me in the kisser, and I got a bum knee and hip. So I throw'd a rock at him. Smacked him right between the eyes. He let me be after that, but he was harassin' other people when I continued on." He looked Tala over. "You're a looker. You're tryin' to hide it, but it's apparent. You be careful in there."

"You know a man named Leathers?" Grey asked.

The old-timer looked at him for a moment, as if the name meant something. "Seen him."

"Chinese guy?" Grey tested. "Short?"

He shook his head as he lifted his shoulders to adjust the pack. "Leathers is a big son-of-a-bitch. Likes to hurt folks."

"He stay in Bamboo Tunnel?"

"Seen him in there before, but I don't think he stays in it." He thought for a second. "You know the Hammer brothers? Saw them on the other end."

"Who's that?" Tala asked.

"The Hammers brothers! Just told you. More nogoodniks, that's all. There's lot of them types out tonight." He threw a mock salute. "Got places to be. Take care, folks."

Grey looked at Tala. "Ready?"

"As I'll ever be." She touched the Morakniv Eldris in its sheath dangling from her neck and patted the Smith and Wesson blade attached to her belt.

Grey unsnapped the sheath of his Mossy Oak Survival knife.

He could feel the weight of his father's Bucknbear tactical chopper cleaver in his left jacket pocket. Still, he pressed his forearm against it for a second anyway.

They walked toward the entrance.

"Will you be wanting to spend the night with us?" the meditator asked, his eyes snapping open and startling Tala, who was about four feet from him. He was sitting on what looked like a sofa cushion. He was wearing a string of Buddha beads around his neck.

"What?" Tala asked. "Spending the night? This a hotel?"

"Yes, ma'am," the man said, with a hint of an English accent. "If you want it to be. We have things for you to sleep on. The price is low: a little food, matches, kerosene."

"Just passing through," Grey said. "We're looking for a man named Leathers."

"Leathers," the man breathed. "He suffers much. I am grateful that I have not seen him in two days. Have a peaceful evening." With that, he closed his eyes.

If the tunnel had been made of concrete, there would have been echoes. But the deep vegetation depressed sounds. Even the man singing operatically from where he was sitting on a thick vine near the ceiling, swinging forward and back like a child on a park swing set. 444

"I love that song," Tala whispered. "Sounds like Pavarotti. You notice that man lying on a platform of some kind high to our ten o'clock? He's been giving us a hard look since we've come in."

"I did," Grey said, stepping carefully on the cluttered ground. "Keep him your peripheral. There are two men twenty-five yards to our front walking toward us, both of them wearing dark overcoats. Also, a lone middle-aged female is walking about thirty feet to our rear. She's carrying a wooden staff, the top of it sharpened."

Tala looked at him then turned her head a couple of inches more to bring the female into her peripheral. "Did you see her first or feel her?"

"Felt."

Tala turned her attention back to her front. "You think I'll ever be that good?" Her eyes widened. "Look to your five o'clock through that pile of sticker vines."

Grey moved his eyes to the right without turning his head to see two naked bodies, male and female, coupling. "Consensual," he said.

"I know," Tala said. Still watching as they passed. "I wish that were us, but not in this terrible place."

"Me too, but right now, you need to focus on looking for Leathers. You know what he looks like; I don't."

The two men to their front were less than 30 feet away now. Grey noted that they were in their late 20s, scruffy, carrying backpacks, and wearing hard expressions. Their faces were similar to one another, brothers, maybe.

Grey moved his eyes near the ceiling on the right side of the tunnel. A long-haired, emaciated man, naked except for white undershorts, sat perched on a cluster of creepers, his butt resting on the heels of his bare feet, both hands clutching a dangling vine. He seemed to be watching the two men—

He launched himself into the air. "Eeeeeiiiieeeee, yaaaaah!"

"What the hell, Grey?"

Gripping the vine with both hands, the man Tarzaned on a straight line toward the two men, his long, thin legs spread obscenely wide as if to capture them in a leg scissor hold.

They reflexively jumped out of the line of trajectory, but it was unnecessary because the vine snapped.

The man's King of the Jungle abruptly ended when his backside landed on a cluster of needle-sharp bamboo spears, less than six feet from the men. A small cloud of dead leaves and twigs lifted into the air around him. The man grunted, either from the impact or from the spears that pierced through his back and punched an inch or two out of his neck, chest, and bladder.

His legs churned in the debris for a moment, then stilled.

The men looked at the dead man for a moment, and then simultaneously looked up at Grey and Tala. "Behind you," the taller one said almost conversationally.

Not knowing if it was trick, Grey turned his head enough to see to his rear while keeping the two men in his sight.

"Duck," Grey said, pulling Tala down with him. They both felt the breeze of the staff passing overhead.

Grey heard Tala rip her dangling neck knife from its Kydex sheath as they straightened and turned.

The woman deftly caught the free end of the staff with her other hand and thrust it toward Tala. She whipped her forearm outward, knocking the weapon aside. If it hadn't been so long, she could have simultaneously stabbed the woman with her 2.2-inch blade. But it was, so Tala closed the gap with a deep lunge and sunk her blade into her shoulder.

The woman cried out but not as loudly as she did when Tala extracted it with a forceful twist of the blade. She thrust the small knife in again, this time penetrating where the shoulder tied into the pectoral muscle, effectively removing that arm from the equation.

Grey knocked the staff out of the woman's hands and grabbed the front of her throat with his beefy fingers. "Do you know who we are," he growled into her wild-eyed face. He squeezed tighter. "Were you sent?"

She tried to touch her stabbed shoulder with her other hand, but Grey knocked it away. "Answer."

Her manic eyes seemed to look through him to some other place. "The goddess of the universe sees you. She will condemn you and…everyone else in this hellish place." The woman grimaced, and her knees dipped as if she were about to drop. "The goddess… sees everythi—"

"She's a rocker," the taller of the two men said, stepping up next to Grey. "We've dealt with her in Sector Three. Crazy as an infected rat."

"Do me a favor, bud," a voice growled from behind the woman. "Kill her ass." Grey looked around her to see the shirtless Buddhist who had been meditating at the tunnel entrance. Blood oozed between his fingers as he clutched his side. "Filthy rocker cut me in my ribs when I asked her if she was staying for the night."

Grey spun her around by her shoulders, generating a cry from her. "Get out of here," he said, nudging her back toward the tunnel's entrance.

"Filthy rocker," the meditator taunted with a jut of his jaw as the woman passed him.

"She stabbed you?" Grey asked, looking at his wound.

The meditator shook his head. "Nah, I was too quick and turned. Scraped me good, though."

"Put on a shirt and keep it clean," Grey said, thinking how quickly the Buddhist's love and peace dissolved. The man nodded and headed toward the entrance, stay a safe distance behind the rocker.

Grey turned around. The two men had to be brothers. The Hammer Brothers, the old man outside the tunnel mentioned?

"That was impressive, girl," the shorter one said, looking at Tala. "Fast as hell."

She was squatting down and wiping her blade with a handful of leaves. She nodded but didn't reply.

"Thanks for the warning," Grey said. He was standing just out of reach of them, his arms hanging loosely at his sides. His peripheral continuously surveyed the tunnel surroundings as he simultaneously noted that the men's overcoats flared out slightly at the waist. They were packing something, but why did the coats bulge on both sides of their bodies?

The tall one nodded and looked over at the dead man. "We might not have gotten off a warning if ape-man there had been successful. What the hell was that about?"

"You from around here?" Grey asked. Tala stood, her hand still gripping her blade alongside her thigh. The shorter man noticed, looked up to meet her eyes, then looked away.

"We're from Sector Three," the taller one said. "We're just looking for someplace where we can drop our guard a little. So far, it doesn't look like Sector Four is any different." He looked around and shook his head. "Man, this tunnel is a circus of the strange."

The shorter one looked at Tala. "A guy told us it was the safest way to get to the next street over." His quick smile was insincere. "He's probably laughing right now at how he set up these two gullible Sector Three guys. Is it any less crazy on the other side?"

"Sometimes worse," Grey said. They told a good story, but he wasn't ready to accept it.

The smaller man said, "You two are headed in the opposite direction as us. But we got no problem heading back to give you some extra security." He looked at Tala. "But after seeing you in action, maybe you should escort us."

Tala looked at him blank-faced until he looked back at Grey, who said, "That's kind of you, but we're good to go. We'll be on our way." He stepped around the men, and Tala did the same on the other side.

Grey looked to his left and right side every few feet to ensure the men weren't following. A minute later, Tala asked, "Not getting warm fuzzy vibes off them?"

He shook his head. "They're a tough read, but I'm leaning toward no warm fuzzies."

"Me neither," she said.

CHAPTER 8

LEATHERS

Leathers was holding the old timer up by his neck with one hand, leaving one foot to dangle, the other barely touching the floor.

"Think carefully. What did he say exactly?"

"Damn, Leathers," the old man managed with his neck constricted. "I practically ran here on my bum leg to tell you about him, and this is how you treat me?"

"Tell me what he said, or I swear I'll—"

"He asked me, 'You know a man named Leathers?' I said I did, and he asked if you hang out in the Bamboo Tunnel. I said no. Could you put me down? Damn, I hurried back to tell you, didn't I?"

"You tell him where I live?"

"I don't know where you live. Come on. Put me down. I have trouble breathing anyway, and now you're squeezing my neck. I'm seventy-seven for crying out loud."

Leathers let go of the man, not out of kindness, but because the strain was making his bandaged arm throb. The old man landed on his feet, then crumpled onto his knees. "Ow. I got a bad hip."

"I'll put a bullet in your good one if I find out you told him where I'm staying."

"You gonna reward me anything? I mean, I ran all the way here through the side streets. There are some bad actors hanging out on them."

Leathers left the man struggling to get up and headed down the street and around the corner. He nodded to the two skinny Asian men working the outside entrance to Hades. Everyone called them The Sumos because they wore topknots on the back of their heads and dark robes, one depicting dragons and the other colorful koi. They knew he lived upstairs and nodded as he approached.

Leathers forgot and reached to pull open the heavy door with his injured arm. He groaned, ignored the looks from The Sumos, and switched to his other hand.

As usual, he was assaulted inside the small lobby by a tangible torrent of throbbing sound that those on the other side of the second set of double doors thought of as music. Leathers knew there were at least 100 people inside the sweat lodge moving to the waves of the bone-marrow-dissolving sound. There was another dozen or two engaged in freaky sex acts, and lots of fights, some leading to death. Leathers found the place repugnant. Still, he occasionally went into the 24-hour debauchery to hook up with a female for 15 minutes in a part of the room called the store.

He unlocked the small door at the far corner of the lobby and made his way up the hot and humid narrow stairs to his apartment. He switched on the lights, but nothing happened. The only thing reliable about the generator, or whatever the landlord used to light the place, was that it was always unreliable. There were occasional 10-second power outages in Hades, but the apartments above were iffy. The heat, however, in his room and in Hades, remained unbearable day and night.

He stretched out on his bed and looked at the dark drips slithering down his window.

Grey. Why in the hell didn't he kill the man when he saw him on the street earlier?

He tried not to think about the answer, but it was right there in his brain flashing off and on like a warning sign back when there were such things.

Several rapid shots sounded outside his window, no farther away than the corner. Silence, then another salvo. He was pretty sure he heard a helicopter, too, but it was hard to tell because of the damn music thumping his floor and his wound. There, he heard it again, and it was for sure a bird, and it was getting closer.

He stood and raised his window, the *thump thump thump* of the rotary wings louder as they bounced off the surrounding buildings. An intense beam of light shot down from the clouds onto a cluster of people, the beam brief, no more than a quarter of a second, making the eye in the sky nearly impossible to track.

Would the idiots in the streets never learn that the helicopters always shot back, and with prejudice? It was—

All hell broke loose outside as the helicopter poured down hot vengeance, the sound of gunfire deafening as it reverberated off the surrounding buildings and shook his window.

It stopped—the sudden silence accentuating the screams of those wounded.

Dumb shits, Leathers thought as he closed the window, not bothering to look down at the casualties. He flashed back to when he was watching Grey work his way down the dark sidewalk. He should have killed him then and there. So why didn't he?

He took a deep breath and eased it out. He knew why.

He was afraid of the man.

There, he admitted it.

Leathers had heard of the father. No one seemed to know his real name; everyone called him "Knife Fighter." He knew of the man's exploits in Vietnam, and that he did covert work in the years after. Who hires a one-armed man to do secret-secret stuff? No doubt people who knew how good he was, even minus an arm. The stories about him in the Green Berets were probably exaggerated. But even if half true, they were still legendary.

Then in the last year and a half, stories started to emerge about Grey. Supposedly, a man abducted a woman's child, not 20 feet from where Knife Fighter's son was standing. Though the abductor released the kid a block away, Grey chased him down into a basement and cut off both of his hands.

Another story had it that he had killed every member of a street gang called NG, New Government. That story had Grey decapitating all 12 members.

Leathers doubted the stories were true.

But maybe they were.

Some tales merged with his father's, and some told about the father were now attributed to Grey. People were even calling Grey "Knife Fighter" now.

The truth was one of the many things hard to determine since The Change.

Leathers took the hit job on the father because the old man was sick and no longer a threat. He didn't know why the people who hired him wanted him dead. Nor did it matter to Leathers.

But now it was all about Grey, a young and healthy man, as far as he knew. And if any of the stories were to be believed—vicious.

Damn.

CHAPTER 9

GREY AND TALA

Grey used his periphery again to check on the two men.

They were gone.

He stopped and turned around. Tala looked at him. "What is it?" She looked behind her. "What the hell."

Tala and Grey had walked about 25 yards since they left the men, both continually making periphery checks. The men were there a minute ago, and now they weren't.

"Unless they have found a place to sit or sleep along one of the walls, they might have found a spot where the bamboo and foliage is thin enough for them to get out of the tunnel."

"I didn't see anything like that when we went past there," Tala said. "Did you?"

"No. But I wasn't looking for it either. If the men found a spot to get out, maybe they did it to get away from the 'circus of the strange' as the one called it. Still, stay on your toes."

For the next few minutes, they passed lots of sleepers perched like nesting birds along the tunnel sides. Tala laughed at a man naked from the waist down, holding onto a dangling vine with one hand, playing with himself with the other, and making monkey sounds. Grey stopped a woman about to smash a heavy iron skillet against the head of another woman sharpening the point of a throwing dart. Tala got another laugh out of a bearded guy sitting on a vine near the ceiling peeing on a sleeper stretched out on a bare patch of cement 30 feet below.

Up ahead, several people stood watching as two men balanced on separate thick stalks of moving bamboo as they struggled to attach opposite sides of a huge American flag. The difficult task accomplished, they climbed down to a warm round of applause from the growing crowd.

Grey and Tala joined them, and they all stood in silence.

Grey hadn't seen an American flag in at least two years, nor

had he thought about it, so preoccupied had he been with finding food, water, pain pills, and surviving the new, cruel world. This one, at least 15 feet across, was frayed on the upper right corner, which Grey thought fitting, and his heart filled, and tears streamed down his face. Every age and race, stood silently, most wiping dirty sleeves across wet faces.

The past 37 months streaked across his mind like a sped-up movie. The shock and awe of the first few months, the daily scraping to survive, the killing, and the ever-present confusion of what was right and what was wrong.

"Folks."

Grey looked up and wiped his eyes clear. An elderly black man, thin, with a scruffy white beard beneath sad eyes, faced the crowd.

"Folks, I'm an old man. Probably not as old as I look, but close. Seeing Old Glory hanging there does my old ticker good, and it inspires me too. Inspires me to do everything I can in the time I got left to help us return to what was good about our country." He wiped away the tears. "I guess I just want to say that we don't have to be brutal to be tough. Human kindness won't weaken our stamina or weaken our will. Compassion for others won't take away what little we have. Nor can we be despondent because that's an emotion that sucks the energy and the determination right out of you. Despair makes you think everything you do is for naught, which can play havoc on your will. Too much despair can take your life. Be inspired, folks, by Old Glory here to keep on keeping on every day. We must all…" He swiped his eyes again, nodded at the people, and turned back around to look at the flag.

A man on his left and a woman on his right patted his back. A voice behind Grey said, "Thank you, sir. Thank you."

Bamboo Tunnel was dripping. It wasn't when they first entered, but now greasy dark drops fell from the ceiling and struck the foliage, the floor, and splattered on Grey and Tala. The top of the tunnel was thinner as they neared its end, and Grey could see patches of murky sky through it. The going was slow because the floor here was thickly covered in bamboo roots and upright six-inch-long spear tips.

Tala said, "I read once where the American Indians used to stake their prisoners over the spears like these, and within a couple of days, the fast-growing things would pierce their bodies."

Grey shook his head. "Humans have always been geniuses when it comes to hurting one another, but not so much at living in peaceful harmony." He looked at the rim of the tunnel exit and the darkness beyond it. "Let's get out of here."

"And just when the place was starting to grow on me," Tala said sarcastically.

The vines rustled to their left, parted, and a man slipped through them, his eyes focused on Tala. "You got some glorious gams, baby," he said, his sneer ugly, his eyes traveling up and down her legs. He was about 30, skinny, with too-large clothes, long hair, and an overall appearance that said he hadn't cleaned himself since the first day of The Change. "And them legs go aaaaall the way up."

"Stop right there," Tala said. "We're leaving."

The man faked a laugh, his teeth nearly black, and kept walking toward them. "She always feisty like this?"

Grey, conditioned to people being threatened by his appearance, was caught off guard by the man's stupidity. Another rocker, maybe.

The man looked back at Tala, his eyes devouring her. "Bet this one guides you around by your nose all day—"

Tala ripped her small knife from her neck sheath and took a step to her left. When her foot caught a vine, she tried to free it, but she snagged another, throwing her off balance. She hopped with her other foot to recover, but it too became tangled and down she went with a grunt.

The man sputtered a laugh and pointed at her. "Now, that's just hilarious." He lowered his arms to her. "Come on sweetness, let me help you up, and we'll go—"

"Back up, now!" Grey blared, moving toward him, albeit awkwardly because of the rough ground. His eyes watched the triangle formed by the man's shoulders and chin, a spot from which he could see all of his body.

The man turned toward him, his hand reaching behind his back. It returned, gripping a kitchen knife, the blade a good eight inches long. "You aren't gonna tell me—"

Grey's hand blurred, his face expressionless.

The assailant's face frowned for a second, two seconds. Then the message his wounded body sent to his confused brain sunk in. He looked down at his hand that was holding the knife, and his mouth dropped open.

His thumb…was gone.

It had been lopped off at the web, leaving a circular stump of red meat, in its center, a smaller circle of white severed bone.

The knife fell from the man's thumbless grip, and an arc of red squirted on his clothing. He opened his mouth to scream, but nothing came out.

Crazed, the man charged Grey, but after two steps he stumbled over a vine and began to fall. Grey managed to sidestep without tripping and slapped the back of the man's head, sending him down hard onto his belly. Grey grabbed a fistful of filthy hair and dragged him a few inches to his left so that the man's face was directly over a bamboo spear.

"I'm holding your head up," Grey said. "You understand the significance of that?"

"You cut off my thumb. I'm going to—"

Grey lowered the man's head until the point of the spear was directly below his right eye. "I'm going to knee drop the back of your head. That spear is long enough to punch through your eye and impale your brain. Think about that. I'll wait."

Tala was standing now, touching her fingertips to the side of her neck where a spear had torn the skin.

"Don't. Please!"

"My arm is getting tired."

"Okay. I'm sorry. Let me up, and you'll never see me again."

Grey looked at Tala. "Got your blade ready?"

"In my hand," she said, showing him.

"And I've got mine ready. I'm going to let you up, pal, and if you even look back at us as you go back to wherever you came from, we'll fillet you for the rats."

"I won't look. Please don't let go of me"—

Grey pulled him to his feet by his hair. "Don't look at us."

"I'm not looking!" the man cried, facing away, his uninjured hand gingerly touching the back of his thumbless one. Without saying a word, he carefully made his way over the roots to the tunnel wall and disappeared into its foliage.

Tala slid her knife back into the dangling sheath as Grey put away his big Mossy. Neither spoke as they worked their way to the end of the tunnel.

They were standing sideways to the tunnel exit to keep one eye on where they had been and the other out into the darkness of the new environment. A massive black space spread out before them, sporadically illuminated by small fires and the occasional lantern. "Sector Three feels like a different world," Tala said. "Weird because we're only two blocks away from Sector Four."

Weak tunnel light illuminated about 10 feet of debris before the darkness absorbed what was beyond. Black clouds hung low as far as the eye could see, but they were a shade lighter than the missile-destroyed downtown skyline in the distance. Grey hadn't seen the dead city since the weeks after The Change. He still found it strange and profoundly sad not to see a single light in its silhouette.

"This was a parking lot, a huge one," Tala said, looking at the mass of black. "There was a Macy's on the far side over there on Sixth Avenue. That way, I think. An Apple store on that side of Belmont, and a yummy place called Chocolatier on the right corner where my mother, sister, and I used… to, uh…"

Grey slipped his arm around Tala's shoulders. Weak light revealed her grimy face and glistening eyes. He wanted to comfort her, but he had no words. Memories of life before were like stabs from a rapier.

He looked back out at the blackness.

He stood here once before a few months after The Change. What he saw that day on one of his early hikes, scorched a place in his memory, one he still sees, smells, and tastes every day.

He hadn't come here via the tunnel but from the north. Or was it the south? He no longer recalled the direction, nor did it matter.

He realized he was holding his breath and released it.

What he saw that day were dead bodies, men, women, and children. Some were stacked atop one another in piles, six feet high, or more. Others were lying side-by-side, so many they nearly covered the entire lot. Their only distinct commonality was the white froth around their gaping mouths.

He counted a half dozen piles of burning bodies. Those tending the fire wore masks or strips of cloth around their noses and mouths, and they used their feet or metal poles to push charred bodies that had rolled down the piles back into the flames.

One man tending a fire in the middle of the lot suddenly threw down his pole and tore away the red shirt he had wrapped around his nose. He extended his arms toward the flames, his hands formed into claws. He bent toward the fire and screamed at it, then laughed maniacally, and screamed again.

All around the lot more piles waited their turn to be cremated.

People watched from the edges of the parking lot, so many Grey couldn't estimate the number. They swatted at the dropping ash that drifted down like gentle snow, and their wails and their cries soared into the smoke-filled air and drowned out the roar of the fires. Others just stared, eyes huge, disbelieving.

A man in the front of the crowd on the right side, took a long step forward, his eyes locked on a raging fire to his front. Grey saw the gun a second before he lifted it and fired a round into his ear. Only those closest to him stepped back as he sagged to his knees, blood squirting from the side of his head. A woman pried the weapon out of his dead fingers and pushed her way through the crowd and disappeared. The man fell over onto his side, each squirt of blood less than the one before.

"Grey?"

He startled from his memory and looked at Tala.

"Where were you? I said your name twice."

"Sorry," he said, taking a deep breath, then letting it out as he spoke. "I was just thinking about our next step." He had never told her what he had seen that day. She probably knew that mass cremations were going on that first year from the deadly viruses that came with the missiles, but why bring it up? Why add that horror to their daily struggle?

"I was wondering," she said, squinting into the tunnel, then looking at him. "Why we were spared. Why was your father spared only to die by Leathers' hand? Why is my sister dying such a cruel death after being spared in the initial attack three years ago? Why do we have to be so violent just to live?" She angrily wiped at her eyes. "Why… I don't even know what questions to ask?"

Grey leaned into her, his eyes ever surveying the dark lot and the tunnel exit. Tala rested her head on his shoulder for a brief moment, then straightened and returned to her duty of watching the tunnel.

Grey said, "I'm guessing there are many more campers in this lot than just those with lights or a campfire. It wouldn't be wise to walk through the middle with people on our four sides. We should head over to the side of the lot and—"

He took a deep breath and blew it out forcefully, angrily. "I'm tired," he said between clenched teeth, his squinting eyes looking into the darkness. "I'm tired of the daily scrounge to survive, of being the prey and the hunter, sometimes at the same time. It's the life of animals."

Grey and Tala were standing side-by-side, their arms hanging at the sides, the backs of their hands touching. "If it weren't for you," Grey said, "I'm not sure that I would want to continue."

Tala caressed the back of his hand with her index finger. "I've thought these things too, Grey. Right now, I want to live for my sister, to help her to…you know. And I want to live to be with you. That's all I—"

Grey tensed. "Remove your big blade now," he whispered as he slid his big Mossy Oak from its sheath. "There's one approaching from our one o'clock and a second from our seven o'clock. If it comes to it, the seven o'clock is yours. The one o'clock is mine."

They stood motionless, both gripping their blades along their thighs. Thirty seconds passed. Forty.

The sky had stopped dripping, and there was no wind. The parking lot, though clearly occupied, was silent.

Sixty seconds passed.

Grey could hear Tala's breathing.

"They still there?" she whispered.

"Yes."

Ninety seconds.

Grey whispered, "Move laterally to your left three steps and face nine o'clock. Do it—*now!*"

Grey and Tala moved in opposite directions in perfect synchronization as two men appeared where he said they would. It was the two in overcoats from the tunnel. Grey wasn't surprised. The tall man's face was blank; the shorter one eyeballed Tala.

"You don't know who we are, do you?" the taller one said. He was standing just out of range of Grey, the shorter one within two strides of Tala. "What we're called."

Grey and Tala didn't answer, their bodies still, their blades held down along their thighs.

The short one smirked as his hands unbuttoned the flaps of his overcoat. "You'll find out. But I'll tell you who you are to us. You're a job. Nothing more, nothing personal."

"You get that?" the taller one asked, turning so he was square with Grey, his hands on the flaps of his unbuttoned overcoat. "Oh, and Leathers says to tell you hello before you die."

Grey almost rolled his eyes, but he managed to restrain himself. Their intimidation technique might work on the untrained and inexperienced. But to telegraph one's intent was a novice mistake, a fool's blunder, especially if they knew who he was. And why didn't they do this in the tunnel? Too many people? Did they think we had allies around? Well, they were here now, and they needed to be killed.

In unison, both men pulled back the flaps of their overcoats to reveal stubby clawhammers, one on each hip riding in short sheaths.

"You got to be kidding me?" Grey said as they simultaneously grabbed their pairs of hammerheads, snapped them up, and spun them until they were holding them by their rubber grips. Grey had to admit they had a flourish, the stuff of silly Hollywood movies.

The two assumed on-guard stances like boxers. The brothers knew Grey and Tala had knives, so this presentation was an attempt at intimidation. Of course, a blow to the head could leave a person drooling for the rest of their life. *This needs to end quickly,* Grey thought.

What followed was an action so fast that the tall man's eyes and brain couldn't possibly register it until it was too late.

Grey lunged low, his empty hand against his chest, and plunged his 15-inch blade into the tall man's lead thigh.

He cranked the blade hard to remove a chunk of meat, then flipped it into the dark like a stir fry chef at a Japanese restaurant flicking a piece of beef onto a diner's plate. Grey was about to interrupt the man's scream by cutting his throat, but he heard a thump behind him and Tala yelp. He took advantage of the tall man's hysteria to quickly look over at her.

Tala had fallen on her knife arm, her entire body weight pinning her weapon to the concrete. The shorter man was bent over her, flailing his two hammers like a cruel drummer, but Tala was deflecting his blows away from her with her one hand.

"Hey!" Grey yelled.

As he hoped, the small man looked at him long enough for Tala to roll onto her back, freeing her knife-hand. Without pause, she sliced her blade across the closest target, the man's hand, cutting tendons and blood veins. The hammer fell from his grip with a clang.

Grey felt the tall man's approach and instinctively stepped to the side. If he hadn't, the hammer would have struck his skull instead of his left trapezius muscle. An electric bolt of pain shot through his trap and neck. It would have been worse if he weren't wearing a thick coat.

He spun without looking, his arm extended, his blade leading the way. The tall man leaned to the side, and the blade sliced only air. Grey snapped his hand over and whipped the knife back on the same horizontal path just as the man straightened.

The Mossy Oak's thin edge neatly sliced across both of the tall man's eyebrows.

He grunted and reflexively snapped his hand up to his forehead, thwacking his hammer into his own face. He cursed, flung the tool to the side, and stepped back on his leg with the fresh hole in it. It buckled.

Grey lunged forward and sliced his big knife across the nerves, tendons, and muscles just above the kneecap of his unhurt leg. As both legs collapsed, the man miraculously managed to swing his remaining hammer at Grey's head. He missed by two feet, probably because of the blood streaming into his eyes.

As the man waved his arms about in a feeble attempt to stay upright, Grey seized the moment to ram the big blade through his chest, directly over his heart and lung.

The man hung there for a moment, his mouth opening and closing like a beached fish. Then he fell backward. Grey tightened his grip on the Mossy Oak as the man's chest slid off it with a sucking sound. The man plopped onto his back, likely dead before he landed. Grey kicked the remaining hammer out of his hand and turned to help Tala.

She was standing—but favoring her right leg, and her left arm was hanging limply. One or more of the hammer blows must have hit her after all, Grey thought. There was a thin bloodline on the side of her neck, a result of falling on a bamboo spear a few minutes earlier in the tunnel. But there was a fresh cut over the side of her forehead, a small trickle of blood thankfully missing her eye.

Apparently unable to advance or retreat, Tala stood her ground, her Smith and Wesson Nine-inch extended, the blade dancing in the air just out of the short man's reach. His hand, the one Tala had sliced, was hanging at his side, blood dripping from his fingertips. He faked a swing at Tala with his stubby hammer, and she faked a thrust at him.

When the assailant cocked his hammer back, Grey exploded across the 10-foot expanse and drove his long blade through the man's bladder. He bawled like an injured animal, then screeched when Grey yanked it out and flowed smoothly into a horizontal slice across his face.

Going against all his teachers' warnings about changing grips within range, let alone in the middle of multiple cutting, Grey rolled the Mossy into icepick grip. He did it smoothly and flawlessly, the result of practicing the technique thousands of times.

He commenced with a flurry of slices, jabs, and hacks that came so fast and furious that the man couldn't fall, though his dying body wanted to.

When Grey finally stopped, the man collapsed to the concrete. His severed tendons, arteries, and destroyed nerves, reacting as if bolts of electricity were coursing through them, twisted and jerked his body. Grey knew his dance would continue for a few seconds after his soul was off to whatever lay ahead.

He looked over to double-check that the other brother was still dead. He was.

Not even breathing hard, he moved to Tala's side, wrapped his arm around her shoulder, and leaned around to look into her wide-opened eyes and gaping mouth. "Tell me you're all right," he said gently.

"Holy shit, man!" she finally managed, looking from the ravaged man to Grey. "Remind me never to piss you off. And just for the record, I was good to go, I was just acting to draw the man in closer. But thanks."

"Sweet Jesus!" a voice that sounded like sandpaper on a rusty pipe said from the dark parking lot. "You killed the Hammer Brothers. Praise be to the Lord, and for that bad mo-fo knife you got."

"Step into the light," Grey commanded. He was about to sheath his blade, but instead he lowered it along his leg, the point toward the sound of the voice.

"I'm getting there," the man said. "Got a trashed ankle."

A set of legs appeared in the shallow light, one of them limping, the torso, which wore a green military jacket, then the head. He wasn't elderly at all, but in his mid-30s, painfully thin, dead facial skin with a yellow tint, and sickly eyes. "Name's Jackson," he said. "Jack Jackson." He jerked his thumb over his thin shoulder. "I got a space out there where I sleep most nights when the dripping isn't bad. Plenty of others all around me, folks who don't get spooked thinking about the time they burned the bodies in the lot after that biological warfare shit they dumped on us. Heard they burned about ten thousand poor souls."

Grey scanned Jackson's hands and clothes for any indication of weapons. He didn't detect any.

Jack Jackson looked down at the chopped up shorter brother. "That's Raul, the shorter but meaner one. The other is Carlos. Carlos kicked me in the throat about a year ago and gave me this voice. A friend who used to be a medic said the blow must have damaged a vocal cord."

"Your limp?" Grey asked.

"Oh, you noticed." Jackson laughed at his own joke. "Yup, these buttwipes. Raul stomped my ankle and busted it good. The wife and I were sleeping in a doorway, and the asshole did it for no other reason than to get a giggle from his brother."

Grey glanced over at Tala to see how she was holding up. She was favoring her leg a little, and her forehead had stopped bleeding, but it had swelled to the size of an apricot. He looked back at Jackson. "We're looking for a guy named Leathers. Heard of him?" Jackson nodded. "Any idea where he might be?"

"His place is two blocks over. Just follow the right side of the parking lot until you hear the worse music ever to assault your ears. That's Hades; he stays above it."

Grey nodded. "Any idea if he's home?"

He shrugged. "Maybe. I was standing across the street earlier, and I saw him go inside. He looked like he was favoring an arm. I heard he stays on the second or third floor." He looked down at the one he said was named Raul, nodded, and smiled.

"Thanks, man," Grey said with a nod. "Stay safe."

"Sure. You too. Mind if I have one of the hammers. My wife and I found some sheets of tin, and we're going to build a little shelter somewhere."

"No problem. These guys don't need it."

Grey eyed him until he disappeared back into the dark. When he was sure he was gone, he turned to Tala. "You okay?"

"Yeah," she said through lips struggling not to grimace. "I checked all but two of his hammer blows. Both hit my forearm. Not bad out of about twenty, if I say so myself. The two weren't his hardest, but they still hurt. But I'm good to go."

"No, you're not. We're going back." He looked at the tunnel entrance. "But not through there again. We can go over a block and—"

Tala shook her head stubbornly. "I told you, I'm good to go." She stepped away from him, not favoring her leg as much as earlier. "When I fell, I landed on my hip, squished a nerve of something. It was hard to stand for a bit, but the numbness is going away." She tried to lift her left arm but couldn't. "I don't use my left much, anyway. Besides, I know what Leathers looks like."

"I got fentanyl," he said, digging into his pants' pocket.

"It makes me groggy, remember? Save it until after our mission."

CHAPTER 10

LEATHERS

Leathers' arm still hurt like a bitch, but knowing the Hammer Brothers were taking care of Grey gave him such relief that he thought he would top off the evening with one of the sluts down in Hades. He wanted to peek under the bandage Christina had done, but he was worried about messing up her good work, plus he didn't want to find out that the wound was worse. Ignorance was bliss, he thought. It sure did hurt.

He hoped the Hammer Brothers made Knife Fighter's son suffer.

It cost to get into Hades, but he didn't want to pay with bullets. He'd need them when he got a gun. He still had a few Quiet Moments Dog Sedative chews left. The K-9 drug didn't work on him, but the sumo guys working the front doors liked them. He got on his knees and searched under the bed until he found the old shoe. He shook out about a dozen pills he kept under the slip-in arch supports. He pocketed three—two for The Sumo and one for the slut—replaced the rest and nudged the shoe back under the bed. As good as a safe, he thought when he found the shoe lying next to a dead man after a helicopter had sprayed Ellis Street a while back.

Leathers still had his seven-inch Ka-Bar on his right side, but his gut was telling him to carry another blade. Always listening to that inner voice had kept him above ground through a lot of shit, so now was no time to ignore it, even if he was just going downstairs. Leathers strapped on his Ka-Bar TDI Tanto with a 3½-inch blade on his left side. His left arm was out of commission, so he carried the knife in its Kydex plastic sheath close to his belt buckle for easy access with his right hand.

He made his way down the stairs to the main floor—the terrible bone-jarring music growing louder with each descending step, every terrible note stabbing again and again at the severed nerves in his shoulder. He pushed open the small door to the lobby and nodded at the two sumo. Leathers thought they were Laotian. But that was irrelevant to street people's inclination to assign nicknames.

On one occasion, Leathers heard a former psychologist pontificate on the subject to a small group of sluts in Hades. He said, "In this new world where only the strong survive, nicknames make it less personal whenever someone meets a quick and violent demise on the mean streets and left to lie in their mess until the Pick-up Crew dumped them in a wheelbarrow for cremation. So whenever someone asks, 'Who's the dead guy,' someone else can say, 'That's Clubber.' Or, 'That's Dogman.' Nicknames make the decaying human a little less personal to the living."

Leathers wondered if that bullshit got the shrink laid that night for free.

"What ju gotch for us, man?" the sumo with the clear complexion asked. He wanted people to call him "Scar," though he didn't have any visible ones. Leathers thought his attempt to sound inner-city sounded silly.

"Some more Chewable Xanax, for you," he lied. "It'll mellow you out for a while. One each for you fellas."

"Only one?" the man with the weeping acne asked. He had been trying to grow a mustache for months.

"You know, times are hard, right?"

"Yeah, yeah, yeah," Scar said, extending his hand. "Gimme dem." He jerked his head toward the door. "You know duh rules. Don't kill nobody unless ju gotta."

"Oh, okay," Leathers said with sarcasm, shouldering open the door.

He compared the initial shock of walking into the place to being suddenly draped in a wet blanket sopped with sweat, blood, semen, and puke. He hated the music, but the smell was an aphrodisiac to him.

CHAPTER 11

GREY AND TALA

The walk, though not far, took them an hour because of the low light conditions and the hard-to-see debris lying all about. Grey tripped half a dozen times, nearly falling flat once when a piece of metal snared his foot and wouldn't let go. After that, he began stepping high as if walking in deep snow and set his foot down carefully for better purchase.

Tala did go down, twice, releasing curses Grey hadn't heard before. Apparently, she was hurting more than she let on from the Hammer brother, but when Grey mentioned they should head back, she snapped at him, "Pain demands to be felt; it doesn't mean you quit."

When Grey told her that she should write bumper stickers, she snorted a laugh, and that was the end of it.

At about the 30-minute mark, a square-headed pit bull, the white froth around its mouth almost luminous, charged out of the darkness and headed for Tala's closest leg. As smooth as if she had been practicing it, she hopped to the side, snapped her knee up high, and stomped down on the dog's head.

The beast shook its great skull, then plopped over onto its side, its eyes blinking rapidly. If the pit had been at its best, the stomp wouldn't have hurt it.

"Should we put the poor thing out of its misery?" Tala asked.

Grey shook his head. "Animals, I don't kill."

"Me neither," she said. "But I suggest we make some distance from Fido."

And they did, looking behind them every few seconds.

At about the 45-minute mark, Grey grimaced. "Is that music from Hades?

"That's earhammer loud," Tala said.

"Howitzer loud," Grey returned.

"Makes me want to cut somebody."

Now, 15 minutes later, they were standing across the street from the source. In the dark intersection to their right, five or six people huddled around a barrel in which licks of fire danced about its rim. Halfway down the block to their left, a small circle of people sat on the pavement around a solo lantern in their middle. Grey once mused to Tala that possessing a lantern required trading, stealing, hurting others, or all three. And the same for getting oil or batteries for it.

If you have it, someone else wants it.

Father.

He shook the thought from his mind. Now was not the time to grieve.

He said, "No one working the doors on the outside, but there might be someone inside."

They looked up but couldn't see a helicopter slowly passing overhead, its rotary blades barely audible.

A burst of gunfire from their right.

Grey and Tala reflexively pressed their backs against the building. The people around the lantern and those around the barrel dashed to the sides of the closest buildings.

"Close, but not that close," Grey said. He nodded at Hades across the street. "Let's see if anyone comes out." A moment later, two Asian men wearing kimonos emerged through the double doors looking in the direction of the gunfire. "I'm betting those two are the doormen." The Asian men reflexively crouched as a salvo erupted from the dark sky.

"Sounds like it's happening around that far corner," Tala said.

"Let's cross to that doorway straight across from us," Grey said.

He stayed at Tala's side as she hobbled as fast as she could. They ducked into the doorway about 20 feet away from the entrance to Hades just as half a dozen shots rang out, sounding like the same ground weapon as before.

The two Asian men, who were focusing their attention in the opposite direction, moved along the side of the building, apparently to see what was happening on the street around the corner. Grey and Tala took advantage of the moment and sidestepped toward the doors to Hades, then slipped inside without being seen.

They were halfway across the foyer to the double doors when the hammering music stopped. They froze, looked at each other. "Did we trip something?" Tala whispered.

They both startled as the all-pervading drum machines and heavy electronic sounds resumed. Tala touched the knife dangling from the end of her neck thong.

Grey said, "We go in the left door and move to the left, our backs to the wall, or whatever is there. Ready?" Tala nodded. He pulled open the left door just wide enough for them to slip into the semi-dark.

Their faces instantly recoiled from the sweltering, wet heat, and the reek of sweating bodies and a dozen other repellant odors. They took two quick steps in and then pressed their backs against a damp wall.

Strobe lights flashed and rolled and danced over the room in response to the horrific thumping percussion. Some gyrated, their arms swaying above their heads; others pushed and slammed into each other as in the mosh pits of years past. A few, completely naked, ground into each other, men and women, men and men, women and women, threesomes, foursomes.

To their left was a sunken area where people sat on cushions, faces nearly touching, screaming at each other to be heard. In one of its corners, two women smashed their fists into each other's bloody faces, while the others paid them no mind.

Someone smarter than him, Grey thought, looking about, found a way to harness power for the lighting and sound system. Generators, maybe, or solar panels. The temperature and the humidity were in the red zone, and Grey wondered if he would wilt or suffocate first.

Taking it all in, Grey incongruously remembered a refrain from a song by The Doors, one of his father's favorite groups. *And all the children are insane… All the children are insane.*

"Hey, you!" a female voice shouted in his ear. Grey jerked his head to the left.

The girl was young, late teens at the most, long unkempt hair, pretty without makeup, wearing only tattered panties. Wet hair stuck to her forehead and sweat rivered down between her bare breasts. She shifted her weight from one dirty foot to the other, and she seemed to vibrate with unbridled energy.

She moved over to stand in front of both of them, her hands fisted on her hips. "My name is Saffron. You know, like the spice? You two are new, I think." She spoke rapidly without pause. "My old man runs the place, so I know most of the regular crazies." She looked Tala up and down. "Yum. An Asian pearl." She looked into Grey's eyes. "You're yummy too. They'd *love* you over in the orgy area."

"The what?" Tala asked.

"Okay, here's the rundown," Saffron said, waving her hand over the room. "The place is separated into four areas." She nodded toward the dancers, now springing up and down as if the floor was a giant trampoline. "The dance floor, obviously," she giggled, turning back to them. "It can get you going, let me tell you. Over in the far right corner of the room, you can't see it from here, is the orgy area. That'll really get you going too." She grinned, looking pointedly at Tala. "They enforce the 'no more than 10 people at a time' rule pretty close in the orgy area. Anything goes, but if someone says no to you, you have to honor it. The bouncers enforce that pretty close too."

She pointed to the left of the room. "You can't see that corner from here either, but it's where you can blow off steam." She giggled. "But in a different way from the orgy area. You can fight. The bouncers there enforce a 'no more than four couples at a time' rule. You can fight any way you want as long as there are no surprises. You can say you want to fight with garden shears or something, and if it's okay with your opponent, then you can use them."

Astounded, Grey asked, "How do the fights end?"

Saffron smiled. "People get hurt, of course, like, maybe about two deaths a night or something. Last Tuesday, six dudes bought it. It was awesome. But that's really not bad considering how many fights there are. People love it. Me? I like the orgy area." She smiled at Tala.

"You're kidding, right?" Tala asked.

"No, I really do like the orgy—"

"About the deaths," Tala snapped. "How can you say 'it was awesome' with that stupid smile on your stupid face? Isn't this

new world bad enough without adding recreational fights to the death—?"

Grey stepped in front of Tala and leaned in so Saffron could hear. "Excuse her; she's had a bad day. Listen, we're looking for our friend, Leathers. Do you know him? We have to get a message to him."

Tala tried to get around him, but Grey reached back and grabbed a wad of her jacket and pulled her flush with his back. When Saffron tried to look around him, he stepped to block her. "Leathers. Do you know him?"

Saffron frowned her disappointment when Grey blocked her again. "I thought the hot one and I had a connection," she said.

"Leathers," Grey reminded again.

She looked at him. "Yeah, I know him," she said, her voice flat. "They shouldn't let him in here. I saw him about twenty minutes ago, heading over to the store."

"What's that?"

"Oh, I forgot to tell you about the fourth place. It's straight back behind the dancers, between the orgy pit and the fighting pit. It's a place for people who want privacy. Customers shop for a man or woman to satisfy them. Very low cost, and there are plenty to choose from. They take bullets, water tablets, salt." She shrugged. "I hear salt is getting scarce. Anyway, the only rule is you can't hurt the worker." She leaned in close. "If you like privacy, I'd be happy to take care of your needs. The girlie too if she's done having a temper."

"Thank you, Saffron. But we want to find Leathers."

She pouted her disappointment. "Okay, follow me."

"Wait. Does Leathers have friends here?"

Saffron made a face. "Well, I'm definitely not one, but yeah, there's a few here tonight. More like people that he pays to do some of his dirty work."

"Where?"

She gestured broadly at the room. "They're scattered about doing their thing.

Grey nodded. "OK, go ahead and lead the way." He looked back at Tala, her frown still bunching her brow. "Stay cool. It's about the mission." She shrugged, but the frown remained.

Saffron led them to the right side of the dancing area and then around the gyrating crowd. There was a narrow passageway on the right side between the dancers and where watchers leaned against the wall. It was darker here as the strobing lights barely reached this side of the room. Grey's head was throbbing from the jet-engine-like sound system, as well as the heat and humidity.

The music stopped.

So did Grey and Tala. They moved their hands near their blades.

Saffron looked back at them. "It's nothing. The sound system is old and stops all the time. It will start again in—" The sound came back on with a vengeance, startling Tala. Saffron pointed at her and giggled and gestured for them to continue following. Tala glared at the back of her head as if it were a target.

They rounded the back corner and stopped. Another sunken area; this one was full of naked bodies, every combination, every act, the strobing light accentuating their squirming sweating flesh. They're like a nest of pink worms, Grey thought, before a wave of nausea churned his gut.

About a dozen men and women watched from outside of the pit, several touching themselves.

"Hot, huh?" Saffron said into Grey's ear, the 'huh,' breathy.

"Show us the store," he snapped.

Saffron spun around angrily and stomped off along the backside of the gyrating dancers. About 20 steps later, she jabbed her finger toward a doorway where a naked girl sat next to the entrance. "There! Now, go eat shit and die," she shouted before merging into the tribal dancers.

Grey turned to Tala. "Let's"— he followed her eyes to the fight pit a few feet away. Two bare-chested men rolled about on the floor, exchanging punches and knee strikes to each other's face and torso. Two other men brawled with broken bottles, the jagged glass shredding wherever it made contact. One had taken a nasty gash across the side of his neck, the artery squirting like a severed hose. He won't last long, Grey thought.

On the pit's landing, a woman lay crumpled and motionless, one arm hanging down into the fighting area. Another female, apparently the victor, was holding her weapon, a bloody stone, in the air as several men pounded her back.

Grey turned away; Tala already had. The degradation of it all was too much for him to process, at least right now. He knew it was the same for Tala.

"How do you want to play it?" she asked, looking at the entrance to the store. "Stealth or barge?"

"Inquire first," he shouted into her ear. "If that fails, we do whichever one fits the bill." He stepped over to the teen sitting naked on a wooden chair by the entrance.

"Three bullets or two water tabs for a two on one time," she said, affecting a nonchalance that belied her years, 15, maybe 16.

"Do you know a man named Leathers?" Grey shouted.

She looked at him without expression and extended her open palm. Tala said something that Grey couldn't hear over the music, but he knew it wasn't complimentary. He dropped a water purifier tablet into the girl's palm.

"He's inside," she said, affecting a yawn.

"Which room?"

She smirked and held out her palm again. "That will cost you another—"

Tala reached around Grey and clamped her thumb and index finger on the girl's nose. "Look, cuteness," Tala snarled, cranking her schnoz a quarter circle. "Which room?"

"Owwww," the girl cried, her hands reaching for Tala's wrist.

"Don't you touch me," Tala growled, then twisted harder.

"Oh God! Sec-second one," she said nasally.

"Thank you," Tala said, releasing her grip with a snap. She stepped into the hall first with Grey on her heels. He started to suggest she try a little more patience but decided it was best not to say anything.

"Bernie! Two no-pays!" the girl called behind them.

"Stand fast, Tala," Grey said from behind her. The first door on the left jerked open, and a man the size of a dump truck emerged, his barrel-like chest stretching a black tank top, arms like tattooed ham hocks, and a neck as thick as a Greek column.

"You can get steroids in these trying times?" Grey asked before the bottom of his foot slammed into the man's closest knee. He bounced his foot off the floor and banged the patella again before the man had fully reacted to the first kick.

The behemoth cried out and extended a shaky hand toward his injured joint. But his cry quickly turned to a snarling growl, and he started to straighten.

As quick as a blink, and before grey could kick the man again, Tala extracted her large blade, spun it into an icepick grip and smashed the butt end into the man's throat.

He went down, one hand clutching his knee, the other clawing at his throat.

Grey knew Leathers would have to have heard the ruckus, but hopefully, he would think it was just routine trouble with a customer. He looked back to the entrance to the hall to see if there was anyone else coming. The naked girl was standing in the doorway looking dumbly down at the big man moaning and squirming on the floor. She looked up at Grey wide eyed, then spun about, no doubt going after more help. "We need to step up the pace," Grey said.

"Barge or stealth?" Tala said, looking at the second door.

"Barge," Grey barely uttered before Tala's foot kicked the cheap door below the knob, splintering the wood and sending it flying open. It struck the back of a kneeling elderly woman's head who was servicing a man leaning against the wall, his pants bunched around his ankles. The woman cried out, and so did the man.

Must have startle bit him, Grey thought.

"That's him!" Tala shouted, sweeping the injured woman over onto her side.

"What the hell!" Leathers yelled, struggling to pull his pants up over his swollen injury. "Who are—" His eyes widened as Grey stepped into the room behind her.

A large arm snaked around Grey's neck, bent him backward, and pulled him back through the doorway.

Tala spun around, her knife still gripped in icepick, her hand cocked at her shoulder. Without missing a beat, she launched the point of her blade as if throwing a baseball toward Grey's face. His eyes widened as it streaked toward him, arced down past his eyes, nose, and mouth to plunge into the meaty part of the thick forearm cutting off his air.

The owner of the big arm squealed and released his hold. He made the same sound again when Grey spun about and whipped his elbow into the side of the man's neck, specifically the cluster of nerves known as the brachial plexus. The man dropped with a thud.

For good measure, Grey stomped on his jaw, another knockout point.

Just as the old woman was struggling to get up, Leathers pushed her back down as he bolted out of the room.

"Bastard poked me," Tala said, making no indication that she was hurt. "He was trying for my face, but I deflected it. He's got one of those curved Ka-bars."

"You good to go?"

She nodded. "It's my left arm; it was in bad shape, anyway. My right one's still good. Leathers' left arm looked hurt too." She headed toward the doorway where the girl stood blocking the exit, her arms folded across her bare chest in defiance.

Tala palmed the teen's face like a basketball and thrust her into the crazed dancers.

"There." Grey pointed toward the fighting pit. "He's heading around to the other side of that."

Leathers shoved people out of his way, jumped over a man lying on the edge of the dance floor, and pointed his knife at a woman who took issue with his aggression.

A huge man stepped in front of Grey, shirtless, thickly muscled, his face seemingly chiseled from granite. Grey followed his eyes down to his sheathed Mossy. His jacket flap had caught behind the knife during his last struggle, leaving it exposed. The big man looked up at Grey. "Knives are only permitted in the fightin' pit. Give it to me."

"Where *do* you guys get your 'roids?" Grey asked before driving his fist into the man's Adam's apple.

"Good one," Tala said. "Big dudes can't toughen their throats." They stepped over him and continued moving around the fighting pit.

"I didn't see which way he went," she shouted over the music. Grey didn't either. He examined the pit area where four new fighters were going at it, one pair with metal bars, the other couple with chairs. Another body lay next to the female he had seen earlier. It looked like the guy with the bleeding neck artery.

Several dancers slammed into Grey and Tala, and it was only their quick footwork that kept them from being knocked over. Tala pushed the dancers aside and jutted her head forward, straining to see into the gyrating crowd and the pulsating light that created disorientating shadows and movement. She pointed at a man.

Grey looked where she indicated. He shook his head.

A forearm slammed against Grey's face, snapping his head to the side, then ground excruciatingly into his cheekbone and sinuses. The attacker's other hand secured the wrist of Grey's knife hand and forced it and the Mossy high up his back. The assailant began dragging him backward, Grey's churning feet trying to keep up. The side of his head was pressed into the attacker's chest, but he was still able to see another man gripping Tala's throat in a tight C clamp. Her knife was gone, and both of her hands were fighting the arm.

The music stopped.

"Tala!" Grey shouted, his voice strained. "Eyes!"

Without a moment's hesitation, she rammed a finger into the man's left socket. He bellowed, but he didn't release his clamp. So she pushed it in deeper, up to her middle knuckle, then stirred, as if her finger were a swizzle stick in a cocktail.

The man released her and clutched his face. "Derek!" he cried, staggered about before falling off the edge of the fighting pit and landing on two of the combatants, one of which was choking the other with a metal bar.

"Jerald?" the man restraining Grey bellowed in his ear. He stopped dragging Grey backward, and his arm reduced its crushing pressure "You bitch! You hurt my Jerald. Jeraaaald?"

The music blared back to life. Grey took seized the distracted moment to slip the Bucknbear tactical chopper knife, his father's cleaver, from his left coat pocket.

Still hanging from the man's arm, Grey swayed his hips to the side, opening a clear pathway to the attacker's groin. He swung the cleaver back with all the muscle and momentum he could muster…

…and chopped the man's package into two parts.

Grey had pocketed his father's cleaver but was still gripping the big Mossy when the small, dark-skinned man holding a rattan stick in each hand came out of the shadows and blocked their way. Grey was getting tired, and he could feel each of his injuries, but he was still sharp enough to deduce that this man, half the size of the last few, possessed skills with the nearly 30-inch-long sticks. He took a step toward the man to feel him out.

The sticks began moving in the air in an intricate, flowing pattern as the man slid his feet dance-like from side to side. He weaved the hard rattan faster and faster until they began to hum. Grey recognized the man's fighting style as Kali, a Filipino martial art. His father had studied aspects of it in the Philippines, and Tala had shown him some of what she had learned when she was young.

"Move to twelve o'clock," he said just loud enough for Tala to hear. "I'll go to six. Do it…now!"

Grey placed his left hand on his chest and held his knife near it as he began shuffling counterclockwise around the man. Tala remained motionless, her blade held close to her upper torso. Her left hand clutched a wad of jacket front, probably because she couldn't hold her injured limb up on its own. The man was now weaving his sticks so fast they were nearly impossible to see.

About 10 feet behind Tala, two women grappled fiercely in the pit, their screams a mix of adrenaline, excitement, and killing intent. A violent shove sent the closest one over the rim of the ring and rolling toward Tala. She quickly side-stepped to avoid getting bowled over, her avoidance inadvertently putting her within striking range of the kali fighter. The first whack struck her closest leg, the next one hit her hip. Then he commenced a hailstorm of blows.

Applying a technique to his father's axiom, "If you're fighting fair, you're doing it wrong," Grey lunged and thrust his big knife into the man's back, just missing his spine. Grey yanked it free and was about to drive in another stab, but the stick fighter spun about with a flurry of strikes on Grey's knife arm, sending his Mossy spinning free.

Tala was weakened from the assault, but the man miraculously didn't hit her healthy right arm. She scooted in fast, her lead hip nearly collapsing under her. Still, she managed to thrust her knife into the back of the Kali man's neck.

He screamed, spun, and whipped a single stick so fast that for an instant, Grey doubted his eyes until it smacked Tala's right biceps. Her knife flew somewhere into the midst of dancers, not one of which was paying attention to the stick vs. knife fight.

Grey snatched his blade off the floor and, as he rose, sunk his Mossy just under the man's ear. He forcefully rotated his hand to the right and left, extracted his knife, and stepped back.

The stick man spiraled to the floor, plopping on his butt, and raggedly exhaling his last breath so loudly that Grey could hear it above the music. His hands slid off his lap and onto the floor, the sticks still in his grip.

Movement out of the corner of Grey's eye.

He reflexively lifted his knife, but he need not have worried. It was only a dancer, a woman, naked as the day she was born, but had filled out nicely in the years since, dashing over to snatch the sticks away from the sitting dead man's hands. She disappeared with them back into the jam of revelers.

"Leathers went through that door," Tala said, breathing hard and moving around the sitting dead man. She was pointing at a door with block letters on it that were too far away to read.

He scanned her body. "Are you hurt?"

"Well," she said, massaging her right biceps, "the asshole did beat the shit out of me with sticks. But I want to finish this. You?"

"I can feel my arm swelling. I'm glad he didn't hit the back of my hand."

She looked over at the dancers. "Man, he was fast… Hey!" She took off at a fast hobble toward a man holding something in his hand for a woman to admire.

Tala's aggression so startled him that she effortlessly snatched away whatever he had in his hand. When he tried to get it back, she thrust the thing toward his face. Grey was halfway there when a strobing light bounced off the blade in Tala's hand. She was tapping it threateningly on the man's lower lip, his eyes wide, frightened. He slowly stepped back into the crush of dancers.

"Got my blade back," Tala said, limping back to Grey and holding up her knife proudly. "Let's get Leathers."

Grey grinned. "Yes, ma'am."

"Stealth or barge?" Tala asked.

They were standing next to the door marked Furnace Room. Tala was looking at the doorknob as Grey faced the other way, watching for any more of Leathers' people. *Please don't let there be more. Just let me have him.*

"Barging has been working for us so far," Grey said, turning around. "You good to go?" He knew she was hurting as much as he was, but he also knew her answer.

"Yes, and with prejudice," she said.

"Okay, you go right; I'll go left."

Grey turned the knob, which was hot to the touch, felt the latch release, and slammed his shoulder against the heavy door. It opened, but not much. A roar and rattle that was the furnace and a wave of intense heat smacked them in their faces. Grey leaned against the door and pushed it enough for him to slip through and go left, and Tala to curl around it and go right.

The two of them were standing on a red metal landing, something akin to a fire escape. They were about 20 feet above the cement floor, on which a monstrous ancient-looking furnace trembled and rattled from the roaring blaze within. It felt as if all the oxygen had been fried out of the room, making each breath difficult. For a millisecond, Grey thought of retreating back out the door.

"Leathers," Tala said, pointing down the slanted metal stairs to where the killer of Grey's father had just stepped out from under the steps. He jerked his head up at them, his face a mixture of surprise and disappointment.

Grey launched himself down the stairs.

Leathers was standing next to a door. He yanked on the knob, but it didn't budge. Grey hesitated on the next to last step, his right hand holding the Mossy in a saber grip. Leathers looked toward the furnace. An exit? Grey wondered. He couldn't see the front of the old boiler where someone's shoulder was moving in and out of view. "There's someone to our right, Tala. In front of the furnace."

"Check." She eased behind him and stepped down onto the floor. She scanned the area before slowly sidestepping along the side of the rumbling furnace toward its front corner.

Grey had been watching Leathers in his periphery, but now he gave him his full attention. The man had maneuvered his right leg forward, a standard-sized Ka-Bar in his right hand with an icepack grip, and in his rear hand, a smaller Ka-Bar, a TDI Tanto with a curved 3½-inch blade. His left arm appeared to hang lifelessly along his leg. The hand holding the weapon was slack as if he couldn't grip it more tightly. A bad day for left arms, Grey thought incongruously.

His eyes burned into Leathers. "One question: Why?"

Leathers shrugged indifferently. "Why do we do anything these dark days? Sustenance. One hundred nine-millimeter rounds, 20 gallons of clean water, and a half year's rent.

"You killed my father for rent?" Grey said, his voice icy. Leathers shrugged. Grey stepped down onto the floor, the butt end of his Mossy Oak against his chest, its point aimed at Leathers. With his weapon hand and empty hand positioned close to his body, it created an illusion that he was farther away than he was. But if Leathers was as experienced as everyone has said, it wouldn't fool him. "Who hired you?"

Leathers looked at Grey for a long moment as if debating whether to answer. He shrugged. "Oh, hell. I don't care if you know because the bastard shorted me half the rounds. I'll tell you, then you go away. Deal?"

Grey shook his head. "No. I'm going to kill you either way."

Leather blinked rapidly. "So why would I tell you?" he said, his Adam's apple taking a trip up and down his throat.

"Not used to people standing up to you?" Leathers blinked rapidly again and shifted his weight from his right leg to his left and back to his right. "Well, Leathers, if you don't, tell me, I will cut off body parts until you do. If you do tell me, I will kill you quickly."

Out of the corner of his eye, Grey could see Tala had stopped halfway along the side of the furnace. She looked behind her, over at Grey and Leathers, then commenced creeping forward.

"That's…" Leather's swallowed hard. "That's crazy thinking. You can't—" his eyes dropped to Grey's left hand as it retrieved the Bucknbear tactical chopper knife. The man's eyes widened.

"Recognize it, don't you? I'm guessing this blade is why your left arm is hanging like dead fruit on a vine." He watched the man squirm for a moment, then, "Who hired you? Tell me, or I will start by cutting off your feet first, and then—"

"Eagle!" Leathers blared. "He goes by Eagle, and I don't know if it's a street name or his last name. All he said was that 'Knife Fighter' killed someone important before The Change, and that other people wanted payback. I was hungry, so I took the job. It was just another job, Grey. It wasn't personal. It didn't mean nothing."

In his peripheral, Grey saw Tala stop at the corner of the furnace. She looked behind her, over at him, then leaned out far enough to see around the corner.

Rage surged through Grey's body. "'It. Didn't. Mean. Nothing,'" he repeated. He circled to the man's dead-arm side, the adrenaline surging through his muscles.

"Oh, my God!" Tala shouted. Grey snapped his head toward her. She had stepped away from the corner of the furnace, her arms trembling as she gaped at something in front of it, something Grey couldn't see from his position. She jerked her head toward him, then back at whatever was causing her reaction. "No, no, no!"

Motion on Grey's left side.

He reflexively sidestepped, feeling the displaced air of Leather's big Ka-Bar slicing vertically where his face and torso had been a hair of a second earlier.

He countered with the cleaver, a quick jab-and-drag down Leathers' face, leaving a two-inch slice on his cheek in its wake. "Short but deep," Grey said as the man snapped the back of his hand up to the bleeding gash, his eyes brimming with fear.

Grey watched him while simultaneously monitoring Tala in his peripheral. She was still standing motionless, her knife hand down at her side, her other one dabbing her eyes. Sweat? Tears?

Leathers was trembling now, but from fear or anger, Grey couldn't tell. He could step in and kill the man in an instant, which would accomplish his grandiose objective of ridding the world of evil. But Grey knew that a quick death wouldn't satisfy his other desire. His need to avenge his father's murder. Yes, it was wrong to think that way, but he didn't care.

"The Hammer Brothers?" Leathers said, taking a step backward.

"Sliced and diced," Grey said, his eyes watching. He wasn't stupid enough to try to run, so why did he step back?

Leathers glanced toward Tala. "You should see what she's seeing."

Grey knew it was a ruse, and he wasn't about to turn and look. She had moved out of his peripheral so he couldn't—

Leathers' snapped the big Ka-Bar up to his shoulder and whipped it toward him.

The half-second it took for the man to cock his arm was sufficient time for Grey to understand what he was doing. But the additional fraction of a second of disbelief that an adversary would actually throw away his weapon was time he should have spent evading.

The hard steel penetrated Grey's jacket, his shirt, and sank into the left side of his belly.

Grey looked in disbelief at the dark handle extending obscenely from his waist. The blade was ice-cold, but it burned, and it shocked his flesh and nerve endings. He fought his legs' desire to buckle.

He had been cut in battle many times but never had anyone been stupid enough—or brilliant enough—to throw a knife at him.

The pain in his gut was excruciating and profoundly weakening, but Grey forced himself to endure. And the blade had to remain.

"Never, ever remove a knife when stabbed," his father had drilled into him. "It's the barrier that slows the blood from leaving the body." *Well, father, it's pouring out pretty good as it is, but I'll do what you say.*

Leathers' expression looked like a big Ooooh shit!

Grey deliberately bent toward the floor; his peripheral perceived Leathers' left hand pass the curved Ka-Bar to his right. Grey moaned, the cleaver still in his left hand and the Mossy in his

right, his arms hanging limply. Leathers took the bait and moved confidently toward him.

Grey waited...

The man paused for a moment, then took another tentative step closer, putting him two strides away.

Grey's legs began to tremble, and he felt his strength waning. *Take another step,* he willed Leathers. *Come on. One more.*

Leathers' K-Bar lifted out of Grey's view... Then he stepped forward.

Still bent and looking as if he were going to sag all the way to the floor, Grey whipped the cleaver from left to right slicing just above the kneecap of Leathers' advanced leg.

Though the pain in his abdomen was greater than anything he had experienced, he whipped the big Mossy from right to left slicing deeply across the already severed leg's upper thigh. Both cuts were done in under two seconds.

Leathers was bent forward, his mouth open as his eyes stared in disbelief at his leg.

Grey straightened a little and simultaneously whipped the cleaver from left-to-right again, slicing across the man's right hip, his crotch, and his other hip.

Leathers' shrieks finally penetrated Grey's haze of pain. The man staggered back a step, but still within range. Grey was nearly straightened now, and despite the terrible fire in his punctured gut, he ripped the Mossy right-to-left across the man's torso at his nipple line. Leathers snapped up his right arm, his knife-holding-hand barely avoiding Grey's blade.

Again, the cleaver was already on its left-to-right course, slicing across the man's chest, this time severing the fingers of his knife hand, sending the weapon and three digits flying.

"Please!" Leathers screeched. "Stop!"

Grey's merciless Mossy slashed right-to-left, severing his neck.

Leathers fell forward, his severed arteries spraying their red contents into the air. His eyes closed in death before his body thudded to the cement.

Grey, his torso drenched in his and Leathers' blood, and his cloudy mind confused that there was still evil to destroy, whipped the cleaver from left-to-right through empty air above the dead body. He started to launch the Mossy, but Tala's shout snapped him out of it.

He wiped the splattered blood away from his face until he could see her standing in front of the furnace, her body motionless, her face frozen in horror. He forced himself, one foot at a time, to move toward her.

She turned as he approached and frowned as if not understanding all the blood. She gaped at the knife handle extending from his abdomen, her eyes trying to compute what she was seeing.

She looked up at his face. "You're... You're..." She turned robotically to the furnace.

He followed her eyes.

"See?" Tala said, pointing at rows and rows of dead bodies. More lay in piles along the wall where an old coal shoot was being used to deliver them to the basement.

Men, living men, were swinging the dead by their hands and feet into the furnace's yawning mouth and the consuming fire within.

Grey could barely hear Tala's distressed cries over the roar of the rumbling old furnace. "The bastards are... God help us, Grey. They're using the dead to heat Hades."

"You're a hell of a date," Grey said for the umpteenth time since they had left Hades two hours earlier. Tala had found two fentanyl tabs in his inside jacket pocket and made him swallow twice the dosage. He had slumped into the large wheelbarrow shortly after she had taken it from one of the furnace workers at knifepoint, and he fluctuated between sleeping and talking drunkenly. Besides commenting on how good their date was going, he had told he loved her at least 10 times, which was just fine with Tala.

She had muscled the wheelbarrow with her bad hip and him in it up the coal shoot to emerge behind Hades into an alleyway where workers were unloading the dead from wagons used to transport them from wherever. Like those she saw in the basement, some of the bodies were bloody, their lives obviously ending from violence. Others looked like they had passed in their sleep, and a few had dried froth around their mouths. Had there been another biochemical attack, and they just hadn't heard yet? Undertaker didn't say anything about it.

Focusing on Grey and their journey back to Sector Four helped Tala, at least a little, not think about the workers swinging the bodies into the blazing furnace on the count of three. When she did see images, she would dry heave, which weakened her even more.

Tala knew she couldn't go through the tunnel again. Instead, she opted to go around it two blocks over to the north. There were a few campers on those streets, and most people were cordial. Most.

Once when she stopped to rest, a man and woman without uttering a word, pushed her aside and started to dump Grey out onto the sidewalk. Though exhausted and physically hurting, Tala stabbed the man in his side with her big blade and squared off with the screaming female. When the woman backed off, Tala quickly hauled Grey away from them. It wasn't until a block later that it occurred to her that she had plunged the knife into his right side, his liver. She didn't mean to make it a potentially fatal stab; she just reacted to save Grey.

She would think more about later.

Two other times people wanted the wheelbarrow but threatening to cut them was enough to drive them off.

With Grey's father gone now and her sister close to passing, she was going to talk to him about moving out to the country. She hadn't heard anything about the conditions there, but they had to be better than the city.

"Take me to Undertaker, Tala," Grey said clearly. For the first time since she had drugged him, his eyes looked focused.

"You're not going to die, Grey. The nurse who's helping my sister can extract the—"

"Undertaker has had medical training too, plus he has some equipment." He looked around to see where they were. "One more block, then turn right. He can patch us up and get this knife out of me. How are you doing?"

"I'm tired of hauling your ass up and down these streets."

He grinned. "Your sweet talk is one of the things I love about you." He closed his eyes.

Tala smiled. That time when he said it, he was completely sober.

EPILOGUE

"I didn't know about the furnace at Hades," Undertaker said after he had finished with Tala and Grey. Tala's injuries—a cut shoulder, a hammered forearm, and stick thumped hip, thigh, and arm—was just a matter of bandaging her shoulder and telling her that time will heal the blunt-force trauma wounds. The forehead wound was not from the steel end of a hammer but from a hard jab with the rubber butt end. "It still hurts like a bitch," she said.

Grey's abdomen was touch and go. Undertaker did the best with what he had, which wasn't much. He had Grey bite down on a fist-sized clump of gauze and had Tala stand behind his head to restrain his arms while the knife was slowly removed.

Undertaker poked and prodded, hem and hawed, and rubbed his chin. "Could have been worse," he said after a while. "If it had been on your right side, it might have punched through your liver. That's a worst-case scenario, especially these days with limited to no medical facilities."

Is that always a fatal wound?" Tala asked, thinking of the man she had stabbed on the way.

"These days, I would say, yes."

Grey looked at her questioningly when she uttered a curse under her breath.

"As for now," Undertaker said, "I think the blade missed everything important. Your blood looks good, which means it's not contaminated from other organs. I've drowned the wound in iodine, which is the only antibiotic I have. It's old school but good stuff. You just need to take it easy to let the wound heal. Don't tear out the stitches." He looked at the Ka-Bar in his tray. "And you got yourself a souvenir."

"Thanks, doc. I owe you big time."

Undertaker waved him off. "Thanks goes to your pretty lady here. If she hadn't gotten you here..."

Grey stretched up and gave Tala a kiss, then groaned and covered his bandaged abdomen with his hand as he plopped back down on the gurney.

"No, no," Undertaker said. "None of that for half a year." He laughed at their shocked faces. "Just kidding. You'll figure out when you can handle it." He organized his work tray for a moment, then, "I picked up your father this morning. The man in the stairway too."

"Thank you," Grey said softly. "I'd like to be here when you… Can it wait until tomorrow? I'd like to get some sleep first."

Undertaker nodded. "But no longer. I don't have a freezer."

After a moment, Tala said, "Hades was awful. An apt name. Hell, for sure."

"I could never do that," Undertaker said, referring to the furnace. "I cremate here, but I do it with respect. I figure we're all on this nightmare ride together, but as terrible as it is, we can all respect that each of us is hurting." He shook his head, his face drawn. "I'm sorry you two had to see that. It must have been terrible."

Tala took Grey's hand.

"I think things might be getting worse," Undertaker said, shaking pills out of a bottle. "Have you heard about Sector Six on the east side of the river?" Grey and Tala shook their heads.

"Give me your palm, son," Undertaker said. "Here are eight fentanyl tabs. I'd appreciate you paying those back when you have a chance."

"I will, doc," Grey said. "Sector Six?"

Undertaker's face tightened. "A serious shortage of food and water. Rioting over the smallest amount. Hundreds were killed in one day, and even the helicopters got involved. I'm afraid things are about to get even uglier."

"Food wars," Grey said. "It was only a matter of time."

Tala looked at him. "My brother lives there," she said. "We need to go to him."

KNIFE FIGHTER 2

"Adrenaline rising knife
fights." ~ AC
"Fans of Mad Max will
love this." ~ KF
"Brutal!" ~ JH

A POST-APOCALYPTIC
SHORT STORY

LOREN W CHRISTENSEN
BEST-SELLING AUTHOR OF OVER 60 BOOKS

ACKNOWLEDGEMENTS

As always, a big hug to my bride, Lisa, for her encouragement, enthusiasm, and support.

And an awkward, manly hug to Kevin Faulk for his edits and input, Karol Krauser Hasegawa for the gift of the Thai sickle, and Mike Schwinof for the use of his Kukri.

"Is the knife evil? Only if
the wielder is evil."

~ Rick Riordan
The House of Hades

WEAPONS FEATURED IN KNIFE FIGHTER 2

Grey carries a very old kukri with a 10-inch blade and a 19-inch ax with a 3 ½-inch cutting edge.

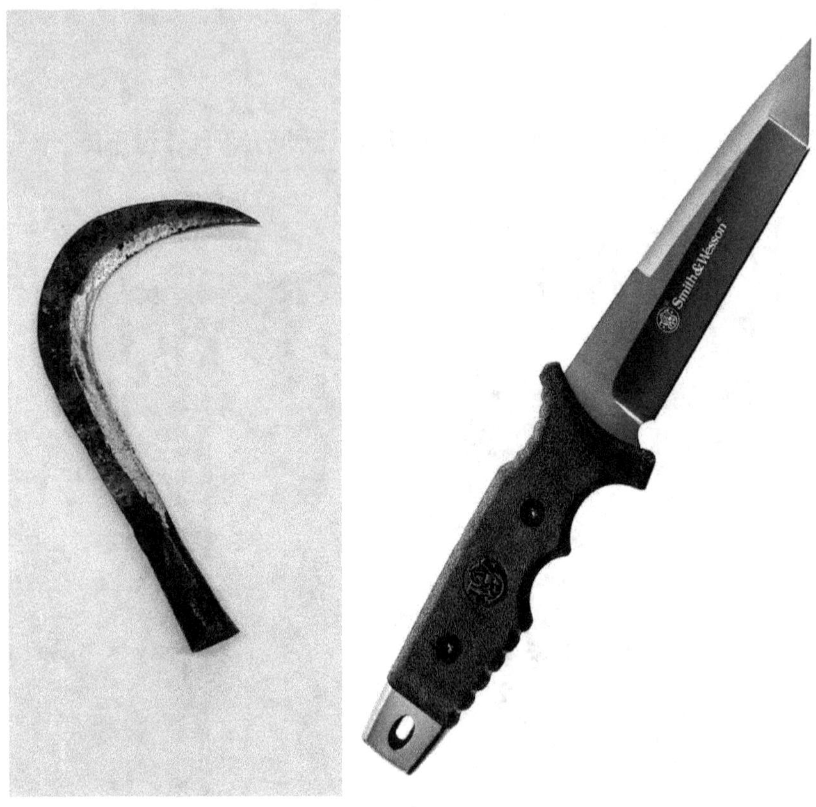

Tala carries a Smith and Wesson 5.2-inch Tanto fixed blade on her hip and a sickle used by farmers in Thailand as a work tool and a weapon.

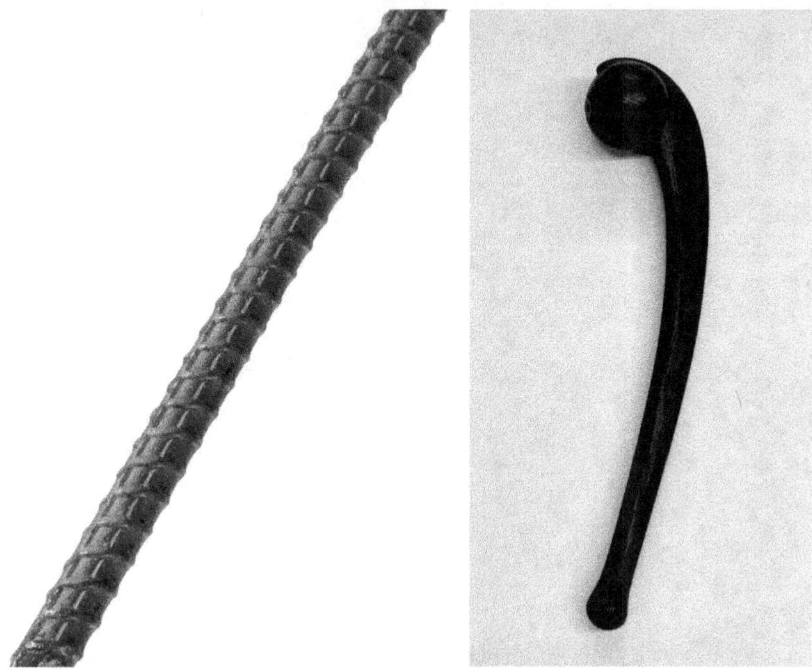

Weapons used by two members of the bandanna gang. A three-foot section of rebar (L), and a modern-day Indian war club made of polypropylene, two feet long, slightly curved at the top, and fitted with a four-inch in diameter ball head.

THREE YEARS, TWO MONTHS FROM NOW

CHAPTER 1

GREY, TALA, AND ROBERT

Tala was leaning her butt against the windowsill and fluidly moving her Smith and Wesson nine-inch carbon fixed blade from icepick grip to saber grip and back. She believed and, wisely so, that it wasn't a good idea to change grips in the middle of a fight. But she also knew from experience, lots of it, that anything can and will happen when the excrement hits the fan.

She had been practicing what she called "rolling the carver" in her right hand for about 10 minutes, fluctuating her speed from fast to dazzlingly fast. Now she was slowing it down, but not too much, and smoothly switching hands to continue rolling the carver with her left. About half the time, there was a millisecond of reconnecting with the new hand. Few people would notice the one-thousandth of a second delay, or care, but she did, and it was pissing her off. A week ago, there was a full second hitch, and this time next week, she anticipated that the delay would be gone completely. But it was there now, and she didn't like it.

The first three weeks of Grey and Tala's recuperation was slow and painful. Undertaker stopped by a few times to check on their injuries, especially Grey's abdominal stab wound. He was astounded each visit at how quickly they were healing despite not benefitting from antibiotics and the proper nutrition so necessary to repair damaged tissue. By the fourth week, they were doing bodyweight exercises—pushups, squats, and slow punches and kicks. By the sixth week, Grey was able to do planks and crunches for his midsection, which at first hurt, but by his fifth session, the pain was tolerable, and he could feel his strength returning.

Soon, they began manipulating their knives. Using her injured left arm "hurt like a bitch," as Tala put it, but she did it anyway. She did too much one day and could barely move her arm for the next two days, but by the fourth, she was at it again. Soon they were practicing drills, offense, and defense, and moving faster and more fluidly with each set of repetitions.

The style of knife fighting that Tala learned from her family in the Philippines and the approach Grey had learned from his father and his knife fighting buddies in the Army, was what many would call basic. It lacked frills, fancy twirls, arm entanglement with the adversary, spinning in a circle here, and somersaulting there. Their approach was based on overwhelming speed and target selection, while filling every beat of time with a storm of slices, dices, and stabs. Grey often said, "When it's time to slice and stab, rain down razor-sharp hell all over the adversary so he can't reach for his umbrella."

The first time he said this to Tala, she rolled her eyes and said, "'Storm. Rain. Umbrella.' Oh, I get it. It's a metaphor."

On this day, Grey was bare-chested on the floor, working his abs and watching Tala manipulate her blade. She placed her knife on the windowsill and rolled her shoulders back and forth to work out the tightness. "Not bad," he said with a subtle smirk.

"Yeah, I got your, 'not bad.' And you just did three sets of abdominal crunches without making your pain face."

He placed a palm over the ugly red abdominal scar where two months before a man named Leathers pierced his belly with a Ka-Bar, all seven inches of its blade. Seconds later, and in terrible pain, Grey filleted him from his knees to his throat. "I was making the 'pain face' internally, but I guess that's an improvement. I did the usual twenty crunches for the first set, added 10 on the second, and pushed it to 40 reps on the last. It hurt, but I think some of it was psychological." He turned onto his side and pushed himself up until he was sitting. "How many pushups did you do?"

Tala picked up her knife with her left hand and jabbed the air a few times, forward to 12 o'clock, then three each to 10 o'clock and 2 o'clock. "My left arm is feeling good today. Maybe seventy-five or eighty percent of how it was before I got hurt. For pushups, I did three sets of 40 each. I could have done 50, but I'm feeling lazy today."

"Lazy isn't a word I'd ever apply to you. 'Cute,' I would. 'Sexy,' for sure. 'Sometimes scary.'"

"'Scary.' I like that." She slashed the air back and forth several times so fast it was nearly impossible to see. "But only with the blade, right?"

"The blade? Okay, sure, with the blade too," he smirked.

"Oh reeeeally," she said grinning and setting her knife back on the windowsill. She put her hand on her hip and exaggerated a fashion model's heel-to-toe walk. Her eyes gazing into his, she straddled his extended legs, pulled off her T-shirt, and lowered herself down onto his thighs. "Well, scaredy-cat," she purred, pushing his upper body back down onto the floor, "you ought to be shaking in your boots right now."

"You got brave pretty fast, big boy," Tala said, her face against Grey's bare chest. Six inches below her face was his angry, four-inch red abdominal scar. In a move of pure desperation, Leathers had surprised Grey by throwing his Ka-Bar and burying the large blade into his abdomen. The good news was that it missed critical organs. They could get fentanyl for the pain, which Grey took sparingly out of concern he would get addicted to it, but antibiotics, sterilizers, and other healing facilitators so plentiful before The Change were virtually nonexistent.

Outside the window, the usual dark night drips slithered down the glass. Would they ever find out what they were?

"It was easy. You inspired me," Grey said. He could feel her mouth smile against his chest. He kissed the top of her head. "We need to get up. Robert said he would be here right after dark."

"Food!" she said enthusiastically. "You'll need the energy

because I plan on scaring you again later." He swatted her bare butt as she scooted off the bed then watched her dress.

For Grey and Tala, the last two months had been an eternity of painful recuperation from injuries received on their journey to find the man who murdered his father. The search had been punctuated with life and death battles with skilled and unskilled assailants, leaving Grey and Tala with wounds that necessitated rest, recuperation, and rebuilding.

Three days after their return to Sector Four and their respective apartments, Tala's sister, Angel, died. Weeks earlier, she had fallen into a nest of rats that had bitten her over three dozen times, infecting her, probably with multiple diseases.

Their friend, Robert, a nurse before The Change, had tended to Angel, though there wasn't anything he could to do without medicine. Nonetheless, he stayed with her and kept her comfortable by singing, holding her hand, and giving her refreshing sponge baths. Three days before she died, she whispered in his ear that she loved him.

To show her appreciation after Angel passed, Tala made an arrangement with her landlord to let Robert have her apartment. She moved in with Grey, and they hired Robert to bring them food while they recuperated. Grey gave Robert 9mm bullets—his father had acquired many boxes of them a few months before he was murdered—to buy food for the three of them. Over the weeks, they had become close friends.

Tala was dressed now and examining her knife as Grey dressed. He smiled at her. "I love you," he said, slipping a sweatshirt over his head. When he pulled it down past his eyes, Tala had moved up within three feet of him.

"I love you too," she said and thrust her Smith and Wesson nine-inch carbon fixed blade at his chest.

He twisted his body out of the line of the blade's trajectory and simultaneously snapped the back of his forearm out to deflect the attack off course. He followed with a snap-punch to Tala's throat, stopping his knuckles on her skin.

"You notice I attacked you with my left arm?" she asked, spinning the knife from saber grip to icepick.

He smacked her knife hand that hadn't completely finished the grip change, sending the knife flying across the room and onto his pillow. "Did you notice that I almost punched your throat with my almost good as new left hand? And how easily I knocked your weapon out of your weak grip also with my left? I hope I showed you again that the fancy grip change should never be done within range of a threat, even when practicing."

"'How you practice is how you will fight for real,'" she said, imitating how he had told her that a dozen times. "I was just showing off." She leaned toward him. "Now, don't punch me; I'm coming in for some lip action."

He puckered, but Tala quickly stepped beside him, hooked his neck with the crook of her arm, and swept the back of her leg into his.

She got me again with her *osoto geri,* Grey thought, landing on the floor with an arm slap to absorb some of the impact. Without hesitating, he spun on his butt, hooked her closest ankle with his foot, grabbed the waistband of her jeans, and yanked both toward him. Tala fell with a grunt on her side. Without missing a beat, she thrust her leg straight up in the air and dropped her heel fast toward his abdomen.

"NO!" he blurted, though she had stopped her foot short of contact.

"I'm so sorry, sweetie," she said, scooting over to him. He pushed himself up, one hand covering where her foot could have landed if she hadn't controlled it—the same place Leathers' knife had sunk into his belly.

Tala cupped his face and kissed him. "It was just reflex. I'm so sorry."

While Grey had mostly recuperated physically from the stab wound, he had progressively become psychologically sensitive to it. If Tala hadn't stolen a wheelbarrow and hurried him through the dangerous streets to Undertaker's place, where the old man had applied his limited equipment and limited medical knowledge, Grey would have been a customer for his cremation furnace.

Grey understood the issue was in his head, but that didn't reduce its impact. A week earlier, Tala accidentally bumped his midsection close to the wound, and a week before that, he unintentionally banged his abdomen against their table. Neither incident hurt him physically, but Grey nonetheless froze for a moment. When he did it to himself, his reaction lasted about five seconds, but when Tala bumped him, he froze for a good 10, probably, he figured, because someone else did it to him. Apparently, it was irrelevant that the perpetrator was the love of his life.

He hoped this would soon pass.

Grey walked over to the window and looked out at the darkness. They liked the new apartment the building overseer had given Grey after his father's murder. It was larger with a view of the street below and an intersection at the end of the block where, somehow, a dim streetlight came on every night. Grey called it "watching TV" because there was always a show going on under the streetlight.

Of course, something was going on everywhere at night in the mostly dark and destroyed city, lit sporadically by lanterns, campfires or, rarest of all, an actual lightbulb powered by a generator, solar panels, or whatever. During their two-month recuperation, they had watched a gang fight in the intersection that left three dead, two packs of dogs chew and claw each other until only four were left to hobble off, and a rocker randomly shooting into the darkness. Rocker was a slang word for an old expression meaning someone was 'off their rocker.' It ended when someone dashed out of the shadows and struck him in the head with a cinderblock, then fled with his rifle. The rocker lay dead in the intersection for two days, then one morning, he was gone.

"What do you think?" Tala asked.

Grey looked at the Amerasian beauty and tilted his head in thought. He knew what she was asking because she had asked it every day for the past two weeks: Were they ready to travel to Sector Six and look for her brother, Juni?

They were feeling better now, though neither was 100 percent. Tala's hip and forearm didn't bother her at all, nor did Grey's left shoulder. Both of their injuries were from blows inflicted by the Hammer brothers wielding stubby hammers. The walnut-sized swelling Tala wore on her forehead—from the butt end of a stubby nail driver—was gone, leaving only a two-inch diameter yellow and brown bruise. Robert had removed the stitches from Grey's abdominal wound a few days back, noting the surface damage was healing nicely. But it was still sensitive to the touch, and his insides still hurt, whether real or imagined, he wasn't sure.

"What do *you* think?" Grey asked.

"My kicks feel good, my punches too." Tala walked over to the table and picked up her newest blade. She found it in Grey's father's knife collection seven weeks ago, and instantly, in her words, "Fell madly in love with it." It was a small sickle used by farmers in Thailand for harvesting rice. The short handle fit her hand perfectly, and she liked that the curved nine-inch blade was, "One nasty mo-fo."

The Thai had long ago determined that the sickle was as effective on human flesh as it was in their rice paddies. When Grey was about 10 years old, his father told him, with a twinkle in his eye, that the Thais also used it to circumcise monkeys and very naughty little boys.

Tala picked it up and slashed left and right, up and down, and diagonally, the fast-moving blade dividing the air with a *whoosh*.

She switched to her left hand and made the same cuts. "With my left arm, I can feel some stiffness and a slight pinch when I move laterally, but considering my condition eight weeks ago, I'm... good."

Before Grey could get a read on why she hesitated before she said 'good,' she turned toward the dark window. She followed a slow crawling drip down the outside glass with her index finger. She looked back at him. "But..."

"But you're hesitant to say you're ready to go check on your brother, and you're hesitant to say you aren't."

Tala nodded. "How about you?"

Three knocks at the door, a pause, then two more. Then, "'Tis moi."

"It's Robert," Grey said, glad he didn't have to answer Tala yet. He released the door locks.

"Hello good looking people," their friend said, breezing in. He dropped his backpack on the table. He was a quarter-inch under five-foot-four but refused to say he was five foot three. He wore his dirty blond hair in a ponytail, and despite the daily struggle, he had an easy smile, twinkling eyes, and was always a ball of energy. Tala told him repeatedly that she was jealous of his healthy glowing skin and green eyes that always seemed to be laughing at everything. His usual response was to wave her off and say, "I exfoliate my face thrice weekly and apply a high-quality skin moisturizer daily," which always made Tala laugh. Of course, neither was possible since The Change. He also liked to say, "I didn't choose to be gay; I just got lucky."

Once when Tala teased him about him liking way too much tending to Grey's stomach wound, Robert said, "He's a lovely man but waaaay too macho for me. I prefer them skinny, pale, and aaaall femboy."

Grey had pretended to be relieved. "Whew, I was worried." Then, "Or should I be disappointed."

Robert had laughed at that and said, "Good, we got that out of the way."

Even with the window closed, they heard a gunshot that sounded like it came from no more than a couple of blocks away. Four shots from a different weapon followed.

"That last was an AR-15, I think," Robert said, without the flamboyant speech he sometimes used around Tala and Grey for laughs. He looked toward the window as he shrugged out of his backpack. "Not sure about the other one." He set it on the table with a heavy clunk. "Some boys were arguing hot and heavy the next block over. It might be them."

Grey moved to the side of the window and looked down. The lit intersection was empty." He looked over at Robert. "Last time you went to get supplies, you said you saw three helicopters buzzing around Hampton Bridge."

Robert nodded. "One each night I was there. This time I saw four. Someone told me that two of them shot the shit out of a group of people on the street that leads up to the bridge. But I also heard that people on the ground shot at a helicopter first."

"How'd you know the make of the weapons just now?" Tala asked.

He waved his hand in the air. "Oh, my knowledge extends beyond moisturizers, honey."

Tala laughed. She stepped over to Robert's backpack. "May I?"

she asked, reaching for the zipper.

"Of course. The good news is I scored lots of food; the bad news is it all expired last year or the year before."

Tala shrugged as she extracted can after can of Campbell's soup. "They always errored on the side of being conservative with those dates." Then to Grey in an over-the-top little girl's voice, "Honey, do you mind taking the first few bites?"

"I heard some news," Robert said, looking at both of them.

"About Sector Six?" Tala asked, looking at Grey, her expression communicating that he didn't answer her.

"Six *and* Seven," Robert said.

Two months ago, Undertaker told Grey and Tala that Sector Six had been experiencing terrible riots because of food shortages. The rumor was that there had been mass deaths from hunger, street violence, and the mysterious helicopters. Grey and Tala wanted to go to Sector Six to find Tala's brother, but until recently, neither felt they were in good enough condition to deal effectively with whatever problems arose on the walk there, plus whatever awaited them in the troubled sector.

During the first month of their recovery, Robert would hear of continuing problems in Sector Six but got few details. Then all news stopped. Robert said his usual source—a man named Ronny, who made the trip to Sector Six every few days to check on his parents, hadn't returned. A week passed and then another, but still, Robert's friend was a no-show.

"I heard from Ronny," Robert said, turning away from the window, his face beaming.

"Good news!" Tala said happily. "What happened to him? Is he okay?"

Robert's face changed to concern. "Not really. The day before he arrived in Sector Six, his father had been beaten to death by a group of men. The sweet man was sixty-nine." Robert swiped his palm across his tearing eyes. "Ronny stayed to take care of everything. Their home was quite large with a big backyard, so Ronnie buried him on the property. His mother couldn't be consoled, and that night after they buried him, she died in her bed. Died from a broken heart, poor thing. Ronny was devastated, of course, and stayed to take care of her body."

"Sad," Grey said. "He's lucky to have a friend like you."

"So are we," Tala said. "So, it's still rough in Sector Six?"

Robert nodded. "Ronnie said he's not going back. There are bodies everywhere, and every day is pure survival. He said people are fleeing, but most don't know where to go because they've heard other places are worse. I know our sector is bad, but it's not anything like Sector Six. I just pray ours won't get like that. But," he shrugged, "why wouldn't it? We've just been lucky so far."

"Had Ronny heard of Juni Santos?" Tala asked.

"Sorry," Robert said. "I asked, but he hadn't heard of your brother."

"Did you have any problems?" Grey asked.

"None I couldn't outrun—twice. One little shit wanted my shoes, and since he was barefoot and the road was littered with broken asphalt, I lost him easily. The other time, three guys were after me, calling me a fag and all that. If I hadn't been fleet of foot, I might have lost my virginity."

Tala and Grey laughed.

"Speaking of Ronny," Robert said: "I think now that he's back in this sector, we can be more than just friends."

Tala gave him a quick hug. "I hope so too. Hey, we can double date."

"Yeah," Robert said wistfully. "We'll all be ancient by the time that kinda life returns, if ever." He looked at Grey. "You have a guesstimate as to when we're going to Sector Six?"

"We're still deciding," Tala said, looking at Grey.

"You said 'we're,' Robert," Grey said. "Like when are *we* going to Sector Six. We?"

"Yeah?" Robert said as if not getting his point.

"You aren't going with us."

"What? Of course, I am, Grey. I'm your nurse. Plus, I can be of help. It's hairy in Section Six. Just getting over the Hampton Bridge would be a challenge. It was touch and go just getting close to the sector, and back."

"Sweetie," Tala said, touching Robert's arm. "Grey and I have trained most of our lives for this new world. That is our purpose. We are supposed to help people. You are too but as a caregiver.

We got healthier and strong because of you, and you were there touching my sister's gentle soul with yours as she weakened and passed. You can't go with—"

Robert's eyes flashed anger. "You think you know me, but you don't," he said. "You don't know me, you've never made an effort, but that doesn't stop you from telling me where my worth lies."

"Robert!" Tala said, her face surprised and pained at the anger in his voice. "I'm sorry if I offended you. I love you. I don't want you to get hurt and—"

"Tala," Grey said, cutting her off. He was looking at Robert as if for the first time. There was something there he hadn't noticed before. Grey had been so focused on his injuries and seeing Robert as the person helping them get better that he had been blind to was right there below the man's surface.

"Robert," Grey said gently. "I apologize. We apologize. We have been so self-focused, first with Angel, then with us." Grey stepped over to where Robert was leaning against the table. "May I ask how old you are."

Robert's face was tight, his anger still apparent. "Thirty-six."

Grey nodded. "You haven't always been a nurse, have you?"

Robert looked in Grey's eyes. "No."

"Soldier? Cop? Bodyguard?"

"What?" Tala said in a small voice.

"Bodyguard."

Grey nodded, his eyes still locked on the short man. "Armed or unarmed?"

"Armed."

"With the weapon you've been carrying?"

"What?" Tala said again. "You have a gun, Robert?"

Robert met Grey's eyes and asked, "How long have you known?"

"About three minutes."

"I've been carrying it the last two trips."

"Where did you get it?"

"Off a man who tried to shoot me with it." Robert pulled the flap of his jacket back to reveal the weapon. "It's a Glock seventeen, nine-millimeter. I carried a nineteen when I was bodyguarding."

"What happened to him?"

"He didn't survive."

"You didn't run from the three guys who chased you, did you?"
Robert shook his head.

"Their status?"

"Two of them didn't survive either."

"So the nine-millimeter bullets I've been giving you to buy food, you've kept?" Grey asked.

"Guilty," Robert said. "I used some thirty-eight ammo and matches that I had to buy our food."

"Damn," Tala said under her breath. Robert looked over at her. "I'm so sorry," she said just above a whisper.

Robert nodded. "Forgiven."

"What kind of training have you had?"

"I trained privately with an FBI range officer in the Glock and Sig Sauer. I prefer the Glock. I trained for two years in general combatives and several months in techniques specific to bodyguarding. I was just starting to teach it when I got shot."

"Shot?" Tala blared. "You got shot?"

"In Ireland about eight years ago. I was escorting a very wealthy man from New York to a compound outside of Dublin when my team was ambushed. Three of my people were killed, and I was shot in the hip as I pulled the principle from our car just before it was riddled. The principle survived, and six out of the thirteen who ambushed us perished.

"I had been thinking about getting out of the business for a while—the travel, long hours, ridiculous demands from self-important principles. It was consuming my life. My mother had been a nurse, and the guy I was seeing at the time was one, so I went to school for it. I graduated, then worked in a hospital for a year before the world turned to shit. Since The Change, I help where I can."

Grey looked at him for another moment, then, extending his hand, he said, "We're idiots. We'd be honored to have you go with us."

Robert shook his hand and accepted a hug from Tala.

CHAPTER 2

GREY, TALA, AND ROBERT

It was nearly 9 a.m. before they took their first steps on their journey. Grey had heard a few strong wind gusts rattle their window before sunup, but at the moment, there was only a slight breeze moving the low hanging dark clouds across the sky.

Once he and Tala decided they were fit to travel and that Robert could go with them, their friend headed back to his apartment to prepare. The two of them slept soundly and met Robert in front of his building, ready to go.

"When I was packing," Robert said by way of a greeting, "I was thinking that it seemed like I just made this trek. Then I remembered that I did just make this trek, yesterday. Except I was hiking back." He was wearing a burgundy ski jacket that hung below his rear, concealing his Glock.

"You still up for it?" Tala asked, knowing the answer. She was wearing her usual olive-green cargo pants and black jacket. Her coat was long enough to conceal her fixed blade on her right hip and her sickle on her left side. She looked over Robert's shoulder at a woman on the same sidewalk a half block away heading toward them.

On the way to meet Robert outside his apartment, Grey and Tala had talked about him joining their two-person team. Tala said, "It sounds like he knows what he's doing but…" She lifted her eyebrows at Grey.

"We watch him," Grey had told her, the finality of his tone indicating that he had already thought about it. He was wearing a long dark brown coat that hid his kukri. "If he's as good as he implied, fine. But you and I have a synergism. We know what each other is going to do, but he won't know it. Likewise, we won't know what he's going to do."

"Gotcha," she said. Then she had bumped his shoulder with hers. "Synergism, huh. I love it when you talk dirty."

Robert didn't hesitate to answer Tala's question. "Of course, I'm still up for it. Is there a plan?"

"We always have a plan," Grey said. "It's called winging it." Grey watched the woman's hands as she neared them.

Robert shrugged. "Winging it works. Plans never seem to work out these days, anyway." Without turning to see who Tala and Grey were looking at walking up behind him, he said, "She's harmless. She fancies herself a medium."

Good awareness, Grey thought.

"Friends," the middle-aged woman said as she pressed her palms together under her chin. "Namaste." She was wearing a tattered brown robe like a monk would wear, with a bright pink threadbare stocking hat, strands of gray hair sneaking out from underneath. Her motorcycle boots were too large for her. She nodded at Robert.

"This is Kathryn," Robert said. "We have talked many times."

To their east, a helicopter was hovering over a tall building. Apparently satisfied all was well with whatever it had alerted on, it continued on its silent way.

Kathryn was studying Robert. "Your backpack, honey. Are you traveling today?" He nodded. She reached out and took his hand in both of hers and looked into his eyes for a moment. "Not a good day to travel, Robert," she said, kneading his palm. "I see four of you…" She frowned, rubbing his hand harder. "Oh my…" She closed her eyes and shook her head. "Stay in your rooms, all of you." She looked at Grey and Tala, then back to Robert. "Heed what I say."

She released his hand, moved around them, and hurried down the sidewalk, her too-large boots clumping.

Grey watched her walk away, then turned his gaze on a man leaning against a corner building at the next intersection. Not perceiving him as a threat, Grey asked Robert. "Your friend ever been right?"

Robert shook his head. "Not once, but she means well." He laughed at his own joke. Then, "I keep forgetting to tell you, Grey. I've heard people—you know, on the street, in my apartment building—talking about you."

"Me?"

"Yes. It seems that everyone knows about what happened to you guys on the way to Hades and in the tunnel. They know your father passed and that you guys were like an army on steroids. They say your father was the old Knife Fighter and that you're the new Knife Fighter now."

Grey puffed his cheeks and exhaled. "Not good," he said, looking down the street. "I might as well have a sign on my back."

"You can handle it," Tala said. "Just stay alert."

"Some have been calling you 'Knife Fighter' too," Robert said, looking at Tala.

"What?"

"'Wonder Woman Knife Fighter,' I heard one guy say."

When Tala looked at Grey with concern, he said, "You can handle it. Just stay alert."

Robert started to laugh but stopped when Tala shot him a look.

"How do you usually go?" Grey asked Robert.

"I've always gone east on Victor for a mile, south on Kennedy to McArthur, then east again to Hampton Bridge. Last night, though, when I was coming back, there was a gang of about six on Kennedy carrying on like they were drunk or something. So I went past that street and cut over on Obama."

Grey reminded them to be mindful of all 360 degrees around them, and if something looks wrong or doesn't feel right, let the others know right away. "If one of us gets into a confrontation," he said, "it's especially important for the other two to protect the one by watching the surroundings for additional threats. If you see an opportunity to help, do it, then immediately go back to looking outward." He looked at both of them. "Okay, let's do a quick weapons check and move out."

Grey pressed his arm against his side and felt the old kukri with a 10-inch fixed blade and a grip made of buffalo horn. He remembered his father saying he got it from a man in 1970, who said he got it from a friend in 1952 who brought it back with him from India. The story was that it had drawn much blood during the county's independence in 1947. Grey carried it in a leather sheath.

Grey had trained with the kukri in the years before The Change, but he had forgotten about it until he was going through his father's box of knives during his recuperation. Since it was a tad heavier than his big Mossy Oak and the weight was distributed differently due to the curved blade, it was perfect for helping him rebuild his strength. After two months of daily training with it, building power, speed, and fluidity, he felt he had recaptured his earlier skill and was completely confident taking the kukri with him on the trip.

This time his left jacket pocket was empty. On the journey through the tunnel and to Hades two months back, he had carried his Mossy Oak on his right hip and his father's Bucknbear chopper cleaver in his coat. In his father's final battle, he had chopped a wedge out of Leather's shoulder with it, putting the man's limb out of commission.

The gods were kind to Grey and allowed him the opportunity to use the chopper to finish what his father had started.

Tala patted her side where she carried her Smith and Wesson nine-inch carbon fixed blade. This trip, she replaced her Morakniv Edris fixed-blade that she usually wore around her neck on a leather thong with the Thai sickle. She made a sheath for it to hang under her arm like a shoulder holster for a firearm. She planned to find a better way to carry it when she had time.

"You carry one in the chamber?" Grey asked after watching Robert check his weapon and replace it into his hip holster. He nodded. "Good. Tala and I have water, do you?"

Robert nodded. "And a potato and some past-date Spam."

"You can't have too much Spam, that's for damn sure," Tala said. "Grey and I each have a can of stew, also expired. So none of us should have a problem with constipation."

"Okay, we're good to go," Grey said, "Let's move out."

They walked side-by-side up to the corner, made a right turn on Victor, and began walking east. The street was like most in Sector Four: broken buildings that once housed name brand businesses, chewed up asphalt and concrete, the ambiance muted and sad during the day, and dark and forbidding at night. A scattering of people leaned against building fronts, sprawled on blankets and tarps in doorways, or wandered on the sidewalks or down streets that hadn't seen a vehicle since the months after The Change.

Despair in monochrome.

"Food," the man said, stepping out from an alley entrance. Fifty feet back, Grey had silently pointed at the upcoming opening and indicated for them to move out into the street to avoid surprises. "Anything would help." Then the ragged, 50-something man with a greying beard eyed Tala. "Niiiice," he said, his tone syrupy, suggestive.

Grey was about to tell him about Fat Phil's a few blocks away who often had food to sell, but when he heard the man's disrespectful tone, he kept it to himself.

"You want something?" Tala asked when the man wouldn't stop staring.

"I'm looking at it, sweet cheeks—"

Tala's foot snaked around his closest one, added a shoulder to chest bump, and down the man went onto his back. She lowered her knee onto his crotch. The man started to push himself up but stopped when she leaned more weight onto him. "Lay back, or I'll crush it." He did, his breathing ragged.

"The world has changed, sir," Tala said calmly. "That doesn't mean that common decency and respect for each other are gone. We're all in this struggle together. It's up to you if you want to add crushed nuts to the mix."

"I'm sorry," the man managed, his voice strained. "I... Please don't... I'm really sorry."

"Grey," Tala said without looking away from the man's scrunched up face. "Tell the gentleman how to get to Fat Phil's."

Grey did, and the man thanked him, then apologized once more to Tala. She stood up and extended her hand to him. He was hesitant for a moment but took it and got to his feet with her help. "Have a good rest of the day," she said. "And be kind. It's not hard."

"I will," the man said, straightening his ragged coat and exhaling a long breath of relief. He nodded and headed off in the direction of Fat Phil's, looking back at them every few steps.

Tala usually smeared dirt on her face before going out to hide her beauty, but she decided not to this time.

Half a block away, Robert moved beside Tala and, in his best *Saturday Night Live* Chris Farley voice, went, "You know that thing you did to that guy? That...was...AWESOME!"

The three of them proceeded east on Victor.

Every 30 minutes or so, Tala and Grey took turns "walking point," as Grey called it, with Robert always taking the rear. As they proceeded, Grey gave Robert a few tips on monitoring people, such as how to see all 360 degrees around them with just a small turn of the head. He emphasized the importance of looking up since people liked to drop things on passersby. He told him to be aware of people's hands, watch the V formed by their chin and shoulders because virtually any movement a person makes is telegraphed there. He said most people will look where they're going to hit, and to always be suspicious of bulges under clothing. It was especially important not to focus so intently on one person that other threats around them are missed."

All good info, thanks," Robert said. "I also monitor everything lying around on the streets, sidewalks, and inside buildings as potential weapons that others can use, or that I can pick up to fight with."

"Oh, man," Grey said, shaking his head and chuckling with embarrassment. "Sorry, Robert. I had a brain burp there and forgot that you know all this stuff given the kind of work you used to do."

"Sure," Robert said. "But I appreciate the refresher. It's been a while."

Grey remembered giving Robert other tips when he began going out to get medicine and food while he and Tala recovered. He didn't know the man's history then, but Robert had listened and nodded. He was definitely not a know-it-all. There were too many of those already.

"Let's keep our chatter down now," Grey said in a low voice. There wasn't anything tangible that he saw in the new block, but in his gut, the vibe felt off. "The sound of our voices carries in these empty streets and attracts undesirables. Let's focus on monitoring the sidewalks and streets in front and behind us, the four-way intersections, rooftops, open manholes, inside doorway insets, behind piles of debris, and windows where people can see us, but we can't see inside."

Their route wasn't a thick tangle of green flora, but it was nonetheless a concrete jungle of unseen dangers.

Ten blocks later, the trio ducked quickly into an empty storefront; its door partially open.

Seconds earlier, the godawful sounds of screams behind them reflexively made them twist about, their hands reaching for their weapons. A half-block back, a woman they had nodded to seconds earlier, was now sprawled on the sidewalk as a pack of wild dogs savaged her arms, legs, and face, their heads whipping from side to side as they tore skin, tendons, muscle, and veins from her body. One of them, an exceptionally large Doberman Pinscher, abruptly stopped and jerked his blood-dripping face in their direction.

The beast launched toward them; two other dogs close behind him.

Grey was the last one in the dark, garbage-strewn room. "The door latch is broken off," he said, pushing the door closed. "We need to put our weight against it."

Tala quickly pressed her back against it and set her feet to brace herself. But before Robert could add his muscle, the dogs hit the other side like a herd of Brahman bulls. The impact knocked Tala away from the door and into Robert. He lost his balance and stumbled over a car tire, landing hard on his butt.

Grey was pushing with all his strength. "Some help here," he managed, his shoulder pressing hard against the quaking door, his feet churning on the cement floor.

A black snout and salivating mouth pushed through the partial opening, forcing the door open a few inches. Tala slammed into it just as a second set of dagger-sharp teeth pushed over the top of the first dog. The two partial heads snarled and growled, their drivel-spraying mouths snapping at the air. Robert slammed his weight against the door, causing the dogs to yelp from the crushing pressure against their snouts. They jerked and tugged their heads free.

Silence.

Grey peered through a crack in the door.

"What do you see?" Robert whispered.

"They've gathered out in the street, and there's four more of them." Grey looked into the dark behind him. Any light that seeped in through the cracks in the door and the grimy windows faded a few feet into the room. "Tala. See if there is a way out of here. A backdoor, maybe." She nodded and quickly disappeared into the dark, her fixed blade in her hand.

Grey pressed one eye against the crack again. "I count six. Big ones, all of them looking at the door. Did you see how many there were attacking that woman up the street?"

"Six," Robert said, bracing his back against the wood near where the door latch should have been.

"Oh no," Grey said. "There… There's a man, a rocker, I think. He's across the street dancing and waving his arms around like he's trying to get the dogs' attention… Okay, he got it. Two of them are bolting toward him."

"Crazy. What are the others doing?"

"Watching this door. One dog hit the man's legs, and the other went high. He's down." Grey turned and scanned the floor. "Grab some of the cardboard that's scattered around. Maybe we can stuff it under the door."

Robert began picking up cardboard when a loud, desperate scream from outside stopped him. "That him?"

"Yeah. The four are standing now, all of them focused on our door. I think they're about to… Here they come!"

Grey braced himself against the wood, his eye still watching through the crack. Robert pressed his upper back and palms against the door, his feet shuffling for a solid purchase.

"All four of them?" Robert asked, his voice quivering.

"All six—"

The dogs slammed against the door, splintering the wood and knocking the men back a step. Grey and Robert recovered quickly and shouldered the door again, pushing it with all their strength. Still, three big dog heads managed to force it open enough that the bottom dog pushed itself halfway in, its body straining, its enormous mouth snapping at Robert's leg.

"Keep pushing," Grey said, his right hand extracting his kukri. "Arch your lower back out a little."

Robert did as he was told. "Why— Whoa! Daaamn!"

Grey thrust the big knife on a straight line between the door and Robert's kidneys, with no more than an inch to spare, and rammed the point through the bottom dog's long snout. Grey yanked it free.

The dog yelped and smashed his head from side to side against the door and the door facing, spraying snot and blood, then pulled itself from the opening.

Another dog replaced it.

"There's a door back there," Tala said, running up, adding her weight between the men. "It's not locked, but on the other side— Is that blood?" she asked, looking at the floor around the door opening. "You okay, Robert? Did you get bit?"

"Stab their snouts," Grey said. "It's the only way we can get them to back off."

Her eyes searched his. She and Grey believed that it was okay killing people for the common good, but harming animals was a whole other issue.

"Do it," he snapped. "We'll talk about it later."

"Shit," she said, then thrust her nine-inch blade between the door and Robert's lower back, and deep into the dog's snout.

The dog howled, and Robert yelped. "Tala!" he snapped. "At least Grey asked me to arch my back. Plus, I didn't even see you pull your kni—"

The lower panel of the door caved inward. Two snouts struggled to push through the broken wood.

"I can shoot them," Robert shouted.

Grey shook his head, grimacing as he pressed against the door with his left shoulder, the effort hurting his abdomen where the knife had pierced. He quickly switched to his other shoulder. It didn't help. "Tala, change places with Robert and stab whatever pokes through the opening."

Again, the dogs slammed into the door, jarring everyone and nearly causing Tala to fall. "Robert, as soon as the pressure on the door weakens, head for the one that Tala found and hold it open. We'll follow you when we can."

Grey's plan was to hurt the dogs enough to make them back off for a few seconds so he and Tala could reach the other door. With only two of them running through the dark, there would be less chance of them tripping over each other. Plus, Robert didn't have a knife. Grey wanted him to only use the gun as a last resort. Twice he had seen wild dog packs become mad with frenzy when someone fired a round. One of those times, the dogs slaughtered seven people trapped in a room like they were in.

Tala hammered the butt end of her big knife on a snout. It had no effect.

"You have to stab them," Grey shouted above the deafening cacophony of door banging. "They are no longer dogs. They're beasts that want to kill us."

"Dammit!" she shouted, looking down at a filthy black dog squirming his head and shoulders through the space between the door and the facing. She rolled her knife into icepick grip and slammed the blade between the frothing dog's eyes. "Dammit!" she shouted and pulled it out of the yelping face. "Dammit," she bellowed as she stabbed it again. The dog extracted its head only to be replaced by a rust-red-colored one, its bloody teeth snapping at the air just inches from Tala's legs.

"Dammit, dammit, damnit, dammit!"

Grey and Tala pushed the door shut after the last dog extracted its wounded face. He peered through the crack in the door, which was now much larger than before. "Two of them are down," he said. "One is over on the far sidewalk running in circles and rubbing its face on the concrete. The other isn't moving. Okay, a new dog just came from somewhere and joined the three glaring at this door. I don't think we should run for it yet."

Tala was peering out at them from a splintered portion of the door next to where the locking mechanism used to be. She whispered, "I've seen some dog gangs before, but this one is batshit crazy. How you want to play it?"

Without moving his shoulder from the door, Grey eyed the cardboard scattered about. "Let me know if they're coming," he whispered. He snatched up four pieces of thick cardboard of varying sizes, the largest about 15 inches by 20. He eyed the bottom of the door, then began folding them in half. When he halved all four, he told Tala to open the door a couple of inches.

Grey commenced jamming the thick cardboard under the half-inch clearance between the bottom of the door and the cement floor. "You think that's going to hold them?" Tala whispered, her tone doubtful.

He shook his head. "I just want to slow them for a couple of seconds." He stuffed the last one under the door, its scraping sound on the cement louder than the others.

"They heard that," Tala said. "Aaaand they're coming."

Grey leaned against the door. "You got enough opening to poke your blade through?" Tala looked, nodded. "Get ready, but wait until I tell you."

Two of the big dogs crept cautiously toward the door, the other two followed. They held their heads high, eyes laser-focused on the slight opening. The smaller of the two in the lead bumped the other dog's shoulder, making the larger one snarl and snap. The smaller one lowered its head in subservience and moved over a few inches.

"Get ready," Grey warned, watching the bigger dog drop its snout toward the opening. "Okay, I lost visual."

"I got a snout," Tala whispered, jabbing her blade in and out of the door opening. "I didn't get him."

"That's okay. Keep doing it; the dogs know what that pointy thing is now, and they jumped back. Here comes another. Jab when you see something." She did. "Yes, that worked. All four are backing up. But it won't last. Let's head for the door."

"We're coming, Robert," Tala called into the dark as she and Grey bolted across the room.

A loud bang echoed through the empty room. Grey looked back. The cardboard kept the door from opening all the way, but he knew another ram would be enough to allow the dogs through.

"Follow my voice," Robert called to them from the dark, his voice barely audible above the sound of the manic barking.

Another crash, wood splintering, toenails scrambling for purchase on concrete.

Grey thought Tala was in front of him until she banged into him from behind, sending her down to the floor.

"The dogs are inside!" Robert called. "Come on."

"Now shoot," Grey called to Robert as he pulled Tala to her feet.

The gunshot sounded like an explosion in the dark, empty room, and it hammered into Grey's right eardrum sending him back to that

mud-brick house in Afghanistan.

Grey and a young sergeant kicked in the door. Grey started to go left, and his partner started to take a knee right just as a bearded man rushed at them from around a door archway, firing a revolver, the missed rounds tearing chunks out of the sod walls. The sergeant fired first, his M4 sounding as if it were no more than two feet from the side of Grey's head. He had forgotten to wear his ear protection, and the explosion felt as if it shredded his right eardrum, and his equilibrium warped—

He was back in the dark room. Tala was gripping a wad of his jacket front and pulling him toward the door. "Come on—"

Grey was slammed from behind and sent sprawling on the floor, the side of his head hitting the cement.

Disoriented.

Something heavy on his back.

Snarls next to his ear; hot putrid breath against the side of his face.

Tala shouting.

Dog claws tearing at his jacket. Grey turtled his head and covered the back of his neck with his hands. He had to stay face down.

He couldn't let the dog get to his abdomen.

The animal dug at his back as if trying to make a hole.

Can't roll over. Keep the stab wound pressed against the floor. Don't let the dog—

Shook Shook Shook

Grey knew that sound.

Shook Shook Shook

There it was again, just inches from his ear.

The sound of a knife plunging into flesh.

The dog wailed, also next to his ear.

Clarity returning.

The weight rolled off or was pulled off his back.

The dog lay next to him, a Great Dane, its breathing ragged, its paws churning against Grey's shoulder.

Protect the knife wound, protect—

Someone grabbed his arm and yanked him away from the dying animal.

"You're okay," Tala said.

"Don't let them get to my wound," he said, his face pressed against the floor, his voice muffled.

"You're okay, baby," Tala said gently. "Robert killed one dog, and I got the big one on your back. The rest have backed up to the front door. But they won't stay there."

Grey lifted his head and looked left and right, tried to stand, but his body wasn't receiving his brain's commands. Robert took his other arm, and they dragged him the rest of the way through the doorway and gently laid him down. Grey could see Tala's feet by his face.

"Oh!" she gasped. "What the hell? I saw the woman before but..."

Grey didn't understand what she was saying. Out of his peripheral, he saw Robert shut the door and engage the lock. On the other side of it, he heard the sound of clicking nails growing louder and louder, then a series of loud thumps against the door. "Don't let them get to my wound."

"It's wood, but it's a strong door," Robert said, as he peered through a small window in the door. He turned around and looked down at Grey. "Are you hurt or—" He slowly lifted his head, his eyes looking beyond Grey. "Holy shit," he whispered.

"What?" Grey said, straining to look up at him. When Robert continued to stare wide-eyed at whatever was behind him, Grey rolled over...

...and looked into the ashen face of a dead woman, one eye partially open, the other closed, her face covered with dried, crusted blood.

On the other side of her—more bodies, lots of them.

Grey had seen many dead bodies in his life, beginning in Afghanistan during his tours, and countless times since The Change. Seeing one or two didn't affect him—God knows he had been the cause of a lot of them—but seeing so many in one place and without warning, never failed to bother him.

Not long after The Change, he came upon over a thousand bodies in a large parking lot. Some were scattered about haphazardly, other lay in long, neat bloody rows and still more were heaped in burning piles. The sight still haunted him three years later. Then several weeks ago, in the basement of Hades, he and Tala saw dozens of them in piles ready to be unceremoniously chucked into a giant furnace to heat the repugnant Sodom and Gomorrah.

When he came upon the parking lot, it revealed its terrible presence a little at a time. It was still ghastly and horrific, but he can't imagine how it would have been if he had just breezed around a corner and been smacked in the face with the ghastly sight. Discovering the bodies in Hade's basement was completely unexpected. He had followed Tala around the edge of the furnace—and there they were.

This time, though, Grey opened his eyes and looked into the face of a dead woman. When he quickly scooted up onto his rear, he saw more bodies, more than a dozen, lying feet to heads along the right side of a long hallway that led to a small door. Unlike the door out in the other room, the one at the end of the hall had a window through which dull light cast a diffused gloom along the length of the hall.

He could tell by the way the bodies had been positioned and the final expression on all the faces that the hallway was a morgue, not a hospital. Blood gathered around the bodies, and streams of it had flowed over the floor to the opposite wall. It would be safe to assume that all of them had died from violence.

The good news was the dogs had stopped banging against the door.

Tala and Robert hadn't said a word in the five minutes they had been in the hall. Robert seemed mesmerized by the bodies; Tala had been staring at the floor after her initial gasp. She told Grey three mornings ago that it was the first time she hadn't dreamed of men swinging dead bodies by their hands and feet into the mouth of the big furnace in Hades.

"Can we leave, Grey?" Tala asked without looking up. She reached over and touched his hand with her fingers.

"I'll lead," he said. "You follow, but keep your head turned to the opposite wall. Robert, watch the door behind us."

She looked up at him. "You okay," she mouthed, looking into his eyes with concern.

He was resting his hands on his abdomen. He shrugged.

The three of them had no choice but to walk through lakes of blood, leaving shoe prints in their wake.

"I can see an exterior wall," Grey said. "Probably another building across an alley or something." He slowed as they neared the door. The bloody streaks on the concrete floor indicated the bodies were dragged inside. He stepped over them as best he could and peered through the glass. He placed one side of his face against the window and looked as far as he could, then the other side. "It's an alley," he said. "Lots of blood on the pavement. I can only see a few feet in either direction, but to the right, I think I saw someone's shadow."

"Any place is better than here," Tala said.

"I'll go right," Grey said. "Tala, you go left, and Robert, you go center with your Glock, but no farther out than us. Let's maintain a line."

A loud bang echoed down the hall, made Tala spin around. "Those dogs haven't given up yet," she said. "They—" More booms followed by the sound of splintering wood.

The door exploded open, spraying wood chunks over the closest dead bodies. "They're in!" Tala shouted, yanking her long knife from its sheath.

"Let's go," Grey said urgently, his kukri in his hand along his leg. "Shut the door behind you, Robert." He gave a quick glance behind him—and wished he hadn't. The dogs, four of them, were rabidly shredding flesh from the dead. "Go, go, go!"

He turned the knob and shouldered the door, expecting it to be one of the hard-to-open pressure types. It wasn't, and it was sent crashing into the wall with a pronounced bang. "Get the door, Robert," he reminded as he slipped to the right of the opening.

"Shitshitshit!" Robert shouted, bolting through the doorway. "A big-ass Doberman is coming!" He ran out into the alley without shutting the door.

Tala cut left, saw what Robert did, and reached for the door. "Slam it!" Grey shouted. She swung it with all her might, sending it on a collision course with the black Doberman Pincher's face.

The dog didn't react to the impact—not even a blink—and the door bounced back open. The animal's black-dead eyes bored into Robert; it crouched to spring.

Grey, his hand covering his abdomen with his left hand, lowered his big kukri close to his knee, then whipped it upward, chopping into the mad dog's neck under its foaming mouth. The animal opened its jaws, releasing a loud hiss before it stumbled back into the hall and crumpled to the floor.

The three of them slammed the lime green door shut a hair of a second before the rest of the pack slammed into it on the other side.

"I'm so sorry, guys," Robert begged. "I lost it for a second. It won't happen again."

Grey nodded, noting an overturned chair where the door had struck it, and a few feet away, a wooden wagon. It had big wheels and a rectangular pull bar on one end that allowed one or two people to push or pull it. Blood had seeped through its bed, forming a partially dried pool underneath. Since The Change, variations of the wagon's design were used to transport dead bodies to crematoriums. The exit to the alley was about a hundred feet away.

"Grey," Tala said from behind him. When he turned to look at her, she pointed to the right.

"What the hell?" Robert said.

The right exit was about a hundred feet away too, but four men stood between it and the trio. Two of them were standing together by a chair at Grey's two o'clock; the other two were standing about

20 feet down next to the same wall as the trio. Grey counted four lime-colored doors like the one they just burst out of.

"Y'all know how to make an entrance," one the two men across the way said without humor. He was tall, late 60s, his beard mostly white.

"If you're here to steal from us," the man next to him said, his voice even and conversational, "we'll kill yuh." He was younger than the bearded man, 50s, skinny as a pole. He looked at the older man. "Right, Harry?"

"We need to kill them just in case, Harry," one of the men farther down the alley said. Those two looked to be in their late 20s. The one who spoke was wearing a greasy baseball cap.

"Just in case," the other one parroted. The two were approaching slowly, cautiously. "I'm damn tired of assholes stealing from us. Stealing what we worked for."

Grey raised his palm. "We have no idea what you men are talking about." He jerked his thumb over his shoulder toward the door. If the dogs were still there, they were quiet now. "We ducked into that storefront out on Victor to get away from the dogs. They chased us through the place and down a hall that led out here. And why are those bodies in there?"

"He's bullshittin'," Harry's skinny partner said, not taking his eyes off of Grey.

"We're not," Grey said. "We're on our way to Sector Six looking for someone. Not out here to steal." He shrugged. "And what is there to steal?"

"The dead," the bearded man said.

"He's bullshittin', Harry."

"Damn straight he is," the one with the baseball cap said.

"Damn straight he is," his parroting partner said. "They need killing, don't they Tom?" Tom nodded as he twisted his cap around, so the bill was behind his head. Grey told Tala once that guys who wore their caps backward let you know right up front that they're douchebags.

Grey shook his head in disbelief at the stupidity and brutality of the men. "Is it that easy for you people?"

"Sure as shittin', pal," the man with the backward baseball cap said. He and his parrot stopped about a dozen feet away. "I got a family I gotta feed, and I'm tired of rats like you three taking what the rest of us work for."

"Sure as shittin'…" The parrot frowned, trying to remember everything his idol just said. He gave up, and said, "Me too."

Grey nodded for Tala and Robert to move up on the other side of him. "We're not thieves. Were on our way looking for a relative. You heard the dogs. We were escaping them. We have no interest in stealing the dead."

"He's bullshittin'," Harry's friend said for the third time. "And we can see that big ol' knife down there by your leg."

"All right, fellas," Harry said, scratching his beard as if he had come to a decision. "Let's let these three be on their way. We all saw how they come burstin' out that door, and how that Dobe came after them. They ain't here to steal no—"

"Shut up, old man," the man in the baseball cap said. "We've got it from here. I'm thinkin' these three were trying to steal from us, and the dogs interrupted them. Why else would they have been in the room in there."

"I told you," Grey said. "We were—"

"He's bullshittin' for damn sure, Harry," the skinny one said. Harry sat down on his chair and folded his arms.

"Start backing out," Grey said over his shoulder. To the men, "We're leaving."

Harry's friend moved to cut them off, and the other two moved toward Grey.

Grey raised his kukri to his chest and continued to back up as the men fanned out to his two o'clock and 10 o'clock. The man with the baseball cap occupying the 2 o'clock, pulled a large knife from a belt sheath; the other man shrugged off a small backpack and extracted an ax. Both were holding their weapons in their right hands.

"Don't do this," Grey said. To himself: *Don't stab me in the stomach, don't stab me in the stomach, don't stab me in the stomach, don't…*

"'Don't do this,'" baseball cap sneered. "Was that a whine?" He rolled his knife into icepick grip. He did it smoothly, although stupidly since he was so close to Grey. An icepick grip was strong, but the operator had to be a little closer to the enemy than when using saber grip. The baseball cap man held it low, about even with his pants belt.

Grey's saber grip on his long kukri gave him a reach advantage. He lifted it neck high, let it descend to his solar plexus, which he covered with his left hand, then slowly raised it to his upper chest. He continued to fluctuate levels as he maneuvered to his right until he had "stacked" the two men: baseball hat in front, his friend behind him. Each time the parrot stepped to get out from behind baseball hat, Grey moved to maintain the stack. Neither man seemed to notice what he was doing.

In his peripheral, Grey saw Tala and Robert in a stand-off with the skinny man. Harry simply watched from his chair; his demeanor tired.

The man wearing the baseball cap lunged and whipped his knife in a wide arc toward the left side of Grey's face.

Grey leaned his head away from the knife's trajectory as he simultaneously snapped up both arms to form a shield, his left forearm impacting the man's lower forearm, his weapon arm striking the nerves near his inside elbow. Before the man could retract his arm, Grey ripped his blade downward, slicing through the man's sweatshirt and deep into the muscles of his upper forearm.

His buddy's face distorted with rage. He lunged around his screaming friend and brought his ax down toward Grey's head.

Grey snapped his left shoulder back to blade his entire torso. The ax ripped through the air, missing. Before he could retract his blade, Grey snapped a fast and tight left roundhouse punch into the man's Adam's apple.

The blow was a deliberate, medium impact snapping blow, designed to make the man choke without sending him stumbling back out of range. Grey had more to do to a man who wanted to kill him with an ax.

He brought the kukri straight down on the left side of the man's face, separating his ear neatly from his head and embedding the big blade in his trap muscle. He yanked his knife upward to free it from the meat, then brought it down on the right side of his head, removing that ear and sinking the blade into that trapezius as well.

Grey executed the strikes so fast that the throat-punched man was just starting to react to the first ear amputation when his other one was removed.

Both landed next to their owner's shoes.

Grey quickly slipped his foot behind the screaming earless man's closest foot, then bumped the man's chest with his shoulder to force him to trip and fall to the asphalt next to his ears. It was Tala's favorite move, and he would use it when the moment was right.

Grey turned to the man with the hat who was crying like an infant about his cut arm. "Pick up your deaf buddy and move back a few feet—"

The stupid man ripped his knife, still in icepick grip, down on a vertical path, which Grey sidestepped, again saving his face and chest.

Frustrated and enraged, the man lifted his weapon up high and slashed it down again. Grey casually sidestepped the other way. Poor or no training, he thought, thankful.

Like the shower scene in the movie *Psycho,* the man raised his blade again high above his head to strike.

When Grey sidestepped for the third time, he whipped his kukri with flawless form—a strong, stable stance, picture-perfect body alignment, a faultless blend of muscle relaxation and seamlessly timed muscle contraction—to slice the man's hand off just above his wrist.

Since he had been gripping his weapon at high 12 o'clock, his hand, the twitching fingers still gripping the handle of his knife, dropped on top of his head, slid off onto his shoulder, and landed on the concrete a few inches short of his friend's ears.

The man looked dumbly at his blood-pumping wrist stump, his eyes blinking rapidly, his face turning white as freshly fallen snow. He curled to the asphalt, unconscious.

Tala and Robert were facing the other man who was gripping what looked like a fireplace poker. Tala was holding her knife along her leg, and Robert's hand was resting on the butt of his holstered Glock. The man looked over Robert's shoulder as Grey approached.

"Yeah, I seen what you did to them two. The difference is, I don't care what you do to me. Kill me; I just don't care. But I ain't letting you leave here because—"

Grey sprang toward the man, his lead foot toe-kicking the man's shin to draw his attention down. When the man grimaced, Grey jerked him around by his arm, then rammed the butt end of the kukri into the boney ridge near the bottom of the back of the skull, known as the external occipital protuberance. Fighters who knew about it called it "that knockout point" because it was easier to remember.

Grey cupped the falling man's unconscious head, so it didn't impact the pavement. "Tala, cut a strip off the one-handed man's jacket and Robert, tie a tourniquet on his arm. No worries about the earless guy. That wound doesn't bleed much. And Tala, confiscate that ax."

He looked over at the old-timer still sitting in his chair, his shoulders bobbing up and down with his laughter.

"That was sure a sight, hell if it weren't," Harry said, slapping his thigh. "You're damn good with your cutlery, mister. And you got more heart in you than I do; I would have kilt their asses."

Grey looked down at the two men and back to the old-timer. "When these people can listen, tell them we deliberately didn't kill them. We could have, but we didn't. Tell them to ponder that." The man nodded. "What's behind those other doors?" Grey asked, already knowing the answer.

"More bodies. All waitin' to get picked up to be cremated or burned somewhere. We get paid in food to watch them until the pick-up fellas get here. Sometimes our competition comes here to steal them from us. That's why the boys were fussin' so much."

"Why are so many of the dead bleeding? It's fresh blood too."

The old-timer shook his head and looked toward the alley entrance. "It used to be just one hallway full a week, most of 'em checkin' out from disease and starvation. But now we get four full halls a week. Shit, one time seven hallways. These ones today are from gettin' killed fighting for food.

"And don't ask me who does the pickin' up. I think it's some do-gooders wanted to keep the street clean, so we don't get too many rats."

"I heard they do it to respect the dead," Tala said.

Harry shrugged. "Maybe that too."

Grey couldn't believe what he was hearing. "We've been held up in a room healing for eight weeks and didn't know it had gotten bad in Sector Four too. We knew it was happening in Sector Six, which is why we're going there to look for my lady's brother."

"Uh-oh," the man said. "You say you're goin' to Sector Six. Well, I think you might be confused like a lotta folks are. 'Cause you're in Six now. Sector Four ended four blocks back."

Grey, Tala, and Robert were standing inside of a doorway inset about three blocks from the scene in the alleyway. Robert had appeared lost in thought during the short walk, and even after they ducked into the doorway, he was quiet.

Old Harry told them that a lot of people thought Sector Six started on the other side of the Battledrum River, but it actually consisted of the three blocks on the west side just before the Hampton Bridge, all of the bridge itself, and the first eight blocks on the east side.

It wasn't that significant that the three of them had been wrong about Sector Six, but it did take them by surprise that it had been closer to them all along. And, as it turned out, Robert had actually been going into Six on his trips to get food, which might explain why he had seen so many dead bodies. But he had never seen the food trucks or food riots.

Harry said he didn't know anything about where the food was coming from or who was delivering it. He said two old green military trucks showed up from time to time, and they wouldn't be seen again for a week or two. The men driving them were as ragged and unkempt as everyone else, and they didn't say much as they handed out boxes of food to the crowd. When things got riotous, the men got back in the vehicles and left.

Two times when the crowd tried to block them—probably to hijack the trucks—the drivers ran over them and continued on their way. Once, that the old man knew of, a helicopter with a door gunner hovered about 50 feet above the action. "That kept folks from gettin' too damn rambunctious," he said with a laugh.

"On a positive note," Tala said to Grey to break the silence since they left the alley, "we made a friend back there. Harry."

"Every little bit helps," he said. Grey peered out at the debris-covered street. The wind had increased a little, whistling around the broken buildings and disturbing the dust. It had been a year or more since he had been this far east. They were about three blocks from the bridge, in an area of 10-story office buildings and the beginning of the city's industrial area. There were lots of people on the street and sidewalks. Grey assumed that most of them had taken up residence in the buildings.

Passersby gave the trio a suspicious glance. One crazy-eyed man stopped, looked Robert up and down, and said, "You're not from around here."

"Your point?" Tala snapped at him.

The rocker smiled large, displaying a mouth full of rotting teeth that had to have been that way before The Change. "Well, now, you're a fine-looking piece. How about you and I—"

Tala ripped her sickle from her makeshift sling, startling the man by the quickness of her draw and how close she stopped its point from his nose. His eyes crossed to see it. "How about you moving on while you still have a nose on that ugly face?"

"I'm outta here," he said, turning on his heels.

Tala slipped her weapon into its holder under her coat and went back to watching the passersby.

Robert looked at each one of them and frowned.

Tala saw the look. "What?"

"Uh…nothing, I guess."

"Robert," she said. "You haven't said a peep since we left the alley. What's bothering you? Are you upset because you had to kill a dog? If that's it, I get it. We like dogs—"

"That's not it…" He looked at Grey. "It's the way you handled the three men in the alley. You had a right to kill them, but instead, you…toyed with them. Tortured them, really. Maimed." He shook his head. "I don't understand your reasoning behind that."

"Instead of simply killing them?" Grey asked, watching two men brawling across the street.

"Well, yeah."

The men were exchanging wild punches, most of them missing, and those that did land were weak and barely noticed by the receiver. Finally, one man went down, and the one left standing kicked him in the head. Two men who had been watching from a few feet away pulled the kicker back a few steps. He shook his arms free and with much animation, said something to the two. Then all three commenced kicking the downed man. Half of a minute later, either out of fatigue or boredom, they picked up their packs and headed up the street. The victim slowly struggled to his feet and walked off in the opposite direction holding the side of his bleeding head.

Grey turned back to Robert.

"I don't like killing, Robert. But I've done it a lot. In Afghanistan and here at home since The Change. I'm good at it…very good at it, but I hate it. I remember all of my kills, and I will carry those terrible memories with me until I fall as a victim. And I'm convinced all of us will die that way. Not one of us has old age in our future.

"Sometimes, when I'm morally justified to take a person's life, I don't. Instead, I leave them with a souvenir at how close they came to death. I'll remove a body part; I'll give them horrible pain; I'll cripple them. My hope, and maybe I'm wrong, is that they will live their life looking at their missing body part, or limping, or in the case of that guy without ears, looking strange, and think twice before they bully, or in some way try to hurt someone else."

Robert frowned. "But—"

"I know," Grey said, cupping his shoulder. "I know, I know. There are a lot of buts to my awkward philosophy. Like, who made me judge and executioner? What about the lack of medical help for those I've maimed and wounded? What about the risk of the person eating the pain and continuing to attack?"

Grey shrugged. "I understand these things, and I've thought about them…" He shrugged again. "All I know for sure is that my actions are always defensive, and if I can avoid killing when I can, I'm going to take it."

Robert studied him for a moment, his face not revealing his take on Grey's words. "Have you killed when you could have avoided it?"

Grey's eyes narrowed, their intensity making Robert look away.

Tala leaned against Grey and looked at Robert. Grey knew she was telling their friend something with her eyes because two beats later, he looked at Grey and nodded ever so slightly. It was an apology.

"You did great with those dogs, Robert," Tala said. "We would have definitely been doggy Milk Bones if it wasn't for you."

"No hard feelings if you want to go back, Robert," Grey said. "We appreciate—"

"I want to continue," he said quickly. "I don't know if I agree with your philosophy; I have to think about it more. But you two are my friends. Friends don't turn their backs on each other over different opinions. Or, in my case, not knowing what my opinion is."

CHAPTER 3

GREY, TALA, ROBERT, AND GUEST

It was a couple of hours before nightfall, and the clouds were hurrying across the strip of dark sky exposed between the tall buildings on each side of the street. The wind had increased in the last few minutes, whipping dust and light debris through the air, forcing the trio to shield their eyes against its force.

Grey and Tala were walking side-by-side, and Robert was following a few feet back.

"Your stomach is really bothering you, huh?" she said loud enough to be heard over the increasing wind but low enough so Robert couldn't hear.

"I'm not in pain, but my wound is got me psyched out. I'm fighting it the best I can."

"We can go back," she said, leaning into him. "My brother is a grown man, and I want to find him to make sure he's okay. But you are my number one priority. If it's too soon, I understand. I'm a little sensitive about my left arm, even though it feels fine."

"You think I'm being a bitch about it?"

"Weeeell," she said, feigning an expression like it was a possibility."

"Funny," he said, punching her arm. "Oh, that's your left one, sorry." And he punched it again.

She reached over and drew her hand back as if to backhand his abdomen. He jerked away from her; his face tight. "Too soon?"

He exhaled. "I guess it is."

A few minutes later, they were walking in a column, Tala in the middle, Grey in the lead. "Who are you people?" a bearded man, leaning against a lamppost, shouted over the wind when Grey was even with him. When he didn't get an answer, he shouted the question louder when Tala was passing by.

She stopped and jutted her head toward him. "Your worst nightmare."

The man blinked rapidly and stepped back, his eyes following Robert as he passed. "A wise decision not to pursue," Robert said. "We're passing through; we're not here to take your food."

A group of people halfway down the block huddled around a 50-gallon drum barrel, the fire within dancing in the wind. The added windchill added an extra bite to the cold; the fire helped warm the malnourished.

Most streets were covered with litter and debris, but the next one was especially dense with bricks, shards of broken glass, loose wiring, and chunks of sheetrock and plaster. Some of the piles were over six feet high.

Grey stepped away from the sidewalk and into an intersection to better see the buildings down each street. That is, what was left of the tall structures. Missile strikes had blown off the front walls of many of them, some all the way to the roofs, others just a few floors. The first building on their left was missing its front walls up to the sixth floor, revealing desks and filing cabinets within the three walls.

Three years ago, when he hiked all over the city after the third and what turned out to be the last wave of missile strikes, the sight of so much destruction devastated him, and it was all he could do to hike back to Sector Four that had been spared from all but a few strikes. Seeing so many mutilated buildings again was chilling. How many thousands had lost their lives in them?

Movement from an upper floor of the closest of the two buildings. Grey locked his eyes on where he thought he saw it. A face…no, two faces peered over the edge of the open sixth floor, its edges jagged. Both heads were topped with long hair, one bright red, the other brunette.

Tiny pieces of something—maybe carpet, floor tile, dirt—fell over the edge and were whisked away in the wind. The two people pulled back out of sight.

Grey looked at Tala and Robert. "I'm not comfortable walking below those open floors above, he said. "I saw two people, and I'm guessing there are many more up there. Is this the way you come, Robert?"

"Twice. The last time, someone up there dropped a computer screen and hit a guy sitting on some rubble. So I went down to the next block, Obama Avenue. There were dickheads there too but none on the roof, none that I could see, anyway."

Tala leaned back and looked up at the top of the building. "There's a guy sitting on the edge of the roof above the eighth floor. Just sitting there enjoying the view, I guess."

Grey looked up at him and then back at Tala and Robert. "Let's eliminate the risk and head on down to Obama and see what that looks—"

"Hey!"

They turned toward the voice, a 40-something Asian man standing on a pile of debris about 30 feet down Kennedy. He was shielding his eyes from the swirling dust and looking up at the building. "Don't do it!" he shouted. "You hear me, punks? Don't do it!"

"He yelling at the guy sitting up there?" Tala asked.

"No," Grey said, pointing at the sixth floor, where the same two long-haired men were struggling with what looked like a tall filing cabinet.

"I see you, you carrot-topped asshole!" the Asian man shouted.

They pushed it over the edge. The drawers opened, spilling papers out into the wind.

"No!" Tala blared, pointing at an elderly female doddering along the sidewalk.

The cabinet clipped the side of her head, bashed her shoulder, and slammed her to the sidewalk.

"Dammit!" Robert shouted, heading that way.

"Stop, Robert!" Grey commanded. He did, looking back at him. Grey pointed at other exposed floors where people began dropping bricks, furniture, assorted garbage. A desk missed two women running to get away, but something large hit a man's upturned face, knocking him to the sidewalk.

"How do we get up there?" Grey called to the Asian man.

"Don't know," he said looking back at Grey. He turned back to watching the upper floors, then looked back at Grey.

"My friends!" a voice shouted from above.

"It's the guy on the roof," Tala said.

The man was standing now, his hands fisted on his hips, his head slowly turning as if scanning the view.

"He going to throw something off too?" Robert wondered.

The wind subsided enough that they could hear the man's next words. "What a beautiful evening," he shouted, sweeping his arm out to emphasize the panorama. "Such a beautiful, beautiful, beautiful, beautiful—"

"A rocker," Grey said.

"—beautiful day to die." The man lifted his arms over his head, palms together. He posed for a moment, then tipped forward until his feet left the ledge. He speared downward like an arrow, floor after descending floor, until his palms-together hands, arms, head, torso, pelvis, and legs compressed into the sidewalk like an accordion next to the man who was stirring awake after being struck in the face with something.

Two women checked on the old woman under the file cabinet, shook their heads, and quickly moved out from beneath the open floors above. The man struck in the face was confused, no doubt from being knocked unconscious but also waking up just as someone slammed into the sidewalk next to him, the jumper's snapping bones louder than the wind. Grey dashed over and pulled him to the corner just seconds before a dropped chair crashed on top of the dead jumper.

As calloused as Grey, Tala, and Robert were to seeing death, they had to get away from the scene. They moved around the corner and kept walking until they were about halfway up the block. The Asian man followed.

"Who are you people?" he asked when they stopped. "Never seen you before. You here to get food?"

"There has to be a way up to those floors," Grey said, ignoring his question. "Those people need to be stopped."

"We think they hop from building to building or something. That's all we know about the bastards, other than they do this all over the sector." He looked down at the debris-covered sidewalk and shook his head. "The jumper, well, that was something new. It'll be tough to get that out of my head for a while." He looked up at them. "Now, answer my question. Who are you people?"

Grey quick-scanned him: fit, commanding presence, something under his jacket.

"We're from another sector," Tala said, her black hair whipping in a hard gust of wind that thickened the air with white dust. "We've come here looking for my brother. His name is Juni. Heard of him?"

The Asian man smiled. "He's your brother, is he? Well, I'm his mother, so that makes us, what? Cousins?"

Grey saw Tala's quick-to-anger nostrils flare. She was desperate to find her brother and in no mood for the man's flippant attitude.

She took an angry step toward the man, her hand snaking under her jacket flap. He took a defensive step back, tripped over a bicycle frame, and fell onto his butt.

"Are you okay, sir," Grey asked, stepping in front of Tala and extending his hand. "Let me help you up."

"No," the man said, getting to his feet.

"Sir," Grey said, kissing up to him. Judging by the look on the man's face when Tala mentioned her brother's name, he knew him. "The lady isn't lying. Juni is her brother. If you know him, look at her. You can see the resemblance."

He looked at Tala and dropped his eyes to where her hand had disappeared inside her jacket flap. "Tell her to take her hand off whatever weapon she has," he said. Grey looked at Tala and nodded. She reluctantly complied. "Yes, I see some resemblance. Juni has a scar."

"Over his right eyebrow," Tala said. "I gave it to him when we were training with knives. He was seventeen, and I was fifteen."

"No one knows his last name but—"

"Santos," she said.

"…but me," the man finished. He nodded. "Okay, I believe you." He looked at her for a long moment. "Allow me to give you some advice." Tala looked at him blankly. "Juni told me how he got the scar and that his sister gave it to him. Tala, right?" She nodded. "He said you're very good with a blade. I assume that's what you were reaching for." He looked at Grey. "You have two, I think. A big one on your right hip and something on your left hip with a long handle." He looked at Robert. "You hold your right arm out away from your side. "You're carrying a knife too."

"Who are you?" Grey asked, impressed, though he guessed the wrong weapon for Robert.

"My name is Sukimoto. I was a police captain in NYPD. I was in charge of training cops to notice things like I just told you. I was visiting my brother in this fine city when the attack came."

"You were wrong about me," Robert said.

"My first thought was a gun, but as you know, they're hard to come by these days." He looked at Tala. "My unasked-for advice, miss, is to control your temper. You've obviously survived this long with it, but the future is not guaranteed, right?" He pulled his jacket flap back to reveal what Grey thought was a Sig Sauer .45. "On even ground, you would have closed the distance before I could extract my firearm. But as you can see, there are many things to trip over here. If it had been you who tripped, I would have shot you dead."

Tala swallowed hard.

The four of them were huddled in a narrow space between two buildings that was cluttered with junk and smelled of shit and piss. Robert, Tala, and Sukimoto stood with their backs to one of the walls; Grey had positioned himself at the front edge of the entrance so he could peek out to check the sidewalk to their left and right.

Grey flashed to Kathryn, Robert's medium friend telling the three of them before they left that they "would be four." Then she saw something, or whatever it was that psychics do, and warned them not to go. He looked back at Sukimoto.

The wind had increased, as did its banshee-like howl that carried white dust and anything else light enough to fly or bounce along the sidewalk. Visibility was reduced, but between hard gusts, Grey could make out several small groups of people across the street huddled in doorways as well.

One woman lay on the sidewalk directly across from them. Fifteen minutes earlier, Grey had noticed her scurrying along, one hand protecting her eyes like a visor. At the same time, he spotted what looked like a four-foot square sheet of something—tin or a piece of roofing—riding the air. It was about six feet off the ground, which is probably why the woman didn't see it given that her shielding hand was blocking her line of sight. Grey shouted at her to watch out, but his voice was carried away by the wind. The sheet of material road a gust on a downward trajectory and struck the front of her neck. She went down hard, blood pumping from her throat.

Robert dashed over to check on her but returned shortly. "She's gone," he said, squinting against the wind. "Severed her carotid artery."

For the last 30 minutes, no one had spoken a word. In less than an hour, they had witnessed three horrific deaths, a murder by a dropped file cabinet, a suicide, and a nature-perpetrated accident.

Grey continually looked behind him to check on the other three, and always they stood scrunched into themselves against the wind, their eyes closed, each dealing with what they had seen in their own way. This time when he looked back, Tala was looking at him. She smiled with her eyes.

Are you okay? she mouthed.

He shrugged. *You?* She shrugged back.

Grey looked at Sukimoto; he was looking back at Grey now.

When the three of them hurried away from the scene of the building jumper and the homicide of the elderly woman, Sukimoto had followed them. When Grey gave him a questioning look, the man said, "Do you mind if I tag along for a bit? Strength in numbers, right? Plus, I might be able to get you close to Juni."

Grey didn't think he was a rocker, and he did have a cop vibe emanating from him, so he might prove useful.

"I'm thinking of that jumper," Sukimoto said to Grey, squinting against the dust in the air. "I probably covered 50 suicides as a cop in New York City. Usually after the act, but a few happened right in front of me. Self-inflicted gunshots, self-poisoning, bridge divers, and hangings. Always tragic, always hard for me to understand."

He shook his head as if trying to make the images go away. "So hard for their loved ones.

"Homicides were often about want. Somebody else has it, the killer wants it. Sometimes want is synonymous with jealousy. That rich guy is wearing a Rolex; Joe, the killer is jealous that the rich guy has it and he doesn't. So Joe kills him to get it. They're rarely big complicated plots like on TV cop shows, and it doesn't take Columbo to figure them out.

"Since The Change, it's about food and medicine. Joe sees a guy with food, and he knows the guy's belly is full. Joe is jealous because he wants his belly full, so he kills the man to get the food."

"What about those people pushing stuff off the sixth floor down on people below?" Tala asked. "What about people who get a gun and randomly shoot other people? Grey and I saw that two months ago."

Sukimoto looked at her. "I've seen it too, twice recently. Maybe they do it because they finally can. There are no laws now, no restrictions, no repercussions. Some kill because it's in their genes and because now—now—they finally can.

"Those men on that sixth floor didn't hate that woman they killed or that man whose face they struck with garbage; they didn't know them, so they couldn't hate them. It was about indifference. Back in the day, I read a lot of George Bernard Shaw. He wrote—I don't remember the book—'The worst sin toward our fellow creatures is not to hate them, but to be indifferent to them. That's the essence of inhumanity.' Those shitheads on the sixth floor were indifferent to the human lives below them. How terrifying that thought is and how often we're seeing it now."

"Indifference and jealousy," Robert said aloud as if he were pondering it.

Sukimoto nodded, folded his arms across his chest, and closed his eyes.

"They bring the food on two old military trucks," Sukimoto said after several minutes of silence in the cramped doorway inset.

"Where did they get the vehicles and gas?" Grey asked. "I haven't seen a moving vehicle in a year."

"Million-dollar question," Sukimoto said with a shrug. "I asked but just got glared at in return. Lots of rumors on the street about a government forming, but that's as far as the stories go. Anyway, I was standing near the top of the bridge three months ago when two trucks came lumbering up the slope and stopped next to me. He looked at Tala. "Your brother eyeballed me for a moment before asking if I wanted to earn some canned soup. When I said, 'Hell yes,' they put me to work unloading and handing out boxes. Juni said they do the handouts on top of the bridge because they can get it to folks on the east side and west side of the river.

"I've helped them six times now up on the bridge, and we haven't had too much trouble other than some fights and a fatal stabbing. Two days ago, they stopped on this side of the river, just before the turn to go up the bridge, and it was a slaughter. Shootings, knifings, and those damn helicopters shot a bunch after some idiots on the ground shot at them. I wasn't there because I didn't know they were coming. But I heard it. Man, did I hear it, and I was about a mile away."

"We saw some of the bodies a while ago," Tala said. "So, they don't do deliveries on a regular schedule?"

Sukimoto shook his head. "Nope. But the word is they're supposed to do a drop tonight on the apex of the bridge again. They usually come around seven o'clock."

"You think Juni will be there?" Tala asked.

"I don't know how the trucks divide up the deliveries, but five out of the six times I've worked for them, Juni has been in charge of a truck."

Tala looked at Grey, her eyes hopeful.

Sukimoto saw the look. "May I be blunt with you?"

Grey thought his politeness quaint, given all the horror of the day. It gave him hope.

When Tala nodded, Sukimoto lowered his voice as if hesitant to speak. "I don't know Juni well; I've only seen him those few times and we talked some. Usually, he was calm and collected while the crowd was pushing and shoving one another to get the handouts. Even when a man was stabbed in the back and fell dead, he showed total self-control as he called for order. He did it with the authority of a good policeman, and the people listened, and things got quickly under control."

"I hear a 'but,'" Tala said.

"Yeah, there is one. The last time I saw Juni, he seemed stressed to the hilt: sweating, face tight and angry. He threw some of the boxes at people, hitting them in the head. Once when a man complained about getting hit, he jumped off the truck and punched him in the face. Then he punched the guy who pulled him off the first guy. Things went sideways fast, and people started jumping into the truck and fighting us. Finally, the drivers of both trucks pulled away, and we had to push people out the back. A lot of them got hurt falling. When I heard gunfire about half a block away, I jumped out of the truck." He shook his head, remembering. "I'm surprised they're coming back tonight, but that's the rumor."

"You don't know why the change in Juni?" Tala asked, worried.

Sukimoto shook his head. "I heard him say something to one of the workers about having girlfriend problems. Maybe that was it. But we've all seen it happen, right?" He pointed to the world outside the doorway inset. "It's because of the way it is now. The inhumanity. One day a person is coping, and the next they're a rocker."

"You think Juni is a rocker?" Tala snapped.

"No," Sukimoto said, touching Tala's arm. "I didn't mean him. Your brother just seemed really stressed."

A strong gust roared down the street, carrying a cloud of dirt and debris. Thankfully it didn't find its way into the small space between the buildings. When the roar died, Sukimoto asked, "You all run into or heard of the bandanna gang?"

"Seen them on the other side of the bridge two weeks ago," Robert said. "About ten of them all wearing bandannas on their heads, around their necks, over their nose and mouths. If they were trying to intimidate, it was working. I ducked into an alley, and they passed by me."

"Who are they," Grey asked.

"Bunch of assholes," Sukimoto said. "Power of the group and all that psychology stuff. But I've heard they're the ones causing all the problems at the food giveaways. So far, not on the bridge, but once on Kennedy Street. I hear one guy has a gun, and the others have clubs and knives."

Grey sighed and looked out at the street. "It's always one more thing." He looked up at the sky. Darkness was coming quickly, the rapidly moving clouds barely visible now. "How is the lighting down here? And on the bridge?"

"Down here, it's the same as most places, I suspect. But the bridge has some good light. It's not as good as it was. Did you ever see it before The Change? All purples and blues. It's not like that now, but it's got some pretty good floods. How and why? I don't know."

Another rush of wind, not as intense as the others, but with enough force to send what looked like a 10-foot square piece of tarpaper fluttering along the sidewalk, catching on the dead woman's head as if it were about to cover her, then riding away on another gust. Dust and bits of garbage rode with it…and voices.

Grey leaned out from the inset wall to look down the sidewalk. "Two people. One with long red hair, the other with long brown hair. I think—"

"The two shitheads who have been dropping stuff down on people," Sukimoto finished for him.

"The ones who dropped that filing cabinet on the old woman?" Tala asked, leaning out to peek. "It kinda looks like them."

"Today wasn't a first for those two," Sukimoto said, his anger evident. "I personally know of two other times, and I've heard there've been more. Like I said, no one has been able to find them."

"Uh-oh," Tala said. She pulled her head back and looked at Sukimoto. "Am I seeing what I think I'm seeing?" She moved out of the way so he could lean out.

He looked, leaned back, and nodded. "Speak of the devil. The redhead and the man beside him are wearing bandannas around their necks. Yellow. There's two black guys behind them too, but they're too far away to tell if they have bandannas."

Robert sucked in a nervous breath.

Grey looked at him. "Bandannas are pieces of cloth, Robert," he said. "Consider the man, not his bells and whistles."

His father had drilled that into him at a young age. "Scary tattoos are made of ink, son," his father told him the first time he had to fight an inked-up competitor in the ring. "Ink can't hurt you. And neither can stripes on a competitor's black belt, big biceps, glaring eyes, and growled threats. Those things are bells and whistles, son, designed to psyche an opponent. Ignore them and fight the man's skill."

It took Grey a few tournaments to understand that, but once he did, he mowed through the menacing-looking competition like a 200-pound lawnmower.

"Hopefully, they'll pass on by," Tala said."

Sukimoto shook his head. "Doubt it."

Grey peeked out again. They were about 15 feet away. The red-haired man, his long locks whipping in the wind, saw him and stopped. Grey leaned back. "They made me. And the redhead is carrying a club."

Grey recognized it as a modern-day Indian war club made of polypropylene, a hard plastic. It was about two feet long, slightly curved at the top, and fitted with about a four-inch in diameter ball head. It could smash blocks of ice, cinder blocks, and skulls.

"We need to move out of this small space," Sukimoto said.

Grey nodded. Acknowledging the man's police experience, he asked. "How do you think we should play it? You have a gun, and so does Robert. And he's experienced with it. Tala and I are good with our knives."

Sukimoto nodded. "We form a line straight out from this building. Robert and I in the middle, you and the girl on each end. You two can flank if things turn to shit. Let's not show our weapons too soon."

"Check," Grey said. "Let me try to talk to them."

A blast of wind greeted them as they stepped away from the protection the mini alley had given them. Grey's long salt-and-pepper hair whipped his face, momentarily blinding him. He turned his head slightly, so it blew away from his eyes. Tala stood to Grey's left, Robert to Sukimoto's right, each far enough away from each other that the line stretched across the street.

Grey thought the two white men, still on the sidewalk, looked startled; the two black men, about five yards behind them, froze in place. The psyche worked, Grey thought, but he knew it was only momentary.

And he was right.

The two long-haired men quickly moved out into the street and faced the blockade, the redhead took two steps forward. The wind slapped at them from their rear, lashing their hair around their heads and into their eyes. A perfect time to attack, Grey thought. But the situation wasn't at that point.

The redhead, gripping his Indian war club in his right hand, used his left to push his bandanna from his neck onto his forehead. A few strands of hair remained loose and whipped into his eyes. The dark-haired man gripped a yard-long piece of rebar along the outside of his leg. He tried to adjust his bandanna with one hand but gave up.

The two black guys, taking their time, moved up, stopping a few feet off to one side of their buddies. Grey used his peripheral to check Sukimoto: calm and collected. As a former NYPD officer, Grey knew this wasn't his first rodeo. He quick-peeked at Tala: confident. He couldn't get a read on Robert.

Grey looked at each of the four and guessed the redhead was the leader. He said, "We want to go in the direction you came from, and you want to go in the other. Let's just do that, and no one gets hurt. What do you think of—?"

"Why aren't you talking to me, boy," the tallest black man snapped. He looked to be in his late 20s, wearing a long black overcoat that billowed and whipped in the wind. "Old habits like marginalizing people is hard to break, even when the world is collapsing around us. You naturally assume a white man is the spokesman here because your innate prejudice is alive and well. As a society, we were already crumbling from within when the rockets rained down on us. Crumbling because—"

"By calling me 'boy,' aren't you marginalizing me?" Grey asked, glad to have a chance to talk instead of fight. "Isn't it true that most

accusations of racism are racist in nature? Didn't you see me first look at the red-haired man, then the dark-haired man, then look your way? Didn't you see this guy standing in front of all you? Wouldn't that be a logical assumption to think he might be your leader?"

The red-haired man stepped toward Grey.

"As you were, kid," the tall black man snapped at him. He looked back at Grey, and Grey returned it, his breathing controlled. The man's 'as you were' was a common military expression often used by leaders to order troops to stop doing something or to quiet down.

Grey sensed something pass between the two of them.

He had felt this on three other occasions when meeting someone after he returned from his deployment to Afghanistan. It turned out that they were veterans too. He couldn't explain it and after a while, he didn't try. Two men who served beside him and kept in touch with after they got home, before The Change, said they had had similar experiences.

"Did you deploy?" Grey asked.

The man eyed Grey carefully before he spoke. "Twenty-Thirteen. Afghanistan. Eighty-Second Airborne." He lifted his chin at Grey as if to say your turn.

"Afghanistan. Twenty-ten and twenty-eleven." He shrugged. "Just a trigger puller, nothing special."

The man studied Grey a moment longer, his head ever so slightly nodding as he read him. "'Just' a trigger puller' you say? No, I think you were deep in it wherever you were." He studied him a moment longer. "Yeah, man. I can see it on you."

Grey returned the look. "And I know you were too." He looked at the two long-hairs then back at the veteran. "Why are you with these assclowns?"

"We're not."

The man with the long brown hair snorted. "We don't hang with no niggers, no slant-eyes, no Jews—"

Sukimoto exploded toward the man, dropped into a deep left-leg-forward stance, and drove his left fist into the man's chest over his heart, the thump loud even in the wind. Grey recognized it as a classical technique straight out of a Japanese fighting art, probably Shotokan.

The man's arms flew up, his right hand sending the piece of rebar sailing end over end. He landed on his back hard enough to lift dust that was quickly carried away by the wind. He moaned loudly and curled into a fetal position clutching his chest. Generally, a straight punch was weaker than a rear cross that employs greater hip rotation, but Sukimoto had clearly mastered the move. The red-haired man took a knee next to his buddy.

Grey glanced at Sukimoto, still holding his deep stance, his left arm and fist extended, his eyes locked somewhere in the distance. Then, as if coming out of a trance, his body relaxed, and he stepped back into their line. His voice barely perceptible, he said, "I had to put up with that racist crap on the job. I don't have to anymore."

"Well done," the tall black man said. "You beat me to it."

"What did you do?" the red-haired man shouted at Sukimoto. The injured man rolled onto his side, his body trembling. He retched, once, twice…then stilled, his fingers frozen into claws, mouth gaping, eyes partially open.

Both sides stood motionless, first looking at the dead man, then looking up at those across from them.

"What did you do?" the red-haired man again shouted at Sukimoto. He was touching his dead friend's chest. "Doug! Doug!" He tried to call him a third time, but it came out as a sob.

"Grey," Tala said. "These men aren't—"

"This didn't have to happen," Sukimoto managed, his voice heavy with regret.

The other two men must have sensed the growing tension because they began moving over to the far sidewalk.

"Son-of-a-bitch!" the red-haired man bellowed, standing up, his eyes on Sukimoto. He swung his Indian club up and rested it on his shoulder. "I'm going to smash your skull in. You hear me? I'm going to cave in your—"

"Stay where you are," Grey barked at him. He held his kukri slightly behind his lead leg. When Grey saw Sukimoto move his hand toward his gun, he deliberately stepped in front of him.

The young man's head was tilted back slightly, chin jutted

forward, his eyes large and wet. Looks demonic, Grey thought.

"Watch the other two, Tala," he said out of the corner of his mouth.

The wind seemed to pulsate in short, hard blasts like an enraged bull. Grey's hair blew away from his face, but the red-haired man's loose strands lashed his eyes. He moved the Indian club to his left, his right arm across his chest. A left to right strike, Grey thought.

Again, the bandanna man's hair whipped across his eyes.

Grey lunged like a fencer, stabbing the point of his kukri into the shoulder of the man's weapon arm. He extracted the blade and stepped back. He hoped an injection of pain would end it.

"Ouch," the man said, as if making a joke, and swung his club at him.

Grey ducked below the weapon's path and simultaneously slashed his kukri under the weapon arm in the opposite direction.

"Ouch," the man said again, looking down at the blood pouring out from his sleeve and over his fingers. He held the club out to Grey as if no longer wanted it.

Grey shook his head. "Just drop it on the sidewalk and—"

A surprise kick smacked into the inside of Grey's forward leg. It wasn't hard, and it didn't hurt. But it did create a two-second gap in his reaction to the bandanna gang member's hand switch, and his downward strike at the top of Grey's head.

With his reflexes back intact, he sidestepped away from the assault, and the deadly black ball at the end of the club missed. Acting on the principle that an opponent is most vulnerable the moment after he attacks, Grey rammed his kukri deep into the man's thigh, hoping greater pain would deter him.

No "ouch" this time from the long-haired redhead; instead, a loud cry. But incredibly, he was still undeterred. He spun his entire body 360 degrees, swinging the club around in a two-handed grip at an ever-increasing speed to deliver a blow meant to kill.

Grey leaped back, the club missing his neck by a quarter of an inch. It was a stupid move out of a movie, but next time the man just might get lucky. He had to end this. Before the bandanna man could recover his violent swing, Grey lunged and drove his big knife deep into his armpit.

The man screeched and screeched even louder as Grey twisted the wide blade to create maximum damage. He yanked it out hard, an arc of blood following. Then, sliding the point halfway down the man's side, Grey gripped the kukri with both hands and applied all his bodyweight to ram the blade through the man's ribs, liver, and heart.

The gang member was dead before his face thudded onto a chunk of broken asphalt.

Grey squinted as the wind howled and slammed him with grit. The knife fighter looked down at the dead man but felt nothing. He would later.

Another rush of wind nearly drowned out Robert's, "Holy shit!"

Tala had moved up alongside Grey. "These guys aren't the two who were dropping things off that building," she said just loud enough for him to hear. "These look to be in their mid-twenties. The ones on that fifth floor looked like teenagers." She looked over at Sukimoto. He was standing motionless, his arms limp along his sides.

Grey glared at the two black men. "You say you weren't with these men?"

The arrogance the tall man had displayed earlier was gone. "Weren't with them, didn't know them."

His friend spoke for the first time. "We were walking behind them on Victor heading to the bridge, you know. We kept two blocks back 'cause they were wearing bandannas. You know, you saw them. When they stopped to look at what was happening on Kennedy—"

The taller man jumped in. "People were up on one of those blown out buildings dropping stuff down on people. Someone said they killed a woman on the sidewalk. Anyway, when those two knuckleheads walked on, we did too. It's first come first serve on the bridge."

"They weren't the same men," Grey said, looking down at the two bodies.

"But dickheads either way," Tala said, quietly. "And this one tried to kill you."

"I could have handled it differently," Sukimoto said, his voice thick with remorse. Then after a beat, "Nah, I'm not sorry."

"Hurricane, you think?" Robert said from behind him.

Grey followed his eyes to the sky. It was nearing full-on night, but the granite-grey agitated clouds were reflecting light from the ground, most likely the bridge, he thought.

"I don't think it's that bad," Grey said. "But it's for sure going to get worse."

CHAPTER 4

GREY, TALA, ROBERT, AND SUKIMOTO

Sukimoto led them to the bottom floor of a building around the corner.

It was two blocks from where thugs had dropped things down on people from a damaged building, a block from where Sukimoto and Grey killed the two bandanna gang members, and two blocks from Hampton Bridge that spanned Battledrum River. There were about 50 people in the place, some sitting in small groups, others sitting by themselves, or staring out a large picture window with a view of the dark sidewalk and street.

Grey and the others found a place to rest against the back wall. It allowed them to monitor only three directions and the entire room. The only indication of what the site used to be was a huge sign on the back wall that read: Silverton Publishing.

The room was partially lit by three lanterns—two in the center of the room where about 30 people were sitting and lying down—and one by the wall farthest from the front windows. The light was eerie, and it cast dancing shadows on the walls whenever someone moved about.

"I stay about a mile from here," Sukimoto said, "but if I happen to be close to this place when darkness falls, I'll find a space on the floor to wait until morning. There's always someone in here, sometimes lots of people. Travelers know that it's usually a safe place to stay when passing through. There were two murders a couple of months ago, one near the left front door over there and one just under that window where those two children are sleeping. Two isn't bad these days."

"You were right about it being a good place to stay out of the windstorm," Grey said. "The wind must be gale-force up on the bridge."

Sukimoto nodded. "It's always windy up there anyway. I wonder if the trucks will even try it." He shrugged. "Maybe they'll take a

chance since the wind intensity is so on and off."

"Do you normally go up on the bridge and wait?" Grey asked.

Sukimoto shook his head. "I never know when they're coming. There are always rumors, of course, most of them false. So I hang around here most nights until it starts getting dark, and if nothing happens, I head back to my place."

"What's your feeling about this night?" Robert asked.

"My gut, for what it's worth, tells me they're coming. If they do, the trucks honk as they pass by outside."

"Any problems with helicopters during the distribution?" Grey asked.

Sukimoto nodded. "There are always the very stupid in the crowds who think it's a great sport to shoot at them."

"And they return fire with prejudice," Grey said.

Sukimoto nodded again. "But it's probably too windy for them tonight."

"Hard to say," Grey said. "I was in Afghanistan and saw them do some amazing things in all kinds of conditions, including windstorms. I saw one do a barrel roll once. On purpose too. I'm not sure what he was doing, but it was impressive."

For the next 30 minutes, the foursome talked about everything from medicine, rumors of a military and a government, and what might be happening on the West Coast and the East Coast. In the end, it was clear that there was no new information, and as usual, most everything was conjecture.

When the conversation had run its course, Grey and Tala scooted a few feet away from the other two to talk in private. Grey leaned back against the wall with his legs stretched out in front of him. Tala sat on his right, cross-legged, bent forward with her forearms resting on her knees.

"We haven't been out this late in weeks," she said. "It's like we're grownups now and everything."

"I wouldn't go that far," Grey said. Then, "We haven't missed anything. The world is still a sad place."

"Maybe sadder."

He nodded and scanned the room. There were about 60 people now, singles and couples sitting along the bare walls, and groups of people who seemed to know each other sprawled out in the center of the floor. Everyone talked in hushed voices, all the while their eyes watched everyone around them. Just as Grey was doing.

Darwinism had long removed those who weren't cautious and suspicious in this new dark world.

"You thought any more about the country, my uncle's cabin?" Tala asked. The cabin wasn't far from the Pacific Ocean and about 50 miles from the city. She had brought it up to Grey several times over the last two months.

"It might as well be a thousand miles," he said the first time she mentioned it.

"But not far for a better life," she quickly responded as if anticipating his negativity. "They have a garden, there are deer, rabbits, fish, well water. No rockers, and I'm betting the sea air keeps the dark clouds away."

"I love your optimism," he said with a warm smile. "I wish I shared it. I talked to people the first year about what it was like elsewhere, and everyone said they had been told that conditions were the same across the U.S. That's not written in stone, just hearsay, but at least one man said he had just come from the coast, and it was bad. That's all I know about it."

"Then we should keep asking," Tala said, her eyes filling with tears. "Isn't it worth it to keep asking? How long can we go on like this? The odds are against us, Grey. We're always one fast reflex away from getting seriously hurt. Or killed. One day, someone is going to be faster than us, or we'll be distracted, or we're just having a bad day."

That conversation took place three weeks ago, and both had brought up the same pro and con arguments as they had two weeks before that.

He felt Tala's warm hand rest on his thigh. He looked away from the room and into her eyes. "You've thought more about it, haven't you?" she whispered. "You're thinking the same thing I am—that it's time."

"You a psychic or something?" he said, losing the fight not to smile.

"No, but I can read you like a book, one with yellow pages and a beat-up, scarred cover."

He looked away for a second, then returned to her. "This day has been a rough first outing."

She nodded and took his hand in both of hers. "It was awful. I…I'm just full, Grey. I don't know how much more room I have in my soul for all this awfulness."

He leaned over and kissed her. "Let's find your brother, go back to the apartment, and figure out how we can make the trip."

"Thank you, thank you, thank you," she said, cupping each side of his face and kissing him. "It's got to be better there; it just has to."

"Hey, get a room, you two," Robert said from a few feet away. He and Sukimoto were both smiling at them.

Grey and Tala ignored them and kissed one more time. "I love you," she whispered.

"And I'm becoming quite fond of you," Grey said, then snapped up his hand defensively when she pretended to slap him. They both turned toward a noise across the room.

Someone had pushed open the street door, and a blast of wind followed him in, scattering blankets and water bottles in every direction.

Dull, yellowish light from a nearby lantern illuminated a middle-aged man—not much over five feet tall, his shirtless torso nearly skeletal, his pantlegs rolled up to his knees, bare feet black with grime. He had something in his hand that looked like a half-gallon metal water bottle. Water dripped off him as if he had just climbed out of the Battledrum River less than half a block away.

"He's soaked," Tala said.

"Gents?" Grey said to Robert and Sukimoto, gesturing for them to get up. "I'm not liking this."

Someone yelled at the man to shut the damn door, but the man ignored the voice. He walked zombie-like toward the center of the room, forcing people to scoot out of his way as he tramped on their bedrolls and knocked their things about.

"What the hell are you doing, pal?" a man boomed.

"Get the hell away from us," another one shouted, stretching his arm out to protect a woman sitting next to him.

"Eew, he smells, mama." A child's voice.

Grey looked at Robert and Sukimoto. "Fan out to your right. Be ready for anything." He looked at Tala. "Let's move over to the left side."

"What the hell?" A woman's voice. "I smell gasoline."

"Who stepped on my leg?" a sleepy male voice said.

"He's dripping gas!" a woman shouted, grabbing her child and backing away.

Another man entered through the open door, his arms extended toward the shirtless man, his palms making small patting gestures. "Brent, no," the new man's voice was soothing as if to calm a wild animal. Without taking his eyes off the man he called Brent, he said, "Everyone, move back. Now!" He stopped two strides away from the dripping man.

"He a rocker, or something?" a male voice called out from across the room.

"Brent," the man said, extending his hand. "Come with me outside. I love you, brother. Don't do this." He took a step closer and stopped. "Let's go back under the bridge and talk about—"

Brent stepped toward him as if to comply, but instead, he sloshed liquid from his bottle into the man's face.

His screams echoed around the cavernous room as he staggered back a step, his trembling hands reaching for his face. He tripped over a backpack and fell to the floor, where he continued to scream and thrash.

Brent tilted the bottle up and poured the liquid into his open mouth. It quickly overflowed and streamed down his neck and over his torso.

"Everyone, move back!" Grey shouted, moving quickly toward Brent. When the man plunged his hand into his pants pocket, he bellowed even louder. "Do it! Hurry!" He heard Tala behind him calling out to people to move, and out of the corner of his eye, he saw Robert and Sukimoto pulling others back.

Brent extracted what looked like a small stick from his pocket. Grey knew what it was before he even scratched it on his belt buckle, setting off a low flickering flame.

The man's body instantly ignited with a *Whoosh!*, and a stream of fire shot from his gaping mouth as if he were a human dragon. He staggered toward the thrashing man whose face he had splattered with the liquid, reached down with his burning hand, and touched his dripping cheek.

Flames instantly shrouded the poor man's head.

Grey stopped 10 feet away from Brent, now silently stumbling about, his burning arms waving as the fire seared into his nerves. Grey sensed that he was looking for another target to burn, but his eyes were cooked away by now. Brent blindly stumbled in the direction of an elderly couple sitting on the floor near the front door. Unable to get up in time, the man maneuvered himself in front of the woman and feebly kicked at the approaching blind human torch.

Brent was less than 10 feet from the couple now, the flames roaring all about his body. Grey extracted the ax from his make-shift holder.

His eyes squinting against the intense heat and the stench of burning flesh, Grey rushed toward the man from behind and whipped his ax horizontally into the side of his charring right knee joint.

But he didn't fall as Grey had hoped. The man only sagged to the right and continued shuffle-stepping toward the elderly couple.

Shielding his face from the intense heat, Grey leaned in and yanked the ax free. The handle was hot; a few seconds longer, it would have been too much to tolerate.

In one fluid motion, he raised the weapon up high, then brought it down hard, chopping into the back of man's blistering skull. Silently, Brent fell forward, nearly taking Grey with him when he tried to hold onto his weapon. The ax was buried too deep, and he had to let go.

It was Brent's now.

Behind him, the man who tried to stop the suicidal man had stopped shrieking.

It was only then that Grey was aware that others in the room were screaming, shouting, and scrambling out the door into the storm.

Twenty minutes later, they were standing in an attached room at the rear of the larger one where the two men had died. People who had chosen to remain in the smoky room had braced open the doors. The windstorm diluted some of the stench and haze, but the acrid and distinct reek of burned meat still hung on, even in the back room.

The smell must be clinging to us, Grey thought.

A rectangle of light from the larger room fell across their feet.

"I was going to shoot the burning man," Sukimoto said, "but you got to him first."

Grey nodded, wishing to himself that the former policeman had done it. "Sometimes, I think I've survived just to kill those needing to be killed." He was aware his voice sounded thick, heavy with…he didn't know what. Maybe just fatigue. "I've done it so many times." He looked at Tala and Robert. "We all have."

"And me," Sukimoto said. "It takes something out of me, each and every time. And it becomes so easy. Like that man I punched a while go. I don't think I meant to kill him. I just exploded, and I wanted … I don't know. Maybe I did want to kill him."

"You think we'll be judged for each life we've taken?" Robert asked.

"Judged?" Sukimoto blurted. "Judged? By whom?"

He stood up and walked toward the open door, his shadow falling within the rectangle of light on the floor. Grey could see the tension in his body. Was this something that had been nagging at him? he wondered. Sukimoto turned back to the three, his face in the darkness, his angry voice making it clear his feelings.

"By *God?*" Sukimoto said. "You still think God cares about us? Shiiiit! How many people did we have in this city before the attack? Nearly three million I read once. How many do you think were killed initially? Who knows, right? But I think it was half; it had to be. How many have died from starvation, disease, murder, and suicide since? Again, who knows? But I'd bet half of the remaining.

"And that's just here. I'm also betting the slaughter happened in every other city, town, village, whatever. And from coast to coast.

Maybe not as much in some places and maybe more in others. Some completely blown off the map. Maybe all around the world. We have no way of knowing.

"The bottom line is God let it happen. The same God you think will judge us for killing a few people who needed killing." Sukimoto looked out the door into the large room for a moment then turned back. "Listen, Robert… If there is a God, he doesn't care about us.

"You know what I saw the other night? The helicopters were shooting people they thought shot at them, but hadn't, so I decided I'd stay in a building with a big room like that one out there instead of risking the four-block trip to my place. Anyway, the room was really noisy with a bunch of rockers, so I forced open a door to a small room, smaller than this one.

"It stunk like rotten meat, but I couldn't see anything. I had two matches, so I went out into the other and collected some paper, brought it back in, and lit it." Sukimoto scrunched his face.

"What?" Robert asked. "What did you…?"

"Someone had nailed three people to the far wall. Two men and a woman. They were hanging upside down. Make that *attached* upside down, you understand? Their legs and feet were nailed together, their arms were out to the sides, nails through their wrists and feet.

"Crucified, get it? But upside down. Whoever did it used blood to paint 'SATAN LIVES' in caps above the people."

Sukimoto looked back out into the big room for a moment, then turned back to the others. Punching his palm to underscore each word, he said through clenched teeth, "God. Doesn't. Care. And Satan is loving that fact." When no one said anything, Sukimoto turned and looked out into the big room.

Grey sighed and thought about the many discussions he and his father had on the subject. His father had seen unspeakable horrors in Vietnam, and Grey had seen the same during his deployments to Afghanistan. Both agreed that they couldn't fathom how a God who supposedly loved his flock could allow so much misery to soak the earth with blood.

"I believe a God created this planet," his father said, "but I don't think he gives one iota about what happens to us."

Grey wasn't sure he shared the same opinion, so he didn't think about it. He wanted to just live his life doing what he thought was right. The simplicity of that philosophy allowed him to function without worrying about how he will be judged. When The Change happened, he chose to stand between the enemy and those he loved and those who couldn't defend themselves. And he still does it.

If he was to be judged for that, well, so be it.

Tala was sitting snug against him. "You did a good job getting those families back," Grey said just loud enough for her to hear.

She nodded and whispered, "You think life will ever get normal enough again for me to see a shrink twice a week?" Grey raised his eyebrows. "Yeah, I don't either," she said.

"They would tell you that it's not healthy to bury it inside you. But that is exactly what we need to do to carry on."

"We'll be able to talk it all out when we move into my uncle's cabin."

Grey nodded. "You think I'd make a good cabin person? I mean, growing veggies, tilling the soil, fixing a fence?" Then in a thick southern twang, "Goin' down to the fishin' hole to snag me some bass?"

She feigned a frown. "Hmm, we might have to rethink this."

He cracked a small smile. "I can learn."

Tala smiled too.

CHAPTER 5

GREY, TALA, ROBERT, SUKIMO-
TO, AND THE BANDANNA GANG

The four of them moved from the small room into the big room and headed toward the still-open doors. There were about 30 people inside—some new faces, Grey noticed—all of them sitting or lying as far away from the bodies as possible. Someone had pushed the dead together and draped them with a tattered green blanket, anchoring the corners down with chunks of brick. Still, powerful wind gusts billowed it up and down as if it were breathing for the two underneath.

"Who are you?" a voice challenged from across the room to the left. Grey looked over and saw two men in the corner, the light there poor, but enough to see yellow scarves draped around their necks. The bandanna gang, Grey thought. He didn't see them earlier, so they must have come—

"I asked who in the hell you people are?" This time, Grey saw the speaker, an emaciated-looking man sitting next to a woman near the front window. He stood and tried to look intimidating by puffing up his shallow chest. "You come outta that backroom back there and—"

"Hey buddy," a male voice boomed, deep and authoritative from somewhere in the dark. "They're the ones who saved a lot of people a while ago from that rocker under the blanket. So knock off the third degree unless you want to deal with me, or them."

The man by the window sat back down.

The gang members moved toward the doors, eyeing Grey as they went. A moment later, they were gone. "They had to know about those bandanna guys a while ago," Tala whispered. "They in here scouting, maybe?"

The increasing wind poured through the open doors with an eerie moan, underscoring the grimness of the room, the dead, the bleakness outside, the world.

Grey stopped in the doorway, leaned out, and looked left and right. Clear. He nodded to the others and led them out onto the sidewalk. The wind whipped their hair and coats and pushed against their backs as if wanting them to hurry.

"The two turds with bandannas are gone," Sukimoto shouted. "They could make it to the corner if they ran, but we still need to be wary of doorway insets."

Grey noted diffused light, probably lanterns, bleeding out from sidewalk-level windows where people were no doubt sheltering.

"Hampton Bridge is to the right down there at the intersection," Sukimoto shouted. "There are probably people gathered on the ramp that leads up to the top." He gestured at the windows along the sidewalk. "Most of the people in these buildings, at least on the ground floor, are waiting for the trucks."

"Two doors down," Tala shouted, "a face looked around the edge and retracted. Also, there are people, about half a dozen, behind that big pile of debris at our eleven o'clock."

"Saw them," Grey said.

"Before that last gust," Robert said, looking up, "I thought I heard voices."

"Sometimes on this street, they drop things down on people at night," Sukimoto said with disgust. "Just once, I'd like to get my hands on them."

Grey watched Sukimoto in his peripheral. The anger he had expressed earlier had tightened him into a coiled spring. It was bad enough that Grey had to keep an eye on Robert, who was new to their way of working, but he had to monitor Sukimoto, a stressed and an unknown.

Grey looked again toward the intersection, then turned to the others behind him. "The street is unobstructed all the way down, so let's stay off the sidewalks. Tala and I will visually cover left and right; Sukimoto, you and Robert monitor our rear." He looked at Sukimoto. "Remind me what's around the corner at the intersection; it's been a while since I've been here."

"There's a short block before the street begins to ascend up to the apex of the bridge. The light's better because they, whoever they are, have figured out a way to light the bridge a little from one end to the other."

"Let's do it," Grey said, then looked up at the sky, thinking he heard a helicopter."

They moved out into the street and commenced as planned: Tala monitoring everything on the left side, Grey the right, and Sukimoto and Robert watching their six.

The wind was between gusts. Grey hoped the break would last, but he wasn't counting on it.

There were as many unknowns on this journey as there were known. This was always the case on Grey's missions during the war. A buddy who was on his fifth tour used to tell the newbies, "Expect the unexpected, but whenever possible, *be* the unexpected."

They had walked about 20 feet when a loud crash made them jerk around and look toward the open doors to the building they just left.

"Someone dropped something," Robert said. "Bricks, I think."

Sukimoto took two angry strides in that direction, ripping his Sig Sauer .45 from its holster. Gripping it in both hands, he crouched and aimed high up the building. "I swear to God," he growled. "That's the second time in two days these assholes dropped something right where I'd been standing." He moved the barrel back and forth, scanning the dark structure's upper floors. "Come on, light a cigarette," he said, his teeth clenched. "Do something so I can see you, and I swear to God I'll put one through your forehead."

Grey gestured for others to stand fast while Sukimoto vented. When he stopped, Grey gave him a minute, then said in a low voice, "My friend, it's just too dark. You ready to keep moving?"

Sukimoto looked over his shoulder at Grey, his gun still pointing at the building. He looked back and searched the building's upper floors once more before holstering his weapon. "Yeah, can't see anything, anyway. Let's go." He breezed by Grey to take the lead.

They passed two doorways, one where a solo man muttered and gestured angrily at an invisible person, oblivious to Grey and the others. A 20-something man and woman occupied the other. Grey watched the couple as they passed.

"Robert," Grey said over his shoulder. "Keep an eye of them until we move around the corner."

"See how the bridge lightens the intersection a little?" Sukimoto said as they neared the corner.

"Look at the moving shadows," Tala noted, pointing at the street surface.

"They're from the people gathering around the corner," Sukimoto said.

Grey nodded. "I got left; Tala, you look right. You two keep watching our six."

They stopped at the corner. Grey quick-peeked. "Left is clear."

"Lots of people to the right," Tala said. "Just milling around."

"Our six is good," Sukimoto said.

The four committed into the intersection, quickly rechecking all directions as well as the rooftops of the new buildings, all better lit than the ones on the street they just left.

"Damn," Tala said, looking at the crowd. "There's got to be a couple hundred people."

"Plus, those waiting in the buildings out of the wind," Sukimoto said. "It's doable if people behave and work together in an orderly fashion."

"That ever happened?" Robert asked.

"Nope."

Grey looked at Sukimoto, "You said the bandanna guys haven't been up on the bridge, but we've seen two pairs on this side of it in the last few hours."

Sukimoto frowned. "You're right. I don't have an answer." Then his eyes turned lifeless, like those of a fish. "Attrition by death is the best way to deal with them."

Grey shot him a hard look. "That's the last resort."

Sukimoto returned the look. "You haven't been dealing with them like I have, like everyone in Sector Six has. That would change your mind."

"No, it wouldn't," Tala said. "We've killed a lot of people, but we're not killers."

Sukimoto looked from Tala to Grey, shook his head as if they were a lost cause, then turned back to the crowd.

Grey and Tala exchanged a look. Grey knew she was thinking the same thing he was: They can only be responsible for their own conscience.

"Okay," Grey said. "We want to stay out of the middle of the crowd. Let's move over to the left sidewalk and work our way up to the intersection before the bridge. If the trucks stop down here somewhere, we're in a good position to observe and check for Tala's brother. If they go up on the bridge, they will probably stop in the far-right lane." He looked at Sukimoto and got a nod that his assumption was right. "We stay on the left side and play it by ear as to how we contact him."

"Wherever it stops," Sukimoto said, "I can work my way over to it. Some of the people know I help distribute and will help me get through to the vehicles. Then I can tell Juni that Tala is over here." He looked at Grey, reading his eyes. "Any plan is better than no plan, right? Even this one?"

Grey nodded. "And watch people's expressions, body language, hands. Robert, you good to go?" Their friend nodded, though he looked tense. Better than overconfident, Grey thought. "Okay, I'll lead, Tala you behind me, then Robert. Sukimoto, you good for the tail end again?" Grey figured as an ex-New York City cop, he had experience in crowds.

"Yes."

"Let's do it."

Grey led them toward the left sidewalk behind the crowd.

People were hunched in threadbare coats or wrapped in soiled blankets, some carrying tattered backpacks to fill with food giveaways. Most looked broken with slumped shoulders, downcast eyes, and melancholy. A few made eye contact with the quartette then quickly looked away. There were suspicious eyes too, no doubt thinking the four were moving behind the crowd because they had some secret knowledge about something others didn't.

As they started up the slope of the bridge, Grey spotted a big man eyeing them. A few seconds later, he stepped into Grey's path.

"Where you shitbirds going?" he squeaked.

Grey had to choke down his immediate response, which was to laugh at the big man's voice that made Mike Tyson's sound gruff. Grey made a quick assessment: 30s, two or three inches taller than him, which meant the guy was about 6'4, and a good 190 to 200 pounds. He looked tired and short-tempered. Well, Grey was too, and he was in no mood to deal with the man. "We're going to sewing bee. You wanna come?"

Grey thought it might be a long shot to get a laugh, and he was right. The man extended a finger to poke Grey's chest, but before it made contact, the knife fighter grabbed the thick sausage and rammed it back toward the back of his hand. The big man yelped, the sound high pitched, still sounding like Mike Tyson, had he ever yelped, which Grey doubted. The man reflexively dropped to his knees to avoid one more ounce of pressure that would surely break his finger at the joint. When the man began to reach with his free hand, Grey applied a half-ounce more. The man quickly dropped his arm.

Grey was aware of Sukimoto, Tala, and Robert circling them and facing outward to watch the crowd. No one seemed interested in what was going on, anyway, as all eyes were looking for the food trucks.

"What this 'shitbird' is going to do…" Grey said, pulling his jacket flap back enough to expose the big curved kukri knife. "…is shove this big blade all the way up your ass, then cut my way out."

The man looked up at him, his eyes changing from pain to fear to…recognition?

"You're *him*," he squeaked. "You're the one they call 'Knife Fighter.' I've seen you around and heard about what went down at Hades. Sorry man. I'm the shitbird, okay? I'm the … Just don't stab my ass, please."

Grey eyed him for a moment. Big, a whole lot doofus in the eyes, and truly frightened.

"What's your name?"

"Everyone calls me Candy."

Grey looked at him. "Why? Is it a nickname?"

"No, 'cause it's my name.

"Of course. Okay, *Candy*, I'm going to keep hold of your finger but back off on the tension. There, that better?" Candy nodded. "Now, I want you to walk backward on your knees until your arm is almost straight… That's it. Now stop. When I say stand, you do so. If you try anything, I'll chop off your finger. We good?"

"Ye-yes, sir."

"Now, get up slowly."

When Candy was on his feet, Grey released his finger. The big man held it tenderly in his other hand and looked at Grey with a blend of fear and awe.

"Do me a favor, okay?"

Candy dipped his head a little as if bowing. "Of course, of course."

"The four of us are heading to the top of the bridge. You walk point and politely scoot people aside for us."

"Oh, sure, sure. It would be an honor." He looked at Tala. "Oh, she must be the one who was with you at Hades. They said she was beautiful." He bowed slightly again. "Nice to meet you, ma'am. Much respect." Tala nodded.

"Okay," Grey said. "Lead the way, Candy."

The big man executed a sharp about-face and bellowed like a drill sergeant for people to make a path for them.

"Politely," Grey reminded. "Politely."

"Whoops. I forgot."

They walked partway up the bridge without incident, though the crowd had increased and spread across the lanes from railing to railing. The wind surges were intermittent, some strong enough to make everyone lean into them to maintain their balance. The foursome continued until Grey determined they were roughly halfway to the apex, a good stopping point since they didn't know where the trucks would unload.

"Right here, Candy."

The big man turned around. "Did I do good, Knife Fighter?"

Grey extended his hand. "You did," he said as they shook. "Thank you. And remember, Candy. Be polite to people. It's never a bad thing."

"Yes, Knife Fighter. Thank you."

"He'll have a story to tell," Robert said, watching the big guy move through the crowd toward the top of the bridge.

Grey leaned over the railing and looked down at the fast-moving water about 60 feet below them. It looked like ink, and it wasn't from the weak lighting. There was a lot of garbage in it— unidentifiable junk mostly, a barrel, lots of bottles, another barrel, a car hood. A face?

Grey leaned over a little more. Yes, a dead body was riding the current. Man or woman, he couldn't tell. There was another…and another.

He straightened and closed his eyes, wanting the wind gust to cleanse his face, his eyes. If only it could wash away everything that he had seen these past many months.

"It's twenty after seven," Sukimoto said. Grey turned around, glad to have been pulled from his thoughts. "The trucks have never been later than eight o'clock." He looked at Tala. "I hope your brother is with them. Like I said, one time, he wasn't."

"Thank you," Tala said. "I haven't seen him in a year…no, make that fifteen months. I'm worried."

The four of them turned toward the sound of shouting from the apex.

Grey stepped up on the bottom rung of the bridge railing to look over the crowd. "Something's happening near the top," he said, squinting against the wind. "Lots of jostling around, some people running back this way. Someone threw something, a brick, I think… And it hit someone in the face."

A woman, her forehead bleeding and crying hysterically, rushed by them, heading down the bridge against the crowd.

"Anyone understand what she was screaming?" Grey asked, watching her elbow her way through the mass.

"All I got," Tala said, "was something about the bandanna gang attacking people up there."

Robert shook his head. "Great. I was hoping never to see them again."

"There's always one more thing," Grey said, stretching to see over the agitating crowd. "They're still fighting up there, but it's too far away to see bandannas."

"Let's go up," Sukimoto said, his tone 100 percent behind his suggestion.

"It isn't our job to police everything," Robert said. "I mean, if it happens right in front of us, sure, we help. But we're not cops on patrol. Besides, we're here to find Juni."

Tala nodded. "I agree. If it happens right here, we deal with it."

Sukimoto scowled.

The protector in Grey wanted to go, but he also agreed that they couldn't jump into the middle of mob violence. They were only four strong, Robert and Sukimoto were unknowns, and even blade skills could quickly be overwhelmed.

The wind subsided just as a helicopter whispered by overhead heading toward the east side of the bridge, its lights off as usual. Apprehensive faces looked up.

Another passed over.

A series of honks from behind them. The crowd cheered.

"The trucks," Sukimoto announced, pointing at two sets of headlights moving toward the intersection below. "If they make the turn onto the bridge, they'll probably head to the top."

The trucks turned onto the bridge.

"Should we move up?" Tala asked, the excitement of seeing her brother shining in her face.

"Yes," Sukimoto said. "The crowd should move away from this side toward the other railing, giving us a clear path up."

"Let's do it," Grey said, stepping down from the rail. "Things have calmed at the top, but I couldn't see why. Maybe the gang went back down the other side of the bridge."

The truck horns grew louder as two large Army trucks pushed their way through the crowd in the far lane. It was difficult to see through the mass of humanity, but it looked to Grey that people were jammed against the other railing. He remembered reading accounts of people in India being crushed to death on bridges when something caused the crowds to panic.

"Stay away from the other railing," he warned the others. He took Tala's arm and drew her close to him. "There is nothing about this I like. Stay close to me, keep your weapon arm free, and watch for rockers. And watch for these bandanna people too. They'll probably bully their way to the front of the line. If we see your brother, let's try to get his attention. But it's his decision if he wants to come to us."

From the east, a helicopter swept over the apex, slowed, then hovered above the trucks, the wind knocking it about as it laboriously rotated 180 degrees. Like all the others, it was black, no markings, the pilot impossible to see. A moment later, it headed back over the apex and disappeared on the other side of the bridge.

"Why are they interested in this?" Tala asked rhetorically.

The trucks were almost straight across from them and appeared to be stopping.

"It looks like they're not going all the way up to the top," Sukimoto shouted behind them as another wind blast slammed the bridge. The crowd chatter was growing louder with anticipation.

The trucks stopped.

The crowd roared and rushed toward the vehicles, pushing, cursing. A length of what Grey thought was a pipe, flipped end over end through the air, and struck a tall man in the back of his head. He dropped out of Grey's sight. Then a stone found a woman's face, followed by a rainstorm of projectiles.

"Let's move down the slope a little so we can see into the trucks," Grey shouted to the others.

"Wait," Tala said, taking his arm. "I think that's him behind the steering wheel of the first truck."

The driver's head was turned toward the passenger side. "Are you sure? I can't see his face." The driver turned back and looked out the driver's window.

"That's him," Tala and Grey said simultaneously. "Wait!" Grey shouted, his hand on Tala's shoulder. He pointed upward.

A mostly silent helicopter dropped down from the black sky to hover about 30 feet above the trucks. The wind rocked it back and forth so hard that Grey wondered if the pilot had control over it.

"I can't believe they're up in this," Robert shouted above the noise.

Tala and Grey looked back toward the lead truck. "Where did Juni go," Tala cried, her tone near hysteria. Grey didn't see him anywhere.

The crowd, ignoring the laboring helicopter right above their heads, rushed in behind the trucks, their hands reaching for whatever was being handed out. Grey saw a man come around from behind the first truck holding a cardboard box high above his head. Someone smashed something into his face and tore it from his grip.

The pushing increased, and a moment later, fists flew.

Someone wearing a red jacket lifted a club of some kind into the air and slammed it down on someone's head. Again, it went up, and again it hammered a skull. When the club went up a third time, multiple hands reached for it and the offending arm. A moment later, the man in the red jacket appeared to float upward as a dozen hands lifted his thrashing body overhead. Then the arms crowd-surfed him, passing him along above their heads as if they were at a rock concert.

The man thrashed harder when he realized where they were conveying him, but the crowd had had enough of the man and thousands of others just like him. The supporting hands hesitated at the bridge railing as if they collectively agreed to let the bully see for a moment his fate. A moment later, they surfed him into the dark to drop into the garbage-choked river far below.

"The bandanna assholes," Sukimoto shouted, pointing at several of them pushing people aside. "Eight...no, ten of them."

Intense light from the helicopter splashed over the bandanna men, then just as quickly went out. Grey thought he heard a gunshot, but it was hard to tell in the wind's roar. A moment later, the helicopter bumped and swayed.

"What's it doing?" Robert shouted.

Sukimoto jabbed his finger toward the group of bandanna men. "Look!"

One of them, the yellow cloth covering his mouth and nose like a bandit, was pointing a semi-auto handgun at the craft. It bucked silently, the sound lost in the wind and the whine of the struggling helicopter.

"Hey, asshole!" Sukimoto shouted, running toward the man, his Sig-Sauer leading the way in his extended hand.

"Sukimoto, no!" Grey shouted, knowing that the helicopter people wouldn't know his intention was to stop the gunman.

Sukimoto's gun bucked in his hand, and the bandanna man grimaced, bent forward, and fell to the asphalt.

"Stop," Grey shouted, but even he couldn't hear his voice in the din.

Bright flashes erupted from the helicopter's partially open side door. Sukimoto's arms snapped into the air, sending his gun flying. His body jerked this way and that way as slugs tore holes in his torso and blew away a chunk of his jaw.

Their new friend was still falling when someone dashed from the crowd and grabbed the Sig out of his hand. It was Candy, the big man who had helped the foursome make their way up the bridge.

"Leave it, Candy," Grey shouted, though there was no way his voice could be heard in the din. "The helicopter will think you're—" Candy pointed the gun at the helicopter that had risen to about 50 feet.

The piercing light from the craft illuminated the big man and the gun as it recoiled, once, twice. Again, flashes emanated from the aircraft's side door. Candy's body twisted and turned all the way to the pavement, where he continued to convulse as more rounds, silent in the storm, punched his dead body.

The light extinguished.

For two eerie seconds, the only sound on the bridge was the beat of the helicopter blades as the wind-whipped crowd froze in place silently staring at the two bodies.

A woman, either very brave or very foolish, dashed out of the throng, snatched the dropped gun, and disappeared back into it again.

Grey grabbed Tala's arm and pulled her with him to the railing.

The helicopter wobbled and whined. Grey rode in them in Afghanistan, but he didn't know if .45 caliber rounds could bring them down. Maybe it was the wind gusts, or it was just old and in disrepair.

Below it, people ran in sheer panic in every direction, their mouths open, their screams drowned out by the cacophony.

A diagonal beam of light splashed down on the two trucks. This one came from a second helicopter descending a short distance behind the last vehicle.

"I still don't see Juni!" Tala shouted.

The troubled helicopter was shaking violently now, and its engine sounding desperate as it slowly rotated 360 degrees.

"Let's move toward the top of the bridge," Grey said, eying the laboring aircraft.

Tala resisted. "I want to look for—"

"No," Grey said sharply, taking her arm. "It's not safe here. Come on. Follow Robert. He's already halfway up—"

The helicopter moaned. A death rattle, Grey thought, looking over his shoulder. "Run, Tala!"

"It's going down!" Robert shouted as thousands of pounds of encased glass, steel, and fuel spun toward the bridge.

"Keep running, Tala!" Grey shouted. "Over the top of the crest. Over the top!"

Looking back one last time, Grey saw the helicopter's rear section whip about like the tail of a frantically dying prehistoric beast, slamming people too slow or too infirm into the railing, some of them over the top rung to drop down into the blackness.

Grey, Tala, and Robert were lying face down slightly below the crest on the east side, their arms covering their heads, debris flying by inches above them. Broken pieces that slid across the pavement and managed to travel over the apex, struck their arms, legs, and torsos without much impact. A few second later, it was over. Grey lifted his head. "Everyone okay?"

"Something cut the back of my hand, but I'll live," Robert said.

Tala looked at her fingers, "Got some nicks on my fingers, that's all. It would have been much worse if we'd been on the other side of the rise."

Grey stretched up to look over the rise. The helicopter had crashed on the open back end of the first truck, crushing people beneath it. The flying pieces of aircraft had carved a path through the crowd, leaving dozens lying on the pavement, some moving, some not.

The crash sealed access to the boxes of food inside, so the able-bodied yanked at the canvas cover and hacked at it with knives.

The truck behind it was covered with shards of glass, twisted metal, and a thousand other unidentifiable pieces of debris.

Behind the last vehicle, at least a hundred people fought, shouted, and screamed over ownership of cardboard boxes of food. Clubs thumped, and bladed weapons slashed and plunged. On the outer perimeter of the mob, people appeared to be fighting over nothing, as if just for the gratification of it, Grey thought. Or maybe for the release.

"Do you see my brother?" Tala asked. "Do you see Juni anywhere? Do you think he got hurt in that?"

"We'll find out," Grey said, climbing to his feet. "But we don't want to wade into that chaos—"

"Well, ain't this something?" a voice said from behind them. Grey, Tala, and Robert turned around to find half a dozen young men, all wearing yellow bandannas walking toward them. They appeared to be in their early 20s, dressed in tattered, dirty clothing. Some wore their bandannas around their foreheads like sweatbands, and others wore theirs as neck scarves. Grey thought they looked absurd, like a corny 1980s gang movie. But he also knew it was the symbol that gave them their unity, their deadly mindset.

He didn't see who spoke, but he assumed it was the tall one leading the others.

Grey recognized him as one of the two in the big room. The smaller man next to him was the other one.

"Whoa!" the smaller one said, looking beyond Grey and the others. "Check it out," he said, sweeping his hand across the death and destruction. The gang probably didn't see the helicopter's impact since they were coming from the other side of the apex, but they for sure heard it. "Lookie that shit, will yuh. Daaaamn. And lookie those poor saps that got themselves killed." He laughed and shook his head. "That's great, aint it, Billy?" he said, looking up at the taller man.

But Billy wasn't looking at the mess. He was staring at Grey.

The six of them had stopped about a dozen feet from Grey and the others. "I've seen you three times now in the last hour," Billy said. "First, in that room where the two dumb shits got turned into crispy critters, a few minutes ago when that Asian dude shot my man, and now."

"Our man was Billy's cousin," the shorter man said. "*Cousin.* Serious heat comin' down, you follow?"

A hard wind gust hammered all of them, sending small pieces of debris from the crash skittering across the street, up over the sidewalk, under the railing's bottom rung, and out into the darkness.

Two of the bandanna men stepped up next to the shorter man on the left of Grey, and the other two moved to Billy's side on the right.

Behind Grey's team, people at the crash site continued to shout and cry in desperation. In his periphery, he was aware of someone slightly behind Tala. He turned enough to see all of the man. Grey smiled to himself.

"Who's this dipshit?" Billy said, looking at the new man.

Unaware that someone was behind her, Tala jerked around. She looked at the man for a two-count, then blurted, "Juni!"

Movement in Grey's periphery…the shorter bandanna man was pulling a handgun from his waistband.

The barrel had yet to clear his pants before Grey took three running steps to cross the eight-foot gap and ram the big knife deep into the man's right eye socket. Grey front kicked him in the abdomen and simultaneously yanked his blade free. The bandanna gang member died on his way down to the pavement.

"Back up, all of you," Grey commanded. But the other gang members were staring down at their friend in disbelief, no doubt shocked at the difference five seconds could make.

The man who had been standing next to the one Grey killed bent quickly to retrieve the firearm from his friend's waistband.

A single shot from Robert's Glock punched through the man's skull an inch above his right ear. His head jerked to the side, and his body sagged as his life diffused into the wind. He dropped across his dead buddy's legs.

"Anyone else want to be stupid?" Grey asked. "No? Good. Now back up until I tell you to stop." They didn't. Whether in shock or defiant, Grey couldn't tell. "Do it now! And extend your arms out to the sides, shoulder high. Lower them, and we'll assume you're going for a firearm, and we'll kill you without warning."

"We don't have no more guns, man," Billy, the tall one said, his arms outstretched.

"Good, then you might live," Tala said.

The remaining gang members glared at Grey and the others. They commenced slowly backing up, all with their arms out.

"How much for the hot chick?" the blond-haired man standing next to Billy asked, eyeing Tala. A large backward swastika tattoo covered over half of his forehead.

"Stand fast," Grey said out of the corner of his mouth when Tala tensed.

"You tattoo yourself in a mirror?" Juni asked.

"I will kill you last," the tattooed one said, staring hard at Juni.

"Not if I kill you first," Juni taunted, his eyes smiling. It had been over a year since Grey had seen Juni, and he had forgotten how the man wasn't intimidated by fools.

"Just curious, Billy," Grey said. "Were your people here to get food?"

The tall one snickered, then the other three followed his lead. "Hell no. We've got plenty. We're here to bash some skulls. For shits and giggles."

"Shits and giggles," the blond-haired man repeated.

Grey shook his head at their stupidity. "Considering your two dead men, how's that 'shits and giggles' plan look to you now?"

"It means it's payback time."

"Back up slowly toward the railing," Grey said out of the corner of his mouth to the others.

A gust slammed them. A bigger one followed, its roar nearly blotting out the cacophony of shouts and screams from the horde only a few yards away. The bandanna men intently watched the foursome, waiting for the right moment.

A half dozen men and women burst past Grey and the others, the sound of their approach covered by the wind. Some were carrying cardboard boxes and looking over their shoulder as if being pursued. The bandanna man, on the far right, laughed and thrust his arms out as if to grab a man's box. The man startled and

swerved toward the far railing, the others following him. A female stumbled over debris, tried to recover, but fell hard.

Four more people ripped by Grey and the others, two of them with bloody faces, and commenced kicking the downed woman.

"Hey!" Grey shouted at them.

The knife fighter was slammed from behind, launching him forward and down to the asphalt. A second later, Robert was sent sprawling onto the pedestrian sidewalk a few feet away. Grey had been gripping the handle of his sheathed kukri, so it remained secure. But in the corner of his eye, he saw Robert's Glock slide under the bottom bridge rail and out into space, while at the same time, a woman ran up to the dead man with the gun, yanked it out of his waistband, and dashed away.

The man on Grey's back, snaked an arm under his neck. Grey pulled on the forearm enough that he could breathe, then violently twisted until the big man toppled off his back. Grey quickly sat up, only to be met by a hard palm-strike to his forehead that slammed him back down onto his back.

He tucked his chin to keep the back of his head from impacting the pavement and snapped up his hands to protect his face. Grey could see the man now, and he was huge. He slapped Grey's hands out of the way and dropped his knee onto his sternum, forcing air out of his lungs.

Grey sucked for oxygen as he tried to buck the man off again, but the attacker's other leg was extended out to the side for balance. He knew what he was doing.

Then the man commenced raining punches down on him.

Gasping for air, Grey managed to block each incoming roundhouse punch. After what seemed like a dozen arm-numbing blows, he swept the man's arm inside and jammed it against the assailant's chest, preventing him, at least for a second or two, from punching with his other fist.

And a second or two was all Grey needed.

He let go of the arm trap to thrust the fingers of his left hand into the man's eyes as he simultaneously unsheathed his kukri with his right. His first thrust with the blade sunk into the man's left kidney; his second penetrated the side of his neck, severing his carotid artery.

Grey turned his head away to avoid the blood geyser shooting toward his face and hip-bumped the dying man off of him. He rolled onto his side and looked for Tala.

She was less than six feet away, holding her bloodied Thai sickle and climbing slowly to her feet as if in shock. A man with multiple bleeding puncture wounds in his face lay at her feet, motionless.

He glanced over to where he last saw the bandanna gang. They weren't there.

Juni was dealing with two men, both of them armed with knives. He was trying to line them up to fight one at a time, but they were on to his plan and continued to separate. Grey moved toward the closest one, a 20-something with fast feet and quick feints with what looked like a kitchen knife.

The man turned toward Grey, his right leg forward and right hand holding the knife in an icepick grip. Grey recognized the distinctive-looking kitchen knife; it was an eight-inch Santoku. His mother had one, gifted to her by his father. It was considered by chefs to be a high-end kitchen utensil.

"You don't have to do this," Grey said. "Why don't you and your buddy just take off."

The man, tattered and unwashed, twisted his mouth into an ugly grin, his teeth black and broken. Apparently, the smile was his answer.

In his peripheral. Grey saw Juni execute a flurry of fast knife stabs into his opponent's torso. The man emitted a weak growl and dropped.

Grey's man lunged with a face-high, right to left slash, but at least two feet short. A kick followed his fake and struck Grey where Leather's knife had penetrated, knocking him back a couple of steps. Grey looked down at his abdomen, his heart thumping; he brushed his hand up and down as if to wipe off the impact.

The man charged him, his hand now holding the long knife in saber grip, the pointy end in a straight trajectory toward his belly. *How does he know?* Grey thought. *How does he...* Grey's brain reeled.

The confused sounds—shouting, screaming, the banshee groan of the wind—seemed to beckon him to cease the struggle, the daily fight to survive. Just let it....go.

The eight-inch Santoku floated through a black void where only the glimmering blade existed, its lone charge to perforate through the scar tissue where another rapier had grooved a terrible path through skin and meat and capillaries.

"Grey!" Tala's cry. "Watch out!"

Clarity.

Grey snapped his torso sideways, and the Santoku only snagged the front of his jacket.

He grabbed the wrist of the man's extended arm with his left hand and hacked down into the top of his forearm with the Kukri. He retracted the knife near his lead leg, rolled his wrist, and executed the next two moves in a fraction of a second: He sliced upward to hack into the underside of the man's forearm, turned the knife over with a snap of his wrist, and chopped down into the forearm again.

The first cut went deep into the nerves near the bend of his forearm. The second into the tendons under his forearm between his wrist and elbow; the third hacked into the radial nerve in his wrist joint.

Grey flashed to his father drilling him on up and down cutting, called *rompida* in Filipino stick and knife fighting arts. The old man nicknamed the cutting technique: "You'll never use your arm again."

At first, the attacker's screams were covered by the wind. But when the wind died for a moment, they were loud and clear. Tala snatched the man's dropped knife and handed it to Robert.

Grey grabbed the front of his opponent's sweatshirt. "Who are you?" The man didn't answer. "Why did you and your buddies jump us?" The man's jaw trembled from the pain and no doubt what he thought was his imminent death. But still, he refused to speak.

Grey nicked the side of his face with his kukri, drawing a trickle of blood. "Answer!"

The man's eyes bugged. "We wanted to join the bandanna gang," he said, his words rushed. "We wanted to impress them."

Grey's anger flashed. "You made us kill your friends because you wanted…" For a nanosecond, he thought about smashing the butt-end of his knife into the man's face. He quickly sheathed it and took a deep belly breath to control himself. He was just so tired of it all.

"Now your buddies are dead," Grey said tightly. He looked down at the blood pouring out of the man's jacket sleeve. "And you've probably lost the use of your arm." He felt his temper surge again. He yanked the man around by his sliced-up arm. "Get out of here," he growled, making the wannabe gang member cry out. "I could have killed you." He pushed him away. "Remember that."

The man dashed off over the bridge crest.

Grey, his breathing ragged, looked down at the man he killed and over at the two Tala and Juni had finished. The waste, he thought, struggling to calm himself. Then aloud, "The goddamn waste!"

"The bandanna guys split," Robert said.

"Did anyone see where they went?"

"They took off when we were dealing with these other guys," Tala said.

Grey took a deep breath and eased it out, feeling his control returning. He again looked at the man Tala had killed, and at the one Juni finished.

"Sorry," Robert said. "My gun went sliding off the bridge when I got tackled. I didn't even see him."

"You hurt?" Tala asked. "Where's the guy?"

"I banged my shoulder on the pavement, but I'll live." He pointed his new knife toward the top railing. "My man went over that. I thought the water might cool him off."

Juni chuckled and jerked his thumb at Robert. "I like this fuckin' guy," he said.

With Sukimoto gone and Juni joining the group, they remained a foursome. Things were happening so quickly that there was no time to mourn Sukimoto's death, celebrate connecting with Juni, or ponder the self-defense killings everyone had a part in. Grey hoped they would be able to do these things later.

Tala was thrilled to find her brother, and she had yet to move away from his side. Grey first met him a few weeks after he met Tala. They liked each other right off. On one occasion, the three of them had trained with their blades for nearly a week. Grey was impressed with Juni's speed, fluidity, and eagerness to learn what he had to teach. Grey enjoyed learning some of Juni's footwork techniques.

Grey could tell that Robert was angry that he lost his Glock. He wasn't a martial artist, and he knew nothing of knife fighting. But he was good with a gun, a useless skill if you don't have one. When Juni saw him looking blankly at the eight-inch Santoku kitchen knife, he went over to Robert, touched the pointy end, and said, "This part goes into the other man." Grey forced himself not to chuckle.

They were clustered next to the bridge railing straight across from where the helicopter crashed on the back end of the first truck, then flopped over onto its side, the whirling blades hacking into the pavement. Most of the injured had been helped away, leaving about two dozen dead and miscellaneous body parts on the bridge. About 20 people stood around looking lost and confused.

Grey couldn't see into the back of the rear truck, but it had to be empty since there wasn't anyone near it. The canvas top on the first one had been sliced open in several places revealing only emptiness now.

Tala moved down the railing a few steps, her eyes studying the helicopter. "You can see the cockpit better from here," she said. "But where is the pilot, the crew?" The others moved down next to her.

"Did someone carry them away?" Juni asked rhetorically. He looked at Grey. "Do you know where they're from? The helicopters, I mean?"

Grey shook his head. He called out to two raggedly looking teenagers standing against the railing a few feet from them. They looked at him. One was crying, his jaw trembling. "Did you see the pilot?" Grey asked.

They shook their heads. The one not crying said, "There wasn't one; I swear to God. We were right over there when it crashed. The door broke off, and there wasn't anyone in it." He frowned. "What does that mean?'

"Holy shit!" Robert breathed. "How can that be? I mean—"

"Maybe he got thrown over the bridge or something," Tala said.

"I was watching," the teenager said. "I didn't see that happen."

Tala continued to look across the way. A moment later, she looked at Grey. "Don't look now, but about fifteen feet to the right of the rear truck, against the railing, there are two bandanna guys. Two from the group earlier. That tall guy is one of them. They're watching us."

"I saw them a few seconds ago," he said tiredly. "They did say they wanted payback."

He looked down at the intersection where no more than 20 people remained. "We need to choose where it's going to go down."

"There might be more wannabes," Juni said.

"That too," Grey said. "I suggest we head down the bridge and go back the way we came. That street was dark, and there are places we can take cover."

This was another 'even a bad plan is better than no plan' situations, Grey thought. He looked up at the black sky.

CHAPTER 6

GREY, TALA, ROBERT, JUNI, AND BILLY

They made it down off the bridge and over to the intersection without incident. Tala was leading the way, and Grey was in the rear watching their six.

"Stop," he whispered after they had turned the corner onto the long street they had traversed earlier in the evening. They looked back at him. "Possible threat," he said, his back to the wall next to the corner, his kukri in his hand. He gestured for them to form a line out from the wall.

A moment later, a man rounded the corner.

Grey grabbed him by his upper arm and swung him in a circle until his chest met the wall with a loud "Ooomph." He C-clamped the man's neck and pushed his face against the graffitied bricks, his blade tip resting against the base of the man's skull. "Put your hands flat on the wall," Grey growled. "If you reach for a weapon, I'll shove my knife into your brain stem."

"I don't have no weapon," the man blurted. "Honest. I wanted to warn you guys."

"Warn us about what?"

"You're hurting my face. Can you slack off a little?" Grey did but left his knife ready to go. "Thank you. Okay, I was standing over by the truck, the one that didn't get hit by the chopper. There were some bandanna guys there, and they were talking about you."

"How do you know they were talking about us?"

"I looked where they were looking. They mentioned the woman and the hard-looking guy. You. You're Knife Fighter, right?" Grey didn't react. "They said stuff about avenging their friends."

Grey turned him around. The side of the man's face was marked with a small abrasion. "How many are there?"

"Four at first then two more joined 'em. I hate those bastards. They hurt my father really bad about three months ago. Stomped him and broke his leg. He wasn't doing nothing. They've hurt a lot of people; killed a lot too. People have been talking about killing them, but no one has had the guts yet."

"Where are they now?"

"About half a block back when I turned the corner. They're walking fast."

Grey quick-peeked around the wall. He looked back at the others and nodded. "Fifty yards," he said.

Grey stepped back and, without looking away from the man's face, sheathed his knife. "What's your name?"

"Reggie." He shook his head. "I can't believe I'm talking to you."

"Thanks for the tip, Reggie. You need anything? I got a fentanyl tablet and some matches."

"No, no, thanks. I just wanted to warn you, that's all."

"You take care, Reggie." The young man nodded, moved into the intersection, and headed in the opposite direction from the bridge.

"Okay," Grey said, looking at Robert, Tala, and Juni. "I'll talk while we head down the street. Now and quickly." As they moved, Grey prepped them. "I want to weaken the gang's strength. There's no time for discussion, so just listen. I want the three of you to walk close to each other, one in front and two side-by-side on the lead person's heels. And change places every two or three minutes. They know there are four of us, but if you walk in a tight group and swap positions, in the darkness and from a distance, it'll be harder to tell that one of us is missing." He shrugged. "I hope."

"Where are you going?" Tala said, gripping his arm. "I want to be with you."

"Trust me on this," he said just to her. She frowned but, after a moment, nodded. "Okay, stay together, keep your eyes open, watch out for the roof on that building where we stayed earlier. Go, and I'll catch up with you?"

Tala squeezed his arm. "Grey…"

"I'll catch up to you," he said softly but firmly.

He watched them head out, Robert in the lead, Tala and Juni walking behind him. She looked back and continued on.

The room was as large as the one in which the man set himself afire. The darkness was dense, broken only by two deep-grey rectangles on the floor on each end of the room. The shapes were formed by the open doorways and the vague residual outdoor light.

He had noticed the open doors earlier when they were walking toward the intersection. There were people in the place then, a few with lanterns, which allowed him to see that it was one large room. If the space had consisted of offices or cubicles, his plan wouldn't work.

His plan had one other requirement; without it, he would have to go to Plan B, which at the moment he didn't have.

Grey heard distant sounds—footsteps and whispering—then nothing. He assumed they turned silent as soon as they rounded the corner onto the dark street outside. They probably spotted the others, and the leader was gesturing and mouthing commands. Was it still the tall one, Billy? Let them be walking single file, spaced apart.

Grey squatted at the inside edge of the first door inset that they would pass. He leaned out just enough to see with one eye.

He could hear their footsteps…their breathing as they got closer… He leaned back and watched the rectangle of dull light on the floor.

A shadow passed through it. One second…two…three…another man passed by, then a third, all single file, in three-second intervals. It was hard to tell by their shadows, but it didn't appear that any of them looked into the dark room.

The fourth and fifth man passed. Reggie said there were six.

He heard a tired exhalation.

A refection of the last man's leg entered the rectangle, followed by his second leg. Then the heel of the first foot lifted to take his next step.

Grey quickly crouch-walked into the outer door inset and swung his kukri hard into the man's Achille's tendon, slicing all the way through. He yanked the blade free and crouch-walked backward into the darkness.

The man's screams echoed through the cavernous room until Grey pushed the door shut. He looked out the large window to check on the rest of the gang members' positions. He could make out all five outside the window, each evenly spaced about three feet apart, all turning to look back at their injured comrade. Unfortunately, the first man in their column—it looked like Billy—hadn't reached the second door. The last two men moved toward the injured one.

Damn, Grey thought. There went his plan to hack the lead man too. Doing both lead and rear men would have had a powerful psychological impact on the others.

"What happened?" a voice that sounded like Billy's asked calmly.

"Don't know," a different voice answered. "He's hurtin' too much to tell us. Looks like a knife cut him. He's messed up bad."

Grey scurried to the back of the room to take cover in the deepest dark. If they all rushed in, he would have some advantage since he was in total darkness, but he could see their silhouettes against the large window and the open door to the left.

"Aaron, you and Thomas check the room."

Something poked Grey in the back. He felt behind him…a doorknob. A storage room, maybe. He opened it, stepped in, and pulled it an inch short of latching shut.

A voice from out on the sidewalk. "Okay. But the door here is closed. Maybe he got cut in front of that door in the first building we passed."

"You think he wouldn't have noticed until he walked this far? Dumb shit. Check the room."

"Okay! Damn. Come on, Thomas." Grey heard them push the door open, then their footsteps on the cement floor.

"Can't see nothin'," one of them said. "Let's check the left wall and move to the back and then along the back wall."

"Okay. But don't talk no more."

A real think tank, Grey thought, hearing them moving along the wall to his right.

"Here's the corner and the back wall. Can't see a damn thing."

"Don't talk no more."

"Okay, I won't."

They were getting closer…closer…

Through the partially open door, Grey saw a figure pass between him and the dull light from the front of the room. The man was about three feet out from the back wall and probably didn't know the door was there.

The second figure walked into view.

Grey opened the door, thankfully without a squeak, and slashed at the second man where the back of his legs should be. His scream was part startle and part pain, a lot of it. Grey knew for sure he severed one hamstring, maybe both legs. He heard the man drop to the floor, his scream piercing.

Grey could barely make out the first man's silhouette turn this way and that way looking for him. Did he raise his arm?

Something slammed into Grey's upper left biceps. The knife fighter ate the pain without making a sound and moved diagonally right to counter stab.

Grey heard air displacement.

He dropped to one knee, scrunching his head down.

The man's weapon, whatever it was, passed just inches above Grey's head, stirring his long hair. With all his strength, the knife fighter ripped his kukri on a horizontal path where he perceived the man's lead ankle to be.

He heard and felt the contact in his hand and arm, but the blade didn't stop as it did when he hacked the first two men. This time it continued until the inside of his arm wrapped around his own chest.

Did he misjudge the distance and only cut superficially?

The man grunted, the pained sound echoing in the empty room, and thumped to the floor.

Grey took advantage of the man's thrashing and desperate sobbing to stand and scan the room for other bandanna people who might have slipped in. But the only other person was the man he chopped two minutes earlier, still down and still carrying on about it.

He looked toward the window. No one there.

Grey looked back at the vague squirming figure of last man he had just cut. When he moved one of his legs from blocking the dull light from the far door, Grey saw something in his hand. It wasn't the weapon he had used, but rather a shoe, in it, an amputated foot, the top of its sock bunched around a bloody ankle.

"My foot came off, mister," the man whimpered. "Can you help me put it back on?"

Grey jerked his head toward a moving light outside the front window. It was a man carrying a lantern, and he was hurrying in the direction of Tala and the others. Where was the rest of the gang?

"Apply direct pressure to the back of your leg," Grey said looking over at the sobbing man whose hamstring he'd sliced. And to the newly made monoped, "Remove your pants belt and make a tourniquet."

As Grey neared the front of the room, he could hear moaning from the man with the severed Achilles tendon. Were the remaining three gang members taking cover behind the wall between the door and the window? Maybe. But Grey's gut said the guy with the lantern was running to where the bandanna guys were clashing with Tala and the others.

He hesitated at the door for a moment, listening, and trying to sense if they were on either side of the door. Nothing. He stepped out of the room into the exterior door inset and listened again. Noise from the left, grunting, cursing. He leaned out an inch to check to the right. Clear, except for the bad tendon guy propped up against the wall down by the other door inset. Grey quick-peeked to the left.

Twenty yards down the block, the man with the lantern acted as a stagehand operating a spotlight.

Closest to Grey, Robert was stumbling backward, his torso twisted and bent over his right side. A man to Robert's front was also bent over, his hands covering his crotch.

On the other side of them, Tala was fighting a bandanna man, both armed with knives. A few feet away, Juni was circling someone, both of them feinting at one another with blades.

Grey never considered himself much of a runner, but he covered the ground in a heartbeat.

Robert lay across the curb. The downed man lay about 10 feet away, writhing on his back like a stepped-on worm. It took Grey a moment to see the handle of the Santoku kitchen knife protruding from between his legs, the eight-inch blade completely buried. He looked at Robert. "Where are you hurt?"

"I'm okay," Robert said. "Took a hard punch to my liver." He nodded at the bandanna man. "Can you retrieve my knife for me?"

Grey quickly braced his foot on the man's lower abdomen and yanked the Santoku free. A small geyser of blood arced from the wound. He handed the knife to Robert, then looked over at the other two.

Juni was deflecting a thrust and countering with a thrust into the man's shoulder.

Tala was in a low crouch, her Smith & Wesson blade in her front hand, the Thai sickle in her left near her chest. Both of her hands were bleeding. The bandanna man, it was Billy, was in constant motion, shifting from one stance to another, his blade making small horizontal figure eights in the air. He knew what he was doing, though a long trickling slit down one side of his face showed he wasn't invincible.

Tala lunged and thrust her knife toward his chest. But the man bladed his body out of the line of trajectory and returned a slash at Tala's weapon arm. She snapped it back, avoiding a deep cut, and whipped her sickle across his forward shoulder, slicing the loose jacket material.

"Billy!" Grey shouted to distract him. The gang leader looked toward Grey, just as the lantern light illuminated small bits of something sifting down from somewhere overhead.

Grey looked down at chunks of broken bricks scattered about the sidewalk in front of an open door. It's the same building where we took shelter earlier, he thought, where someone dropped something right after we left.

A bottle smashed on the sidewalk to Grey's left, then something small hit Tala's shoulder.

Grey lunged at her, hooked his arm around her torso, and pulled her against the wall with him. Billy leaped into the doorway inset less than 10 feet away as sheetrock and white bricks crashed to the sidewalk right where Tala and Billy had been standing. A puff of wind pushed the white cloud of dust away; Billy was gone.

"That other guy went into this building," the man with the lantern said.

Out in the street, Juni was cupping his chin, blood oozing through his fingers, and dancing away from the bandanna man's trained attacks.

"You okay?" Grey asked Tala. She nodded, her breathing ragged, the sickle still in her left hand, the fixed blade in her right. "Help your brother. End it quickly."

Grey looked at the man with the lantern. "Stand closer to this door, so some of that light gets inside."

Grey stepped over to the inset—the thick stench of burnt meat wafting out the open door—and quick-peeked around the door frame. The lantern light was faint but helpful. He could see the mounds on the floor that were the covered burnt bodies, and he could barely make out the door to the small room where he, Tala, Robert, and Sukimoto had rested. It was open. He didn't see the bandanna man in the big room; he had to be back in the smaller one.

"This doesn't need to happen, Billy," Grey said to the empty room as he made his way past the bodies. Earlier, when the four of them had walked out of the little room, the smell of gasoline and burnt meat was diluted from the wind streaming through the open doors. Now that the storm had died, the profuse stench was tweaking his gag reflex.

"Just come out with your knife put away and your hands empty, and you can go on your way."

No response,

Grey heard movement in the small room and quickly moved over to the side of the entrance. Then he waited, left empty hand over his chest, right hand gripping the kukri in the lead, its point off to the left side of his jaw.

"I'm going to leave you on the ground to bleed out," Billy said from somewhere in the little room. "And that's a promise."

The arrogant confidence of the young, Grey thought. "Come on out, Billy. There's no reason to—"

A beast-like scream echoed throughout the room.

Grey dropped into a crouch, his knife slightly extended, the point of the blade aimed at the door. But the bandanna gang leader didn't show.

Nice psyche, Grey thought.

Another ear-damaging scream. Grey's muscles tightened. Billy didn't come out.

"Grey?" Tala's voice from behind him.

"Watch the street doors," he said, without looking away from the doorway. He assumed she and Juni had taken care of the other gang member.

He heard a low sound come from the small room. Cloth on cloth?

Billy streaked around the door facing, his blade slashing neck high. Grey leaned away to his right, which put his weapon arm in an awkward position to counter strike. But his left hand was close, and he scooped Billy's rear ankle as it came off the floor and lifted it just high enough to throw him off balance. The gang leader tried to recover but failed, and he sprawled belly first.

He was on his feet before Grey could reach him.

They squared off, Billy's stance similar to Grey's—lead weapon-arm bent, knife pointing, rear hand open and near his chest. Grey didn't recognize Billy's blade, though it looked similar to a Ka-Bar. The last real Ka-Bar he'd seen was thrown into his belly.

Billy faked a thrust at Grey's middle. The knife fighter inhaled sharply and felt his body tighten. He took a deep belly breath and circled to his left. Relax, he told himself. His muscles responded.

The kid looked good, Grey thought. There wasn't going to be any disarming going on. He had always taught that taking a blade away from a skilled fighter is a falsehood spread by teachers who haven't a clue that most disarming techniques don't work in a real battle. "He who tries often gets stabbed for their effort," his father used to say.

Billy was wearing a heavy coat and cargo pants, making slicing techniques a second option for Grey since the thick material diminished the cut. Stabs were first—vital targets such as the groin, liver, femoral artery in the inside of the thigh, and the side of the neck into the carotid artery or jugular.

Billy feinted again, and Grey's knife flicked out like a serpent's tongue biting the back of his hand. It was his psyche move to show the gang member his speed, and a warning that he could do damage whenever he wanted. He wanted the man to turn around and walk away.

Billy flipped the blood drip off the back of his hand, then rolled his blade from saber grip to icepick, and back to saber again. He did it with speed and was clearly trying to dazzle Grey with his finesse, but it was a stupid move since they were so close to each other. He rolled his knife again, but before he made it to icepick, Grey lunged forward and kicked his lead thigh.

Billy fumbled the knife for a second but managed to recover it in saber grip.

"Leave now," Grey said. "You're out of your element; you're not as good as you think you are. I don't want to kill you."

In Grey's periphery, he saw Juni and a man he hadn't seen before fall through the doorway and crash onto the floor in a squirming pile. Tala, both hands armed, danced around the men seeking a target.

Billy lunged, his left hand leading high, his right cocking his weapon along his side.

Grey recognized the move. He was attempting a prison-style shanking technique: grab the target around the neck, move in almost chest to chest, then rapid-punch the blade into the gut multiple times. When the move was executed explosively, it was nearly impossible to defend against it.

But Billy was attempting it without first setting up a fake to hide his intention.

Grey simultaneously tucked his belly, whipped the back of his left arm into the inside of Billy's knife arm to stop its forward trajectory, then slammed the butt of his kukri into his tender biceps muscle. Billy grimaced and tried to muscle through for an instant before Grey headbutted the gang leader's nose.

Grey was going to follow with a stab, but Billy stumbled back out of range. He tripped over some garbage and fell onto his back, his head thumping one of the covered burn victims.

Grey quick-glanced over to check on Juni. No worries. Brother and sister were bent over the man, Juni plunging his knife into his belly as Tala sliced her sickle back and forth across the man's neck. He must have pissed them off.

Billy got up on shaky legs, swiped his jacket sleeve across his bleeding nose, and advanced on Grey, his knife leading the way.

"Come on, Billy. Leave. Just walk out the—"

The gang leader lunged with a left to right slice, his swing unnecessarily too big. Grey, too close to back away, stepped diagonally and punched the man's ear. He hoped the blow was hard enough to mess with the gang leader's equilibrium and make him throw in the towel. It wasn't. Billy slashed his blade at him, missed, but not by much.

Time to end this.

Billy charged him, rapidly slashing his blade back and forth. Grey sidestepped out of the weapon's trajectory, stepped in a splash of gasoline, and went down hard on his butt. Billy rolled his knife into an icepick grip and danced around Grey, looking for a place to enter to finish him off.

Sitting on his butt, Grey turned in whichever direction Billy tried to get close to him. On the gang leader's fourth attempt, he stepped within range.

The knife fighter quickly hooked his left foot behind Billy's to prevent him from escaping. Grey yanked his foot back, pulling Billy's with it. As planned, the man's leg straightened, and his knee locked. Grey kicked the joint with all his power.

Billy went down with a loud howl landing on one of the covered bodies, inadvertently pulling the blanket off the deceased's head. Billy's face was no more than a couple of inches from the charred face.

His shriek was that of a horror movie's scream queen.

Grey leaped up, only to realize that one of Billy's legs was between his feet. When Grey went to step over it, the slick gasoline punished him again, and down he went, landing on all fours.

He exhaled sharply. He had been stabbed once and cut many times over the years, so the knife fighter instantly recognized the sensation of a cold razor-edged blade slicing across his calf. He jerked his head around, surprised that Billy was sitting up within range, his weapon arm backhand slashing toward his face.

Grey leaned back and brushed his attack arm aside. But instead of disengaging his grip on the limb, Grey took hold of it and pushed the man's arm hard, ramming the gang leader's blade through his own throat.

Billy fell over onto his back, his hand still gripping the handle of his faux Ka-Bar. His throat gurgled, his eyes bulged, and his blood squirted. By the time Grey climbed to his feet, Billy had stilled.

"You guys okay?" he asked, moving slowly across the room. He could feel his bleeding calf leaking into his sock. It felt superficial. Every last ounce of energy had drained from his body. For a moment, he felt as if he might weep, but he didn't have the strength even for that.

Juni and Robert were leaning against the doorframe. Robert was still favoring his right side, and Juni was holding a rag against his cut chin. They nodded.

Tala was standing next to the dead man she and Juni had fought. He wasn't wearing a bandanna. A wannabe? He would ask her later.

She slipped into his arms and rested the side of her face against his chest.

"Let's head back to Sector Three," he said.

EPILOGUE

Five days had passed since their time in Sector Six. Incredibly and happily, the return had been uneventful.

The four of them were exhausted when they reached Grey and Tala's apartment. Robert tended to everyone's injuries, then Tala and Grey fell into their bed, Robert slept in a chair, and Juni curled up on the floor.

Grey was the first to awaken six hours later, the overcast daylight filling him with joy and gratitude that they had all made it back with only bruises, sprains, and minor cuts. Robert awoke next. He told Grey he would be back to check on them in a day or two.

Tala and Juni finally had an opportunity to catch up with what they had been doing for the past several months. Juni's girlfriend had stormed out of their apartment about 10 days ago after they had had a big argument. He told Tala that he had taken it out on people during one of their deliveries, something he wasn't proud of. Grey remembered what Sukimoto had said about him being out of sorts one night.

Sukimoto. If he hadn't lost control of himself…

Juni said he had been so busy gathering and packing food for multiple deliveries that he hadn't had time to look for her. He wasn't worried, anyway, because she had two girlfriends where she stayed the last time, as he put it, "had a hissy fit."

Juni had no idea who supplied the trucks—that happened before he worked for them—but he sensed that they were given to his group by some kind of paramilitary organization based out in the country. The rumor was they were training people to establish order in the city. Like everyone else, he didn't know if the helicopters were part of that mission, nor could he explain how the downed one appeared not to have a pilot.

He liked the idea of Grey and Tala going to their parent's cabin, but he worried about the journey.

"It can't be any more perilous than our daily existence here," Tala said.

"Why don't you come with us?" Grey asked.

Juni shook his head. "I appreciate you coming to Sector Six to check on me, and I'm very happy to see my beautiful sister is good and being taken care of. But I got to go back and find Rosario. She's a short-tempered Filipino, like me, but I love her. When I do find her, I'll talk to her about joining you."

Two days later, Juni left to return to Sector Six, and Tala cried for nearly an hour after. They spent the next few days resting and packing the absolute necessities.

And laying out their favorite knives.

Grey his Mossy Oak, his kukri, and Bucknbear tactical chopper. Tala would take her Morakniv Edris fixed blade that she sometimes carried on a leather thong around her neck, her Smith and Wesson nine-inch carbon fixed blade, and her Thai sickle.

Yesterday, Robert stopped by to say goodbye. He said he met up with his friend Ronny and "things had been going ultra, ultra-splendidly." When Tala told him that he and Ronnie were welcome at the cabin, Robert hugged her and said he would talk to him about it. But it wouldn't be for at least a month. Tala showed where it was on her map. He said he knew the area well.

Tala and Grey slept soundly, and in the morning, they were raring to go. Fully armed and with their backpacks strapped on, they said one last goodbye to their apartment before stepping out into the hallway.

"I have to make a stop first," Grey said.

Tala glanced down the hall at his old apartment. She nodded, her eyes understanding. "I'll meet you at the bottom of the stairs."

Grey stopped in front of the apartment where his father had died at the hands of a man named Leathers. The door was still smashed in and would probably remain that way. Grey reached out and laid his palm on the splintered doorframe.

"Thank you, father. Your teaching has saved my life and the lives of others, so many times. I will honor your guidance with the blade and your example of being a good man. I know you loved Tala too, and I promise I'll take good care of her. Please continue watching over us."

On the first floor, Tala unlocked the outside door, and Grey peeked out through the partial opening as he had every day before leaving the building. The street was clear.

Two gunshots greeted them as they stepped outside, but the shooter was a few blocks away, so no concern to the travelers. The low-hanging clouds were the normal color of ash. "Good hiking weather," Grey said.

As reluctant as he had been to leave the city and move to the unknown of the country, he felt a need to hurry now. A need to escape the horrors of the place they had somehow managed to survive for over three years.

So many questions remain.

What were the thick black drips that fell from the sky at night?

What were the helicopters about? Do they even have pilots?

Why did he survive, and so many, many others perished?

If his job was to kill people so that others live, does that mean there is a future? That there was a game plan for this? Would he be part of it? Tala too? Would their children help build the new world?

They had one stop to make: the manhole where Doctor Feelgood sold fentanyl, the best pain killer around. Hopefully, they wouldn't need it other than to buy necessities.

They headed down the street.

"Are we there yet, daddy?" Tala asked, bumping his shoulder with hers. "Huh? Are we? Are we?"

Grey sighed. "This is going to be a loooong trip."

Tala smiled.

A helicopter passed overhead heading in the same direction as them.

ABOUT THE AUTHOR

Loren W. Christensen has been involved in law enforcement since 1967. He began as a 21-year-old military policeman in the U.S. Army, serving stateside and as a patrolman in Saigon, Vietnam during the war. At 26, he joined the Portland, Oregon Police Bureau working a variety of jobs to include street patrol, gang enforcement, intelligence, bodyguarding, and academy trainer, retiring after 25 years.

In 1997, Loren began a full-time career as a writer, now with nearly 60 books in print with seven publishers, as well as magazine articles and blog pieces. He edited a police newspaper for seven years. His non-fiction includes books on martial arts, police work, PTSD, mental preparation for violence, meditation, nutrition, exercise, and various subcultures, to include prostitution, street gangs, skid row, and the warrior community.

His fiction series *Dukkha* was a finalist in the prestigious USA Best Book Awards. Two of his books have been printed in multiple languages and two are also in audio books format.

As a martial arts student and teacher since 1965, Loren has earned a 1st-dan black belt in the Filipino fighting art of *arnis,* a 2nd-degree black belt in *aiki jujitsu and, on* October 23, 2018, the American Karate Black Belt Association in Texas, awarded him a 10th-dan black belt in karate. Loren was inducted into the Masters Hall of Fame in 2011.

OTHER TITLES BY LOREN W. CHRISTENSEN

The following are available on Amazon, from their publishers, and through the usual book outlets. Signed copies can be purchased at LWC Books, www.lwcbooks.com

Street Stoppers
Fighting In The Clinch
Fighter's Fact Book
Fighter's Fact Book 2
Solo Training **(Bestseller)**
Solo Training 2
Solo Training 3
Speed Training
The Fighter's Body
Total Defense
The Mental Edge
The Way Alone
Far Beyond Defensive Tactics
Fighting Power
Crouching Tiger
Anything Goes
Winning With American Kata
Total Defense
Riot
Warriors
On Combat **(Bestseller)**
Warrior Mindset
Deadly Force Encounters
Deadly Force Encounters, Second Edition
Surviving Workplace Violence
Surviving A School Shooting
Gangbangers
Skinhead Street Gangs
Hookers, Tricks And Cops

Way Of The Warrior
Skid Row Beat
Defensive Tactics
Missing Children
Fight Back: Self-Defense For Women
Extreme Joint Locking
Timing In The Martial Arts
Fighter's Guide to Hard-Core Heavy Bag Training
The Brutal Art Of Ripping, Poking And Pressing Vital Targets
How To Live Safely In A Dangerous World
Fighting The Pain Resistant Attacker
Evolution Of Weaponry
Meditation For Warriors
Mental Rehearsal For Warriors
Prostate Cancer
Cops' True Stories Of The Paranormal **(Bestseller)**
Seekers of the Paranormal
Policing Saigon
Musings on Violence
Street Lessons, A Journey

Fiction

Dukkha: The Suffering
Dukkha: Reverb
Dukkha: Unloaded
Dukkha: Hungry Ghosts
Old Ed, Omnibus
Boss, Omnibus
The Reincarnation of Kato the Monk

Short Story Fiction

Old Ed	Parts	
Old Ed 2	Knife Fighter	
Old Ed 3	Knife Fighter 2	
Old Ed 4	Boss	
Old Ed 5	Boss2	Boss 3

DVDs

Solo Training
Fighting Dirty
Speed Training
Masters And Styles
Vital Targets
The Brutal Art Of Ripping, And Pressing Vital Targets

Note: On Combat and Policing Saigon are also available in audio from Amazon

OLD ED
The Omnibus
Edition
5 Short Stories by
Loren W
CHRISTENSEN
76-years-old, Sweet, Kind, Lady Charmer ...
HITMAN
OLD ED
A SHORT STORY
76-years-old, Kind, Caring, In Love ...
HITMAN
OLD ED
76-years-old, Domestic Problems, Memory Issues ...
HITMAN
OLD ED 3
A SHORT STORY
76-years-old, out of retirement with a trainee ...
HITMAN
What could go wrong?
OLD ED 4
77-years old, nice guy, back problems, forgetful, very good at his job ...
HITMAN
OLD ED 5
A SHORT STORY

You Might Also Like

Everyone at the rest home knew that Ed was pleasant, caring, funny, and popular with the women there. What they didn't know was that he was also a hitman and, over the past 35 years, had eradicated 71 evil men and women. Ed didn't use a firearm because he believed there was already too much gun violence in the world. No problem. He knew many, many highly effective ways to do his job.

The five-part short story series, *Old Ed,* can be purchased individually in a short story format or all together in an omnibus.